TERRACE IN THE SUN

Anne Weale

Justine Field was twenty-three, dominated by her father, unable to make the best of herself and a stranger to any emotion. But it didn't help when she overheard David Cassano pointing all this out to a friend! So why did she have to fall in love with him—the one man who could hurt her more than her father had ever done.

TERRACE IN THE SUN

Anne Weale

OCT 2 6 1990

Curley Publishing, Inc
South Yarmouth, Ma.

Library of Congress Cataloging-in-Publication Data

Weale, Anne.
    Terrace in the sun / Anne Weale.—Large print ed.
        p.   cm.
    1. Large type books.   I. Title.
[PR6073.E125T47   1990]
823'.914—dc20
ISBN 0–7927–0320–0 (lg. print)

90–33792
CIP

© **Anne Weale 1966**

Published in Large Print by arrangement with Harlequin Enterprises B.V.

Printed in Great Britain

TERRACE IN THE SUN

CHAPTER ONE

'OH, Richard, you misguided man! You'll wreck that poor child's life. It really is too abominable!' Mrs. Hurst exclaimed suddenly, in an excess of exasperation.

She and her husband were having tea in the rather dilapidated summer house at the end of the Rectory garden. But although there was no one else present, it was not Canon Hurst who had provoked her indignant outburst. She was apostrophising her brother, who was hundreds of miles away on an island in the Mediterranean.

'What has Richard done now?' her husband enquired, folding and putting aside the local newspaper.

'Nothing new,' she answered vexedly, taking off her spectacles and passing across the airmail letter which had come by the afternoon post. 'But every time I hear from Justine, my blood boils for her, poor darling. It's monstrous the way he treats her, Charles. It really is wicked to bend her to his will as he does. Where will it end? What on earth is going to become of her?'

Canon Hurst read his niece's letter. Then

1

he handed it back to his wife and sat absently pulling the lobe of his left ear, a habit of his when pondering a difficult problem.

'Well?' Mrs. Hurst prompted, after his contemplation had lasted for several minutes.

He roused, and reached for the cup of tea she had poured for him. 'Yes, it's wrong . . . very wrong indeed,' he agreed with her, frowning. 'But I'm afraid there's nothing we can do to help her, Helen. The remedy lies with Justine herself. She's not forced to stay with him, you know. She's of age now, and I'm sure she would have no difficulty in obtaining a post and supporting herself. But no one can make her stand on her own feet. If she wants her freedom, she must fight for it.'

'How can she?' his wife protested. 'You know she adores Richard. She'll never go against his wishes . . . however unhappy he makes her.'

'Are you sure she is unhappy?' Canon Hurst asked. 'There's nothing in her letter to suggest it.'

'Of course she's unhappy, poor child!' Helen Hurst retorted positively. 'She doesn't say so . . . wild horses wouldn't make her admit it. She's fanatically loyal to Richard. But how can she possibly be happy when all her natural instincts have been repressed?

2

She's twenty-three years old, Charles, and she's never had a decent dress . . . or a date with a young man . . . or even a lipstick. It's absolutely criminal the way Richard denies her every vestige of femininity. Oh, if only he had let us adopt her when Cathy died. Had I known what was in his mind, I would have moved heaven and earth to get her away from him.'

'Yes, it's a great pity he wouldn't let us have her. But, to give him his due, he has never neglected her, my dear. In his own eccentric way, he's as devoted to her as she to him.'

'Eccentric!' Mrs. Hurst expostulated. 'Most people would call him unbalanced . . . and I think he must be.'

'Perhaps . . . he is a very brilliant man. *Great wits are sure to madness near allied, and thin partitions do their bounds divide,*' her husband quoted reflectively. 'But Justine herself is no ordinary girl, Helen. It may be that she doesn't care about clothes and cosmetics in the way most young women do.'

'Richard has never allowed her to be ordinary,' Mrs. Hurst replied impatiently. 'I don't believe she's exceptionally clever at all. She's intelligent, yes. And she's been made to study intensively. But I'm sure she's not a born intellectual. It's a wonder to me she didn't break down years ago, the way he kept her nose to the grindstone. She was never allowed to play like a normal child. She was force-fed with knowledge like one of those poor Strasbourg geese.'

'Yes, the curriculum Richard set for her was much too exacting, in my opinion,' her husband conceded. 'But you can't deny she seemed happy enough as a youngster. She was quiet and well-behaved, but she wasn't unnaturally subdued.'

'Perhaps not—as a child. But now she's a woman,' said Mrs. Hurst. 'You didn't see her when they were in London for those few days in March, Charles. After we'd had lunch together, we walked down Regent Street. There was a lovely chiffon evening dress in one of Liberty's windows. She stopped and stared at it like . . . like a child gazing at a toy it knows it can never have. It was pathetic. I could have wept for her.'

She sighed, and made a gesture of helplessness. 'I tried to persuade her to let me buy her some pretty things,' she went on. 'But she made some lame excuse about having plenty of clothes, and not needing anything new. I honestly believe that, if I had insisted on buying her something, she would have dumped it in a waste basket on the way back to their hotel. It's incredible the hold Richard has on her. His word is law. She accepts his views on everything. I simply can't understand it,' she ended distressfully.

'Now don't start upsetting yourself, my dear,' Canon Hurst said gently. For his wife sometimes suffered from migraine, and the attacks were often triggered off by her anxiety about her niece. 'The situation may yet resolve itself. Consider the case of Elizabeth Barrett—and her predicament was a good deal worse than Justine's. I've no doubt that one of these days Justine will meet someone who will exert an even stronger influence than Richard.'

'But she never meets any men, Charles. And if she did, they wouldn't be interested. It isn't that she's a plain girl. She could be very attractive, if she were allowed to make the best of herself. But she isn't—quite the reverse. When I saw her in London, she was looking so drab and dowdy that nobody even glanced at her.'

'Someone may be drawn to her. There are more important qualities than a pretty face.'

'I daresay—but a nice disposition is not usually what attracts a man in the first place,' Mrs. Hurst observed dryly. 'It's not like it was when we were young, Charles. Beauties were born, not made, then. But nowadays, what with colour rinses and false eye-lashes and so on, almost any girl can look charming. Yes, I know you dislike a lot of make-up, and too much of it does look horrid. But it doesn't have to be laid on with a trowel and, skilfully done, it makes all the difference. Apart from her appearance, Justine's whole manner is against her. She wasn't really at ease with me—and I'm her aunt. She isn't shy exactly. It's something more complex than that. She's become so reserved that, unless you keep asking her questions, she hardly opens her mouth. I'm sure she's incapable of giving a man any encouragement.'

'Well, she may not have much small-talk, but I expect she's more forthcoming on her own subject,' said Canon Hurst.

'Yes, but who wants to talk about ancient relics all the time—except other archaeologists? And they're all old fogies,' said his wife.

'On the contrary, there was one on television the other night who was both young and extremely personable,' he told her, with a twinkle. 'His sphere is the ancient Mayan culture, so he is not likely to cross Justine's path. But I expect there are others, equally eligible,

6

in the classical field. I should think it would be best if Justine were to marry an archaeologist. I can't see her settling down in a suburban semi-detached, after the nomadic life she's led with Richard.'

'I doubt if she will ever marry anyone,' Mrs. Hurst said pessimistically. 'Richard will never let her go, and by the time he dies it will be too late. She'll be an embittered, frustrated spinster, with nothing to look forward to but the curatorship of some museum.'

'Single women are not necessarily embittered or frustrated,' the Canon pointed out mildly. 'And marriage is not *ipso facto* a state of bliss—witness Richard's marriage to Cathy.'

Mrs. Hurst waved a fly away from the buttered scones. 'Richard should never have married at all. When a self-centred bachelor of forty-five marries a girl young enough to be his daughter, it's bound to turn out badly. Apart from the difference in their ages, they had nothing whatever in common. Cathy was lovely to look at, but she hadn't a brain in her head. Not that that was any excuse for Richard treating her so shamefully once his mad infatuation began to wear off. The way he snubbed her whenever she said something silly was unforgivable. I used to cringe with embarrassment when he was so cruelly sarcastic to her. And if he was like that in front of other people, what must he have been like in private?'

'He knew he had made a fool of himself, and for a proud man that kind of humiliation must be almost unendurable,' said Charles Hurst. 'I must confess that even I found Cathy's triviality rather irritating. She must have driven Richard to distraction. Though if he had been a little more tolerant, and she had had the sense to chatter less, they might have dealt tolerably well together. There was some improvement in their relationship when she was expecting Justine.'

Mrs. Hurst did not reply. She was remembering the day Cathy had died, without ever seeing her new-born child. Richard Field had set his heart on having a son, to be called Justin. But the baby, a puny little thing, had turned out to be a girl.

Taking for granted that her brother would be only too glad to be relieved of responsibility for the infant, Mrs. Hurst had offered to take charge of her. Her own youngest daughter, Margaret, had been still in the play-pen then.

To the Hursts' astonishment, Professor Field had refused even to consider their offer.

In spite of war-time conditions, he had managed to find a capable elderly woman to keep house for him and look after little Justine.

Helen Hurst had always been uneasy about her brother's motive for keeping his daughter. It seemed very strange that a man of his fundamentally cold temperament should saddle himself with an unwanted girl child when the Hursts would willingly have taken her into their home.

Charles had suggested that perhaps his brother-in-law was expiating a sense of guilt about the way he had treated his young wife after his brief passion had burnt itself out. But Helen had never been convinced by this explanation, and her misgivings had proved to be well founded.

For what Professor Field had done was to rear his daughter as if she were the son he had wanted. As soon as she was old enough not to need constant supervision, he had dismissed the housekeeper and replaced her with a daily woman.

Justine had never gone to school. That would have exposed her to other influences, and ruined his extraordinary experiment. He had instructed her himself. He was well qualified to do so, and there were no grounds for the authorities to intervene as long as the child was receiving an adequate education.

When she was only ten years old, he had resumed his field work—interrupted by the war, and forgone for some years after it—and taken her with him on the first of an almost continuous series of expeditions.

During their infrequent visits to England, he had never permitted Justine to stay with the Hursts for more than one night. Indeed, short of actually shutting her up and keeping her a prisoner, he had managed to exclude from her life every influence but his own.

And, because she had never been neglected or ill-treated in the legal definition of the terms, and had always seemed content with her lot, there had been nothing anyone could do about it.

*　　　*　　　*

While her aunt and uncle were having tea in their peaceful country garden far away in England, Justine Field was sitting under a canvas awning close to the site of her father's latest excavations on the island of Pisano.

It was a burning day and, although the awning cast a patch of shade on the dusty earth, it gave little relief from the heat, which was up in the nineties.

10

Justine was alone that afternoon. There was a tray of what were known as "small finds" on the trestle table at which she was working, and she was carefully marking or labelling them, and recording the particulars in the Site and Objects registers. To a layman, the collection of potsherds would have seemed of little interest or value. But to her, they were pieces of an infinitely complex jig-saw puzzle which, if correctly assembled, might reveal something of very great interest.

It was painstaking work, marking the smaller fragments with a mapping pen and waterproof ink on their broken edges. From time to time, she sat back to flex her fingers, or to fan herself or to take a drink from her vacuum flask.

Pisano was a half hour sea-trip by motor boat from the south-west coast of Corsica. Professor Field had gone to Ajaccio, the capital of Corsica, for the day, and would not return till late that night. Among other errands, he was going to go to a chemist's shop for something to relieve his dyspepsia.

Justine had urged him to see a doctor, for he had never suffered from recurring indigestion before. She was worried in case the pain might have a more serious cause. The irritability with which he had rejected her suggestion made her even more concerned. It was not like her father to be so short-tempered.

She had stopped working, and was lost in anxious thought, when someone said, 'Good afternoon.'

Justine jumped, and drew in a startled breath. Less than twenty feet away, a man was watching her.

He did not belong to the island. There were not many people on Pisano, and she had met them all. But even if she had not, she would have known at once that he was a stranger.

The majority of the islanders were fisherfolk. The girls were slim and graceful until they married, but soon lost their figures as their families increased year by year. The men were short and wiry, and kept their cheap best suits for Sundays and Saints' days. Some of the older ones did not own a lounge suit at all, but still wore the traditional black corduroys and brightly coloured cummerbunds. They were likeable people—poor but not servile, reserved but innately courteous.

The man standing out in the blazing glare of the sun was too tall and too well dressed to be one of them.

'I'm sorry . . . I'm afraid I startled you.'

His voice was English, and his dark hair was cut and brushed in an English way. Yet

12

there was something foreign about him. He was wearing smoked glasses, so she could not tell the colour of his eyes, but his skin was almost as swarthy as that of the island men.

'You must be Professor Field's daughter. He is a very distinguished man. I am looking forward to meeting him. I understand he is in Ajaccio today,' he said.

Justine nodded. She had not yet recovered from her surprise at his sudden appearance. Where had he come from? The "dig" was more than a mile from the village, and the way was mostly uphill. Yet although his shoes were a little dusty, his shirt was not clinging damply to him as hers was to her, and his expensively well-cut trousers looked as if they had just come out of a press. His whole appearance was one of fastidious cleanliness, unaffected by the enervating heat.

Conscious of her own dishevelled state, Justine said awkwardly, 'You have the advantage of me, *monsieur*.'

'I am David Cassano.'

Justine had an excellent memory, and she was sure she had never heard the name before. Yet something in the way he announced it made her feel she ought to recognise it.

It could have been a trick of the light, but

13

she thought a slight smile curved his mouth.

'Well, I can see you are busy, so I won't disturb you.' He gave her an un-English bow, and moved away to follow the winding track which led to the other side of the island.

Justine watched him go up the rising ground with a long, limber, sure-footed stride. At the crest of the incline, where the ground fell away again, he paused for a moment to survey the surrounding landscape. Then, as if he knew she was still watching him, he turned and raised his hand, and passed out of sight.

I am David Cassano.

She nibbled her pen, and searched the recesses of her mind for the reason the name seemed to strike a chord.

She had been right about his not being English. His surname sounded Italian . . . or possibly Corsican or Sardinian. But David was Hebrew in origin, Welsh by adoption, and popular in England and America. It was not, as far as she knew, common in Latin countries. So he must be of mixed descent.

On the question of what he was doing on Pisano, she could not even hazard a guess. The island was private property, owned by the di Rostini family since the days of the First Empire when the Corsican-born

Emperor, Napoleon Bonaparte, had bestowed it on Ludovico di Rostini, one of his *aides*.

Although Justine stayed at the site until six o'clock, she did not see David Cassano again. Either he was still over on the western side of the island, or he had returned to the village by another route. Looking forward to her evening swim, she packed up her belongings and made her way back to the villa.

Usually, she and her father lived under canvas when they were on a "dig." But Madame di Rostini, to whom they had had to apply for permission to excavate, had insisted they should live at her villa for the duration of their stay on Pisano.

She was an old lady of over seventy, the last of her line and, for several years past, a semi-invalid. She lived alone, except for her housekeeper, a widowed island woman. Madame had taken lunch with the Fields on their first day as her guests, but they had seen little of her since then.

Justine thought the villa must be one of the most beautiful houses in the world. It had been built on a rocky headland, jutting out between two crescent bays. The Fields had their morning and evening meals on a terrace where, by leaning over the sun-baked balustrade, it was possible to look down into the crystalline depths of the sea.

In contrast to the dazzling southern light out of doors, the interior of the villa was restfully cool and dim, with marble floors and slatted shutters at the windows. Justine had the impression that the house had once been full of rare and beautiful furniture and *objets d'art*, but that most of them were missing now. Perhaps they had been looted during the war, when Mussolini's troops had occupied the island. Or perhaps Madame had been obliged to sell them.

Everything used in the construction of the villa must have been brought there by sea, for the only other access to the promontory was by a steep and rather dangerous pathway down the face of the cliffs which reared behind the two bays.

When Justine reached the edge of the cliffs, and the villa came into view, she was surprised to see a large ocean-going yacht lying at anchor in the deep water of the larger bay.

It was a magnificent vessel of the kind which could only belong to someone immensely wealthy . . . a Greek shipping magnate, or an American oil tycoon.

Justine knew instantly that this yacht belonged to David Cassano. With an irrational prickle of hostility, she wondered if he had obtained permission to berth and look over the island, or if he had simply done so, as if by right.

She had had a slight headache since midday. When she reached the villa, she decided not to bathe after all, but to rest in the cool of her room for a little while. She had washed at the old-fashioned washstand, and was brushing the dust out of her hair, when there was a tap at the door and Sophia, the housekeeper, came in. Even before she spoke, Justine could tell she was excited and pleased about something.

'Ah, you have returned, *mademoiselle*,' she said, in French. 'What a pity Monsieur le Professeur will not be back until late. Madame requests the pleasure of your company at dinner tonight. It is a special occasion, you understand. Monsieur Julien has come home.'

'Monsieur Julien ... who is he?' Justine asked blankly.

'He is Madame's grandson,' Sophia explained, beaming. 'He has been in Paris for the past year, and we did not expect to see him for some time yet. You have noticed the yacht in the bay? It belongs to his friend, who will also be present tonight.'

She clapped her hands to her temples, and

17

rolled her eyes. 'So little time, and so many preparations to be made! The other gentleman is someone of great importance. He will be accustomed to the finest cuisine. It will not do to offer him anything but the best.'

'I'm sure he won't be able to find any fault with your cooking, Sophia. The food here is always delicious,' Justine said warmly. 'I didn't realise Madame had any family. I thought she was quite alone in the world.'

'Oh, no—as well as Monsieur Julien there is his sister, Mademoiselle Diane,' the housekeeper told her. 'Their father, Madame's only son, was killed in the war . . . God rest his soul,' she added, crossing herself. 'Such a tragedy! It nearly broke Madame's heart when she heard of his death, poor lady. He was such a fine man. But you will see for yourself tonight. Monsieur Julien is very like him.'

'It's very kind of Madame to invite me to join them, but I don't want to intrude,' Justine said doubtfully. Indeed the thought of attending a formal dinner party without her father filled her with apprehension. 'Couldn't I have supper on a tray up here in my room?' she suggested diffidently.

'Oh, no, that would not do at all, *mademoiselle*,' Sophia said, looking quite shocked.

18

'Madame would be most offended. Dinner will be served at eight o'clock, but you must come down a little earlier to take wine with Madame in the salon. Now I must hurry back to the kitchen. I have two girls from the village assisting me, but they are not used to handling fine china and glass. I dare not leave them alone for more than a few minutes.'

After she had gone, Justine took a couple of aspirins, and lay down on the bed and closed her eyes. But it was difficult to relax now that she was faced with the ordeal of the dinner-party. What worried her most was that she had nothing suitable to wear. Archaeological excavation was dirty work, and she and her father always changed before their evening meal—but only in the sense of putting on clean shirts and trousers.

Justine had spent so much of her life in trousers that, on the rare occasions when she did wear a skirt, she felt self-conscious and ill at ease. She owned two skirts, a pleated (and seated) tweed one to wear in England, and a grey denim one with large patch pockets for hotter climates. She had never had a pair of sheer nylons, and her footwear consisted of one pair of stout walking shoes, two pairs of serviceable brown sandals, and some rope-soled canvas *espadrilles*.

However, in spite of her nervousness, the quiet of her shuttered room presently lulled her to sleep. She was woken by the sound of voices from the terrace below her window. For a moment she was afraid she had over-slept. But a glance at her watch showed that her nap had only lasted for twenty minutes. Nevertheless her headache had gone, and she felt considerably refreshed.

As she yawned and stretched herself, she could hear the conversation on the terrace quite clearly, and recognised one of the speakers as David Cassano. Presumably the other voice was that of Madame's grandson.

They were speaking French, and were dis-cussing the merits and faults of various cars. Most of their remarks were too technical for Justine to follow, and would have been equally meaningless in English.

And then, suddenly, the younger man changed the subject, and said, 'So you have met the archaeologist's daughter? What is she like? Pretty? It must be very boring for her, hanging about here with no amusements while her father searches for antiquities. No doubt she will be glad of some company.'

Justine stiffened, wondering how to let them know they were being overheard. But before she could make some kind of warning sound, David Cassano spoke again.

'Don't raise your hopes, my friend. You will have no luck in that quarter. Miss Field is what is known in England as a blue-stocking. She is much too busy assisting the Professor to have time for flirtations.'

'A blue-stocking? I do not know this expression. What does it mean?' the other man asked, in a puzzled tone.

'It means she is clever—but not clever enough to disguise the fact,' Cassano explained dryly. 'Such women are not interested in men.'

'How can you tell if you have only exchanged a few words with her?'

'I have met her type before,' was the careless answer. 'If she is to join us at dinner, let us hope she will retire early. The erudite English female is never at ease in male company. Either she suffers from the curious delusion that, if she relaxes her guard, improper advances will be made to her. Or she feels compelled to prove that she is not merely equal to men, but of greatly superior intellect.'

Justine heard the other man laugh. He said, 'You make her sound formidable. But my grandmother said Miss Field was quite young . . . a pleasant girl. Is it possible you are

21

piqued because she did not respond to your advances?'

'My dear Julien, unlike you, I am past the age of regarding every woman in sight as a potential conquest,' Cassano answered sardonically.

'In your case a conquest isn't necessary. You have only to show interest, and they fall into your arms, lucky devil,' the younger man said, with a chuckle.

'Unfortunately, they frequently presume interest when it does not exist,' Cassano replied, in a bored voice.

Justine had guessed he was an arrogant man after their brief encounter earlier. It showed in his walk, in his whole bearing. But the superlative conceit implicit in his last statement was beyond all bounds.

There was a pause, and the clink of a glass being set down on a table.

'I have never met one of these serious-minded brainy girls before,' the younger man said thoughtfully. 'I am intrigued. I wonder if she is really so different from the rest of her sex. It might be amusing to find out.'

'Try by all means—but I think you will change your mind when you see her,' Cassano warned him. 'And if I were you, I shouldn't try to draw her out by asking about her work.

If you do, we shall probably be subjected to a long and extremely dull discourse on Etruscan funeral rites, or something equally boring. Come on: we had better get changed.'

For some moments after they had gone, Justine lay very still, her long brown hair fanning out over the square French pillows.

Then, in one explosive movement, she sprang from the bed, ran to the window, and flung wide the louvred shutters. Sunlight poured into the room, dazzling her. She put her hands over her eyes and leaned against the sill, trembling.

In all her life, she had never before experienced such a wild surge of anger as that which had swept her a moment ago. It had welled up inside her like a sudden spasm of nausea, overwhelmed her for an instant, and left her shocked and ashamed. She had not known that anger could be a physical thing . . . an almost ungovernable impulse to lash out, to scream, to snatch up the nearest breakable object and smash it to smithereens.

The discovery that she was capable of such a violent and primitive reaction was horrifying to her. She had been brought up to believe that emotions, like physical appetites, must always be rigidly disciplined. According to her father, the measure of a civilised person was the ability to subordinate feeling to reason.

Until a few moments ago, she had thought she had this ability. But now, although the full force of her anger had spent itself, and she could see that it was wholly unreasonable to let what she had heard upset her, she found it impossible to control the fierce resentment which still smouldered inside her.

It was no use telling herself that David Cassano's opinion should be a matter of complete indifference to her. Nor did it help to admit that most of what he had said about her was true.

She knew she wasn't pretty, or even attractive. She knew she had none of the social graces. But it was one thing to know and accept her limitations—and quite another to hear them put into words by someone else.

Hateful man! she thought hotly. *What right has he to criticise me? Just because he has money, and owns that ostentatious yacht, he seems to think he is some kind of superman. I wish Father were here. He would soon cut him down to size. Etruscan funeral rites! I'm surprised he's even heard of the Etruscans. I'm sure he knows nothing about them.*

By now it was half past seven, and time for her to dress. But first she had to put her hair

24

up. She had never had it cut. As a child, she had worn it in a single thick waist-length pigtail, but since her sixteenth birthday she had coiled the braid into a bun and secured it with strong black hairpins.

Because it would have been easier to wash, and not so hot and heavy on her neck, she had once suggested having it cut. But her father had pointed out that they were seldom within convenient reach of a hairdresser, and it would be difficult for her to crop it tidily herself. So she continued to wear it in a bun, although sometimes, at the end of a long day, she longed for bedtime so that she could let it loose and massage away the feeling of strain at her temples.

Tonight, however, she plaited it even more tightly than usual, and thrust the pins into place as if she were jabbing them into a wax effigy of David Cassano.

When her hair was done, she put on a plain white shirt blouse, and the denim skirt, and buckled the straps of her sandals.

If I had a dinner dress, I wouldn't wear it, she told herself defiantly.

But then, unbidden, came the memory of the dress she had seen the day she had lunched with Aunt Helen . . . sea-green chiffon flowing from a high beaded bodice. The window dresser had attached invisible threads to the hem of the dress, so that the skirt had swirled out as if the model were dancing. Light from concealed spotlamps had made the crystal-scattered bodice glitter and gleam like the path of the moon on the sea.

In a dress like that almost anyone would look lovely, she thought wistfully.

Her eyes grew dreamy as she imagined herself floating gracefully down to the salon, her hair arranged in an elegant Grecian coiffure, her lips and eyelids tinted with delicate colour like those of the girls in London. How astonished they would be when they saw her, poised in the doorway. Even David Cassano would lose his aplomb for a moment.

She caught sight of herself in the mirror— a tall angular girl with scratches on her bare brown legs—and the daydream burst like a bubble.

Despising herself for her lapse into such fatuous wishful thinking, Justine squared her shoulders and went down to dinner.

The salon, on the ground floor, was the most beautiful apartment in the house. It was fully eighty feet long, with six tall glass doors leading out on to the terrace. Between the doors, and all along the opposite wall, were alcoves designed as settings for classical statues. Only four of these life-size figures still looked down from their ornate pedestals. Similarly, it was evident that three magnificent crystal chandeliers had once hung from the richly plastered and gilded ceiling. Now only the central one remained.

Since Justine and her father had been at the villa, the furniture in the salon had been shrouded in dust covers. Tonight, these had been removed, revealing some of the finest French eighteenth-century furniture she had ever seen. There was not much of it—several brocaded Louis XV chairs, a *chaise-longue*, two black lacquer commodes, and a *bureau plat* lavishly adorned with ormolu. They were arranged in the centre of the salon, where an Aubusson carpet covered the marble floor, and they looked pathetically sparse in the vast room which must once have contained many more fine appointments. But, in the soft flickering glow of the candlelight, even these few remaining pieces evoked some of the formal grandeur of the villa's past.

Madame di Rostini was seated on one of the *fauteuils*, with her feet on a footstool, and a young man standing beside her. David Cassano was sitting on the silk-covered *chaise-longue*. Justine did not glance at him, but she was aware of him rising to his feet as she entered the room and advanced, stiff with nerves, towards her hostess.

'Good evening, Miss Field,' said the old lady, with a gracious inclination of her head. 'Allow me to present my grandson.'

Justine offered her hand. 'How do you do, *m'sieur*.'

Julien di Rostini was not much older than herself, and very good-looking. As his smiling dark eyes appraised her with frank curiosity, a wave of colour suffused her thin sun-browned face.

'*Enchanté, mademoiselle.*'

To add to her embarrassment, he did not shake her hand, but stepped forward, bowed, and raised it gallantly to his lips.

'And this is Monsieur Cassano, whose yacht you will have seen in the bay, and who is to be our guest for a few days,' Madame went on, indicating the older man.

'Good evening,' Justine said stiffly, avoiding his eyes.

'Miss Field and I have already met, *madame*. She was at work near the excavations when I walked over the island this afternoon,' he explained.

Then he added, 'But of course we have not been formally introduced,' and he held out his hand, so that Justine was forced to take it.

28

As he must have seen her foolish blush, she thought he meant to mock her gaucherie by also kissing her fingers. To her relief, he confined himself to a firm English-style handshake. But his clasp did last rather longer than was strictly necessary, and he made her look directly at him.

How he did it, when she meant to keep her gaze on his tie, Justine did not understand. All she knew was that, as their hands met, she found herself impelled to look up at him.

To her surprise, his eyes were not dark like Julien's, as she had expected. They were grey—the same colour as her own.

They were set under drooping lids which gave his face, at first glance, a look of cold world-weary indifference. But the lazy lids were misleading. The eyes beneath them were alert and shrewd and calculating.

As he released her hand, Madame said, 'You will take a glass of *pastis*, Miss Field?'

'Yes . . . th-thank you,' Justine said unsteadily. For she had an unnerving conviction that, if David Cassano had not wished her to escape his scrutiny, he could have held her in a kind of trance, like a snake hypnotising a rabbit.

Julien brought the *pastis* to her. 'You must be very tired after working in the heat of the sun all day, *mademoiselle*. Surely you do not dig the ground yourself?'

'Sometimes . . . but not today. I don't mind the heat. I'm used to hot climates,' she told him, forcing herself to smile. 'Last year we were working in Tunisia where it was even hotter than here.' She turned to his grandmother, and said awkwardly, 'I hope you will excuse my clothes, *madame*. We need so much equipment that we can't bring much personal luggage. I'm afraid I have nothing more suitable.'

'There is no need to apologise, Miss Field. I understand,' Madame di Rostini said kindly.

But she herself was wearing a long dress of stiff black silk, with lace at her throat and wrists, and both men had changed into lightweight lounge suits.

Feeling wretchedly out of place, Justine sipped her drink and listened in tongue-tied silence to the smooth exchange of conversation which the other three carried on until Sophia came to announce that dinner was served.

Julien helped his grandmother to rise. Although she always sat very erect, she walked with short faltering steps, and needed two sticks to support her. Tonight, she left one stick beside her chair, and took the young man's arm, smiling up at him in a way which made it very clear he was the apple of her eye. Justine wondered what had taken him to Paris, and where his sister was. She was glad the old lady was not alone after all. It had seemed to her very sad that Madame should have no one of her own left to care for her, and that, after her death, the villa would stand empty, falling into decay.

As Madame began her slow shuffling progress towards the imposing double doorway, its elaborate architrave surmounted by an Imperial eagle, David Cassano turned his attention on Justine.

It occurred to her suddenly that, with his hooded eyelids and prominent high-bridged nose, he was not unlike the bronze eagle over the door. There was something predatory about him . . . something which alarmed and repelled her. Sophia had said he was "someone of importance." She wondered how he had attained his position—and how many people he had crushed to achieve his eminence.

As if he could read her thoughts, his hard mouth curled into the enigmatic half-smile which she remembered from their first encounter.

'May I take you in, Miss Field?' He bowed,

and offered his arm.

Justine felt herself flushing again. Even if she had been more appropriately dressed, the gesture would have embarrassed her. In the circumstances, she felt it was a deliberate attempt to shatter what little assurance she did possess.

Reluctantly, she slipped her hand into the crook of his arm, sensing the malicious amusement which her lack of *savoir faire* afforded him. Slowly, interminably slowly, they followed the others to the dining-room.

'What time will your father get back?' he asked her.

'I'm not sure. He went over with some men from the village. He'll have to wait till they are ready to come home.'

He said, 'You should have gone with them. Ajaccio is a pleasant town.'

'I know. We spent a few days there before we came to Pisano. But I was behind with the indexing, so I couldn't spare the time to go today,' she said stiffly, trying not to be so aware of the warmth of his arm through the expensive mohair cloth of his sleeve.

'Do you always put duty before pleasure?' he asked, with a hint of mockery.

She gave him a brief upward glance. 'My

work is a pleasure, Mr. . . . Monsieur Cassano.'

She had hesitated over the title because somehow, in spite of his surname and dark complexion, the French form of address seemed wrong for him. As she had noticed earlier, there was no trace of a foreign intonation in his idiomatic English. On the other hand, he spoke French equally fluently. Her mouth tightened as she remembered his remarks on the terrace.

When they reached the dining-room, Madame di Rostini invited him to sit on her right, with Justine on her left, and Julien at the foot of the table.

As Cassano drew out her chair for her, Justine quailed at the thought of sitting directly opposite him for an hour or more. She had never missed her father's presence more.

The meal began with *pâté de merle*, a Corsican speciality which was unquestionably delicious, but which Justine could never really enjoy because it was made from blackbird flesh. As her father had pointed out, she did not shrink from eating chicken or pheasant. But blackbirds were songbirds, and she could never quite overcome her illogical scruples.

It was during the second course—freshly

caught *langoustes* served with an oil and vinegar dressing—that Julien drew her into the conversation by saying, 'Have you found any valuable relics yet, *mademoiselle*? What kind of treasure are you looking for?'

Justine happened to have her mouth full at that moment and, before she could speak, Cassano said, 'Archaeology is not a treasure hunt, Julien. Miss Field and her father are seeking information—not gold.'

'Information?' the younger man queried, raising an eyebrow.

'As I understand it, archaeology is a scientific reconstruction of the manners and *moeurs* of past civilisations. The discovery of what you call treasure is incidental. Am I right, Miss Field?'

'Yes—quite right,' Justine agreed.

'And that surprises you?' he asked, with a glint in his eyes.

She managed to hold his glance. 'It is surprising how many people do think we are looking for buried treasure,' she answered evenly.

'I should not think you will find much information about the past on Pisano,' Julien put in. 'Until my family came here, it was uninhabited.'

Justine turned to him. 'There were people

34

here long before your family, *monsieur*. I expect you know about Aleria, the Roman city which French archaeologists have excavated on the east coast of Corsica. The Romans were here, too. We've found coins and ceramics which prove it. Aleria was built on the site of an even older Greek city, so perhaps the Greeks—' She stopped short, remembering Cassano's quip about the Etruscans.

'The Greeks . . . you think they came here also?' the young man prompted.

'It's a possibility,' she said, looking down at her plate. 'However, ancient history isn't a subject which interests most people, so I won't bore you with our theories.'

David Cassano said, 'On the contrary, we are fascinated. Do go on, Miss Field. What are your theories?'

Justine glared at him. She could not help it. He had said she would be a bore and, to prove his point, he was deliberately inciting her to be one.

'They aren't mine . . . they are my father's,' she said coldly. 'If you are really interested, I'm sure he will be pleased to explain them to you,' she added, unable to resist the small thrust of sarcasm.

He lifted his wineglass to his lips, his grey

eyes narrowed and appraising. As he drank, watching her over the rim of the beautiful antique goblet engraved with the di Rostini crest, she felt the same disturbing sensation she had experienced when they shook hands—as if he were exerting some kind of will-power upon her.

It was an absurd notion, for she knew that even professional hypnotists could not use their powers unless their subjects were willing to co-operate. Yet, absurd as it might be, the fact remained that when he looked at her in that peculiarly intent way, she felt a queer tightness in her throat, and was quite unable to avert her eyes from his.

He replaced the glass on the table, and stroked the stem with the tips of his long brown fingers.

'I noticed this afternoon that you are confining your excavations to one relatively small area,' he said. 'What made you decide that particular place was likely to be more fruitful than any other?'

Since she could not avoid answering a specific question, Justine said frigidly, 'Before we asked Madame's permission to work here, we took some aerial photographs of the island. It's a common preliminary nowadays. As you seem unusually well informed about archaeology, *m'sieur*, you may know that the position of all the Etruscan tombs north of Rome was plotted by air photographs.'

'No, I didn't know—how interesting,' he said impassively. Perhaps he had already forgotten his jibe about her earlier.

But Julien had not. Glancing at him, she saw the corners of his mouth twitch.

He said, 'I do not understand. Of what use are these pictures from the air, *mademoiselle*?'

'They sometimes show the rough outlines of buried buildings, especially where the land is being farmed,' she explained. 'In a cornfield, for instance, the corn will grow taller on top of an old ditch because the soil is deeper. Where there's a buried wall, the corn may be rather poor.'

'But can't this be seen from the ground?' he asked.

'Yes, occasionally, in certain lights, you can see cropmarks. But not nearly as clearly as from the air.'

'And your pictures of Pisano have shown you the right place to dig?' Julien asked, with seemingly genuine interest.

'No, but they did show certain irregularities which my father thought worth

37

investigating. We used another method to decide where to start digging. But it's rather technical, so I won't try to explain it.'

At this point, the two village girls came in to serve the next course. One of them was an exceptionally pretty little thing with curly black hair and large long-lashed mischievous eyes. She was obviously well aware of her own charms and, as she removed the men's crayfish plates, she gave them each a provocative smile.

Julien responded with a grin and the flicker of a wink. But David Cassano gave the girl the briefest of glances and turned to speak to his hostess.

This surprised Justine, for it did not tally with her unflattering assessment of his character. Then, watching him as he spoke to Madame di Rostini, she decided that his taste was probably too sophisticated for a peasant girl, however comely, to appeal to him. She remembered women she had seen in London—beautiful, scented, supercilious creatures in furs and *chic* hats, who waved imperiously for taxis, and spoke to sales assistants in a condescending drawl, and swept through shop doors without bothering to say thank you to whoever had held it open for them.

They were the kind of women with whom a man like Cassano would amuse himself, she thought caustically. For, after what he had said to Julien on the terrace, she had no doubt that his relationships were never more than transient diversions.

During the main course—wild boar meat cooked in wine, with a chestnut sauce—Julien made several polite remarks to her. In spite of his good looks and charm, she found him much less intimidating than the older man.

The meal ended with creamy *brocciu* cheese and dried figs, and then they returned to the salon for coffee and liqueurs. Now that the evening was nearly over, Justine relaxed slightly. She wondered if David Cassano would be staying in the villa overnight, or if he would sleep on board his yacht.

About half an hour after their return to the salon, she felt it would be permissible for her to excuse herself. But, before she could do so, Madame di Rostini forestalled her.

'I am sure you will forgive me if I retire rather early, Monsieur Cassano,' the old lady said, in her gracious manner. 'Julien, will you help me to my room, please? Miss Field will entertain our guest in your absence. Good-night, Miss Field.' She turned to Cassano

39

again. 'It is a pleasure and a privilege to offer you our hospitality, *m'sieur*. I shall see you again tomorrow.'

Trying not to show her dismay, Justine murmured her thanks for the evening's entertainment, and bade her hostess goodnight. David Cassano walked with Madame to the door, where he bowed and kissed her thin veined hand.

As the others passed into the hall, and he closed the doors behind them, Justine braced herself for this unexpected and unwelcome tête-à-tête. She was puzzled by Madame's use of the word privilege. Was it merely an expression of flowery old-world courtesy? Or had she meant it literally? Who was this man? . . . and why had he come to Pisano?

As he strolled towards her, some of her apprehension at finding herself alone with him must have shown in her face.

He said dryly, 'There is no need to be nervous, Miss Field. I will not bite you, you know.'

Her face flamed, and she lifted her chin and gave him a withering look. But he did not see it, for he was picking up the cigar he had left in an onyx tray.

With the cigar in one hand, and a glass of *fine* in the other, he seated himself in the chair nearest to hers, and said, 'Madame must have been a very handsome woman when she was young.'

It was an observation which had often occurred to Justine, but she was surprised that he had the perception to see the traces of long-ago beauty in the old lady's time-ravaged face.

'Yes,' she agreed stiltedly.

There was a long nerve-straining pause in which she tried to think of something else to say, but found her mind a complete vacuum. How long would Julien be away? Not more than a few minutes, surely?

Her companion crossed his long legs and idly swung one well-shod foot. He was perfectly at ease.

'Allow me to compliment you, Miss Field,' he said suddenly.

She flashed a wary glance at him. 'For what reason, *m'sieur*?'

'For your unusual, indeed rare, ability to keep silent when you have nothing of moment to say,' he explained smoothly. 'I also find nothing more tiresome than an exchange of banalities between people who have no basis for a proper conversation.'

She bit her lip, hating him for pretending to be gallant while, inwardly, he was laughing

41

at her. If only she had the wit to think of some clever riposte which would puncture his insufferable conceit.

She reached for her glass of Myrte, a Corsican liqueur made from myrtle berries, which stood on the little table between their chairs. But her hand was unsteady and, to her horror, she knocked the glass over and sent it flying.

With incredibly swift reaction, Cassano caught the glass before it could hit the floor and shatter. But it had been half full, and some of the liquid splashed on the valuable carpet and on his trouser legs.

'*Oh, no!*' Justine gave a cry of dismay, and sat staring in paralysed mortification at the result of her clumsiness.

'Don't panic. There's no great harm done.' Cassano produced a handkerchief, and mopped first the carpet and then the floor. He then took a second handkerchief from his breast pocket, wetted it with a spurt of soda water from a siphon, and used it to sponge any stickiness out of the carpet.

This done, he casually tossed both handkerchiefs into a waste paper box beneath the *bureau plat*, and said, 'I don't think the carpet will be marked.'

'I'm m-most terribly sorry. Th-thank good-ness you caught the glass,' she stammered wretchedly. 'But your handkerchiefs . . . and your suit . . .'

He glanced down at the spots on his trou-sers. 'They can be removed easily enough, and the handkerchiefs don't matter.' He spoke as if expensive linen handkerchiefs were as expendable as tissues. 'Don't look so upset, Miss Field. Everyone has accidents.' He sat down, and took up his cigar again.

'I'm not usually so clumsy,' she said huskily.

'I'm sure you aren't. Your work must call for considerable precision and delicacy. It was not your fault. It was mine.'

'Yours?' she said blankly.

He turned his head to look directly at her, and this time he did not veil the amusement in his strange grey eyes.

'You were on edge, were you not? Your hand was shaking.'

She remembered his remark on the terrace. *The erudite English female is never at ease in male company. She suffers from the curious delusion that, if she relaxes her guard, improper advances will be made to her . . .*

The anger which had blazed inside her a few hours earlier flared up again, almost as

43

fiercely. To stop herself blurting out something she might regret, she jumped up from her chair and walked quickly away to the glass doors. She knew it made her look even more foolish, but at least is saved her from abusing Madame's hospitality by telling him what she thought of him.

Her clenched hands thrust deep into her pockets, she stood staring out at the moonlit terrace, willing Julien to come back and let her escape.

She heard Cassano leave his chair, and come towards her. Her nails dug into her palms.

'Shall we go outside?' He opened the door and held it for her.

Justine stepped through it, without looking at him. She walked across to the parapet. It was a perfect Mediterranean night. The calm sea shimmered under the moon, the warm still air was heady with the scent of the *maquis*, and the only sound was the soft lapping of water against the rocks fifty feet below them.

Usually, the beauty of the scene filled Justine with inexpressible longings. She often sat at her window till past midnight, watching the rugged coastline, or gazing far out to sea and conjuring secret fantasies which, next day, she preferred not to remember.

But tonight she was only aware of the man beside her, and of the intense dislike he aroused in her.

He said, 'Perhaps I was mistaken, but I felt you were being a little evasive when we were discussing your work at dinner. You mentioned a method you had used to decide where to dig. Is it something your father has devised? Something you prefer to keep to yourselves?'

'There's nothing secret about it. I wasn't being evasive. I simply felt it wasn't a very scintillating subject for conversation,' she answered shortly.

'Perhaps not—but I think it might interest me. Or do you doubt my capacity to grasp the technicalities?' he asked mockingly.

Justine gave a small shrug. 'Very well—if you insist. We used the electrical resistivity method.' She paused for a moment. Then in a deliberately flat monotonous tone, she went on, 'Soil resists an electrical current. Shallow dry soil has greater resistance. Deep damp soil has less. We inserted steel probes into the earth and passed a current between them. The resistance was recorded on a meter, and then transferred to a graph. After we'd made a series of traverses, the graph showed a pattern which appeared to be the outline of a building.'

He said, 'But surely this is revolutionary? It must cut your labour costs by half.'

'Yes, it does reduce them considerably,' she agreed. 'Of course, until quite recently, the gear was much too heavy to use on this sort of site. We'd have had to import a generator, and a lorry to carry it. But, since transistors came out, a much simpler portable apparatus has been developed.'

Against her will, a note of enthusiasm had crept into her voice. She said hurriedly, 'Monsieur di Rostini seems to have been delayed. I expect he and Madame have a lot to talk about as he's been away for a long time. But we get up early, so I'll have to leave you, *m'sieur*. Goodnight.'

As she turned to go back to the salon, he caught her hand and stayed her. Her instinctive reaction was to jerk free, but somehow she managed to check it.

Rigid with indignation at his effrontery, she waited for him to explain himself.

'It's not late . . . only ten o'clock,' he told her lazily.

'It's late for me,' she retorted.

There was a faint tinkle as something fell on the flagstones at their feet. Still holding

46

her hand, Cassano bent to retrieve it.

'A pin from your hair,' he said, giving it to her.

'Thank you.' She slipped it into her pocket. Pointedly, she repeated, 'Goodnight, *m'sieur*.'

He shrugged and smiled. 'As you wish.'

Then he lifted her hand, and kissed it—not as Julien had done, on the knuckles, but on the back of her palm.

Justine did snatch her hand free then, and almost ran back to the salon. In the hall, she met Julien coming to join them. With a mumbled 'Goodnight,' she hurried up the stairs to her room.

A few moments later, as she was leaning against the bedroom door, breathing as hard as if she had run a hundred yards, she heard Julien emerge on to the terrace.

He said, in French, 'What is the matter with Miss Field? She rushed by me just now as if she had seen a *mazzero*'—using a Corsican word she did not understand.

Holding her breath, Justine waited for Cassano's answer, and heard him say, 'I expect she is agitated because I kissed her hand when we said goodnight.'

'Surely that would not upset her? One can see she is very shy, but not to that degree. I

47

also have kissed her hand. She wasn't distressed. It is a commonplace.'

Justine heard David Cassano laugh. He said, 'The circumstances were different. You were not alone with her. She is remarkably inhibited. At the moment I daresay she is feeling as outraged as if I had tried to make love to her, poor girl. She'll get over it. There's a bar in the village, isn't there? Let's walk down for a drink. I need some exercise after that excellent dinner.'

* * *

Very early the following morning, before it was fully light, Justine crept out of her room and stole through the silent house to the terrace, and the rock-cut stairway leading down to the sheltered *plage* on the southern side of the promontory.

She had had only a few hours' sleep, having lain awake long after her father's return, and woken again about four. She had a swim before breakfast every day, but usually the sun was up, and Sophia had begun her day's work, when Justine came downstairs. Today, apart from the village fishermen, she was probably the only person astir on the whole

48

island, and the feeling of having the world to herself for a little while was strangely soothing.

As she took off her cotton dressing-gown, and dropped it on the fine white sand, she was tempted to shed her bathing suit and go into the water without it. The air was relatively chilly first thing in the morning, but the sea was always warm during the summer months, even on the rare dull days.

For a moment, she hesitated. There was not the slightest chance of anyone seeing her. David Cassano's yacht was lying on the other side of the headland, and there had been no sign of life on board when she had paused to look down at the vessel on her way across the terrace.

Nevertheless, she knew that her father would be markedly displeased if he ever found out that she had bathed in her skin. He had strong views on the subject of modesty, a quality which he considered deplorably lacking in most of his daughter's contemporaries. Justine had never dared to argue with him; she herself could see no harm in scanty sunsuits or even bikinis. Her own bathing suit was a decorous black wool garment which she had had for so long that it had become felted and rather scratchy. It was also heavy to

49

wring out, and slow to dry. She would have liked to replace it with a nylon suit, and had looked at some on her last visit to London. But they were all too clinging and low-cut to pass muster with Professor Field, besides being too expensive. The allowance her father gave her was barely enough to cover essential purchases.

There'll be no one about for at least an hour yet. I'll be dressed again long before then, she thought. And, in a sudden fit of recklessness, she pushed the broad straps off her shoulders and wriggled out of the suit.

The sea was like liquid silk. When she had waded in up to her waist, Justine plunged forward and struck out with a strong rhythmic crawl stroke.

By the time she had been swimming for about twenty minutes, the eastern sky was streaked with pearl and rose light, and the last faint stars had flickered out. She rolled on to her back, and propelled herself leisurely shorewards, kicking up a fountain of spray.

She was about fifty yards from the beach, and still well out of her depth, when a sound made her jack-knife into a crouching position, unwilling to believe her ears. She had thought she heard someone shouting to her.

Treading water, she paddled herself round

to face the island. And what she saw made her set her teeth in dismay. For she was no longer alone and unobserved. Julien di Rostini was standing at the sea's edge, waving to her.

'Good morning, Miss Field. May I join you?' he called. And, before she could reply, he stripped off a terry towel robe and came bounding through the shallows towards her.

Justine experienced a moment of petrified panic in which the only escape from her predicament seemed to be to sink quietly under the surface and never come up again.

At the point where the beach shelved, Julien took a standing header and disappeared for some seconds. He came up about twenty-five feet away, shaking his head like a dog, and grinning at her.

'Good morning,' he said again. 'Do you always rise so early?'

Justine recovered her wits. She saw that, at any moment, he would start to swim closer. She said briskly—and with a composure which astonished her—'Good morning. Would you please turn your back for a few minutes? I'm not wearing a bathing suit.'

She saw his jaw drop in surprise. He said, 'Oh . . . yes . . . yes, certainly, *mademoiselle*,' and began to swim away towards the groyne of rocks on the other side of the bay.

There was a changing cabin at the foot of the cliffs. Emerging from the water, Justine did a fast sprint across the sand, snatched up her things, and ran on to the sanctuary of the cabin. She had brought her clothes down with her. Ten minutes later, she was dry and dressed, with her towel wound round her wet head. Peering out of the window, she saw that Julien was still over by the far rocks, and showed no sign of returning to the beach. Her first thought was to hurry back to the villa and hope he would have the decency to forget the incident. But then she felt sure he would not be able to resist mentioning what had happened to David Cassano.

I've discovered something rather amusing, she could imagine him saying, with a broad grin. *The blue-stocking has a guilty secret. She sneaks out very early in the morning and bathes in the nude. It's true, I assure you. I caught her in the act, poor thing. She dashed back to the house as if the devil were after her.*

As she visualised them laughing at her expense, Justine knew that if she ran away now she would never be able to face them again. It was even possible that David Cassano would take a sadistic delight in twitting her about it—and that would be unendurable! The only way to avert such an ordeal was to stand her ground, and pretend to be quite calm and unflustered.

It took all her moral courage to stroll out of the cabin, and sit down on the sand to wait for Julien to finish his bathe. If she had had to wait long, her resolution might have failed her. But, fortunately, he looked in the direction of the beach a few moments after she sat down, and she forced herself to wave to him. He waved back, and started swimming for the shore.

The sun had risen above the horizon by now, and the colour of the sea was changing from amethyst to vivid blue-green. Normally, this was Justine's favourite time of day. As the sun rose, and the dew on the hillside brushwood began to evaporate, the salt air became fragrant with the delectable scent of the *maquis*. The aroma of lavender and thyme, cistus and arbutus, and a dozen other sweet-smelling shrubs, was always present. But it was especially pervasive at sunrise and sunset. Napoleon, ingloriously exiled on St. Helena, had said he would recognise Corsica blind-folded by the unique perfume of the *maquis*. The same could be said of Pisano.

This morning, however, Justine was only aware of the bronzed and handsome young man coming out of the sea to join her.

'Ah, that was good!' he exclaimed, picking up his towel and giving himself a cursory rub down. 'Me, I do not like to get up early—but it is good on such a morning as this. I feel—what is the expression?—like a million dollars?'

With what she hoped was a nonchalant smile, Justine said, 'Sophia tells me you've been in Paris for a year. Didn't you miss all this . . . the sun, and the sea and everything?'

'Miss it?' He threw back his head and laughed. 'No, I did not miss it, Miss Field. I could not wait to get away from it.' He spread his robe on the sand, and sat down. 'What is there for one to do here? Nothing!'

'But it's so beautiful . . . and it's your home.'

'It is where I was born,' he corrected. 'It is not where I wish to live. I must come back to visit my grandmother sometimes—but I have no other reason to return here. Paris is my home now.'

'But surely when you are older . . . when you marry—' she began.

'I shall never come back to Pisano,' he said with conviction.

Justine was startled and rather upset by this statement. Did he really mean it? Or was it just that he was young and restless, and temporarily infatuated with the sophisticated pleasures of city life? Perhaps he would change his mind in a few years' time.

'What do you do in Paris? I mean what is your work?' she asked.

He shrugged, and made a wry grimace. 'I am a student of law,' he told her. 'It is not what I would wish to be, but it was my father's profession, and it pleases Grand'mère that I—how d'you say?—follow his footsteps.'

'What would you have preferred to do?' she asked.

He leaned back on his elbows, and gave her his wide, charming grin. 'Nothing,' he said candidly. 'You know what I would like? To have much money, and to do nothing but enjoy myself.'

'Wouldn't that become rather boring after a time?' she suggested.

He chuckled. 'That is what David tells me, but I do not believe it.'

At the mention of the other man, Justine stiffened slightly. She unwound the towel from about her head, draped it over her shoulders, and began to unplait her braid so that her hair would dry more quickly. She had never been able to find a bathing cap which would fit over her long thick pigtail, and had to swim without one. This meant that, to prevent it becoming unpleasantly sticky, she had to shampoo her hair two or three times a week—another reason why she wished she could have it cut.

'Do you mind if I say something personal, *mademoiselle*?' Julien asked, as she spread her hair out over the towel.

'No—what is it?' she asked curiously.

He said, 'It changes you when your hair is loose in this way. It is more becoming. A *chignon* is too severe for you.'

'I can't have it loose when I'm working. It would get in my way,' she replied.

He cocked his head on one side, and studied her for a few moments. To her surprise, she did not blush under his scrutiny. Indeed, analysing her feelings, she discovered that she was no longer pretending to be at ease—she was! In the space of a few minutes her agitation had completely dissipated. She was even beginning to see that what had happened was really rather funny.

Julien said, 'It is beautiful hair, and perhaps you would not like to have it cut. But I think you would look very charming with a different *coiffure*. I cannot explain in English. Do you understand French?'

She nodded, and he said in French, 'I am

sure it would suit you the way they are wearing it in Paris this season—very short, with soft curls and a little fringe across the forehead. You have an excellent profile, you know.'

'Have I?' she said, taken aback.

'Yes, I noticed it at dinner last night. And your skin too is lovely.'

She did colour at that. 'I'm too brown,' she said, looking away. 'English girls are supposed to have pink and white complexions.'

'You are not brown—you are golden,' he told her.

The tone of his voice sent a queer little tingle through her. And then she remembered what he had said to David Cassano the previous afternoon. *I have never met one of these serious-minded girls before. I wonder if she is really so different? It might be amusing to find out.*

Was that what he was doing now? Flattering her to see if she would rise to it? Hoping to get a laugh out of her gullibility?

Julien said, 'Are you hungry? I have some chocolate, if you would like some?' He took a bar from the pocket of his robe, snapped it in halves and offered one of them to her.

'Thank you.' She took it, and watched him peel the silver paper off his portion.

57

Somehow, in spite of his good looks and debonair manners, he didn't give her the impression that he was a hard-boiled young man, with the streak of ruthlessness and cynicism which she sensed in David Cassano. Julien must be aware of his looks, and he was probably a tremendous flirt. But there was something disarmingly boyish about his broad grin. He didn't seem the kind of person who would get a kick out of playing on other people's weaknesses.

She said, reverting to English, 'How long will you be staying here, *m'sieur?*'

'Oh, please—you must call me Julien,' he protested.

'All right . . . my name is Justine.'

'Justine? But that is a French name.'

'Is it? In my case it's a feminine version of Justin. My parents were expecting to have a son. They hadn't thought of any names for a girl.'

'Your mother does not come with you on these expeditions? She prefers to stay in England?'

'My mother died when I was born.'

'Oh, I am sorry. I also do not remember my mother.' He hesitated, and then went on, 'After my father was killed in the war, my mother was very unhappy here. She came from Ajaccio, and was not accustomed to the dullness of Pisano. One day, when my sister and I were very young, she went away and did not return. It was a great scandal because my father had been a leader of the Resistance in Corsica, and everyone said it was very wicked of her to betray his memory and desert her children. But I understand how it was for her.'

'Do you know what happened to her?' Justine asked.

'Yes, she is married and living in Paris. I have met her there. This is a confidence, you understand. My grandmother does not know I have seen Juliette. She has never spoken her name since the day she left Pisano.'

'Where is your sister now?'

'She lives in Nice with her *belle-mère*.'

'Her mother-in-law? You mean she's married. But Sophia called her Mademoiselle Diane.'

He smiled. 'Sophia forgets we are grown. Always she thinks of us as children. My sister is a widow now. Her husband was many years older. They were married for only a few months before he died with a heart attack. Diane also wished to escape from Pisano.'

'How strange that you should all want to leave the island. I'd be happy to spend the rest of my life here,' said Justine, half to herself. 'We have no proper home,' she explained. 'I've spent most of my life in tents or hotels. Staying at the villa is a wonderful experience for me.'

'But it is so out of date,' he objected. 'No electricity, no hot water from a tap, no television. And in winter, when there are storms, it is sometimes very cold here. My *appartement* in Paris is much more comfortable.'

Justine laughed. 'You're obviously a born sybarite, Julien. For me, the view from the terrace is worth a dozen television sets.'

'What does this word sybarite mean?' he asked perplexedly.

'It means someone who puts luxury and pleasure above everything,' she explained.

'Oh, I see.' He sat up and leaned towards her. He said, in French, 'It is the first time I have seen you laugh. You should laugh more often. It becomes you.'

For the second time, Justine felt a kind of tremor somewhere deep inside her. And this time she thought, *I don't care if he doesn't really mean it. He won't be here long, and when he goes I'll never see him again. What does it matter if it is only empty flattery? I like it. I like him. What harm can it do to let him flirt with me? It's probably the only chance*

60

I'll ever have.

Aloud, she said lightly, 'I can't laugh when there's nothing to laugh at.'

He sprang to his feet, shrugged on his robe, and held out his hands to pull her up. 'Then I must see that you have many things to laugh at. First, we will have breakfast together on the terrace. You can look at the view, and I will look at you. No, no, don't tie up your hair. I like it the way it is.'

Holding hands, they ran across the beach to the foot of the staircase and then, laughing and panting, up the steep winding flight to the terrace. About half a dozen steps from the top, Justine's energy gave out, and Julien put his arm round her waist and half carried her up the remaining steps.

'Oh, I've got such a stitch!' she gasped, leaning weakly against him, her cheeks glowing, her unbound hair wildly dishevelled.

He was out of breath too, but grinning from ear to ear. With his arm still round her, he lifted his free hand to smooth back her tumbled hair.

And it was then that they both sensed they were not alone. A few feet away from the opening in the balustrade, at a point from which he must have witnessed the whole childishly exuberant scramble up the staircase, stood Professor Field. With him was David Cassano.

CHAPTER TWO

FOR a long moment, nobody moved. They stood like figures in a tableau, the two young people facing the two older ones whose presence they had only just noticed.

Julien was the first to speak. Unaware that all the colour and animation had drained from Justine's face, he said cheerfully, 'Good morning. We have been swimming.'

'That is self-evident, young man,' the Professor observed acidly.

Even then Julien failed to realise that the atmosphere was charged with tension. Evidently he thought the tall, thin, grey-haired Englishman had addressed him in that tone because he had omitted to introduce himself.

'I beg your pardon, sir. I am Julien di Rostini,' he said, stepping forward to shake hands.

For one appalling instant, Justine thought her father was going to ignore the gesture. It might not be apparent to the others, but she could tell he was very angry—angrier than she had ever seen him.

He shook hands, then addressed his

daughter. 'We are waiting to begin breakfast, Justine. I trust it will not take you long to compose yourself?'

The bite in his voice made her flinch. 'I'm sorry, Father,' she said, in a low chagrined voice.

'Go to your room, then.'

'Yes, Father.' Not daring to look at the others, she hurried indoors.

It took her five minutes to put up her hair, and another five to nerve herself to go downstairs again. She could not remember her father ever speaking to her in so glacial a tone before, and her humiliation was intensified by the fact that David Cassano had been present, not only to see her reprimanded, but to witness the hoydenish conduct which had provoked her father's censure.

How could I have behaved in that silly vulgar way? she thought miserably, realising what she must have looked like with her hair all over the place, and her face scarlet with exertion. Most shaming of all was the recollection of how she had let Julien put his arm round her, had even hung on to him for support—a man she had met only yesterday.

The three men had already begun their breakfast when she joined them. Julien and David Cassano pushed back their chairs and

64

stood up as she approached the table. But her father ignored her arrival, and went on buttering a newly baked *croissant*.

'Thank you,' Justine murmured huskily, as Cassano drew out the fourth chair for her.

There were several tables on the terrace. The one which Sophia had spread with a clean gingham cloth was shaded by the dense foliage of an orange tree growing in a large white-painted tub known as a *caisson de Versailles*. There were half a dozen of these tubbed citrus trees on the terrace, and many smaller plant boxes containing camellias and azaleas.

'How do you like your coffee, Miss Field?' Cassano asked, when he had seated her.

'White, please,' she answered, without looking at him.

He filled a cup for her, and saw that everything she might want was within her reach. Then he resumed his conversation with her father.

Usually, Justine ate three or four of the warm, flaky crescent-shaped rolls, with butter and some of Sophia's delicious peach preserve. But this morning she ate only one roll, and that tasted like sawdust to her.

'An orange, Miss Field?' Cassano lifted the basket of freshly picked fruit from the centre of the table and offered it to her.

'No, thank you.' Still she could not bring herself to look at him.

'May I have your permission to smoke?'

'Of course, *m'sieur.*'

Warily, alert to look quickly away if he should turn his face towards her, she watched him light a thin dark-leafed cheroot with a more pungent smell than the richly fragrant Havana cigar he had smoked the night before.

He, she noticed, had not touched the *croissants*. His breakfast had consisted of a cup of black coffee and an orange.

Something nudged against her foot under the table. She realised Julien was trying to attract her attention. Unwillingly, she glanced at him, and received a conspiratorial wink.

Pretending not to have seen it, Justine said to no one in particular, 'Excuse me, please. I may as well go and get ready.'

It was a wretched morning. As she had feared, her father continued to ignore her, speaking only when it was essential to give her a curt instruction.

She had been a docile little girl and, on the rare occasions when she had committed some misdemeanour, he had shown his displeasure by appearing not to see or hear her. It was a

66

form of punishment which, in childhood, had frightened and distressed her far more than a conventional spanking, or an angry dressing-down.

But it was more than twelve years since she had last been subjected to this treatment, and now, as the long hot morning dragged by, her penitence became tinged with resentment, and a mounting sense of injustice.

Had her race up the steps with Julien really been so deplorable? Undignified—yes. But no worse. And surely the sarcastic rebuke delivered in front of David Cassano had been sufficient punishment? There was no need to treat her as if she had done something disgusting.

At noon, she discovered that, although she had brought their two vacuum flasks, she had forgotten to pack the napkin-wrapped package of bread, black *figatelli* sausage and hard-boiled eggs which Sophia provided for their lunch each day. The housekeeper had not been in the kitchen when Justine went to fetch the lunch pack and, in her upset state of mind, she must have put the flasks in the knapsack but overlooked the food.

When she told Professor Field about her oversight, he said coldly, 'You will have to fetch it then, won't you?'

67

Justine bit her lip. For a moment, she felt she hated him. It was the same sudden upsurge of emotion as that which she had experienced the day before, only this time it was directed, not at an arrogant stranger, but at her own father—the man who had loved and cared for her all her life, and to whom she owed everything.

'I'll be as quick as I can.' Turning away from the place where the Professor was working, she hurried towards the path leading back to the coastline.

Hot tears stung her eyelids and blurred her vision, making her stumble over stones and exposed roots. Her mind seethed with confusion and remorse.

The day was even hotter than yesterday. As she passed the grotesquely shaped wild olive tree where the track forked in different directions, she felt suddenly dizzy and a little sick. Feeling that she must rest for a few minutes, she slumped down on a convenient boulder and closed her eyes.

She was on the point of getting up, when she heard footsteps approaching from the other side of a dense thicket of *maquis*. She expected to see one of the village men, but it was David Cassano who presently came into view. He was carrying a basket in one hand,

and a plastic bucket in the other. The bucket contained a bottle of wine, packed round with chunks of ice. There was no refrigerator at the villa, or anywhere else on the island, so he must have obtained the ice from his yacht.

'Hello,' he said pleasantly. 'Are you on your way down to fetch your lunch? Sophia told me you'd forgotten it. I have it here. If you and your father have no objection, I'll have mine with you. I've brought some extra food along.'

Justine stood up. At that moment, it seemed to her that, in the past twenty-four hours, the whole placid orderly progress of her life had been abruptly jolted out of kilter—and that it all stemmed from the arrival of this man, and was caused by his disruptive influence.

'If you wish,' she said distantly. 'But we only take a short break for lunch'—and then the ground seemed to tilt under her feet, and she thought her final ignominy was going to be staggering behind a bush to be sick.

But she was not sick. And, after he had made her sit again and pushed her head down between her knees, the giddiness and faintness passed off. When she straightened and opened her eyes, David Cassano held a glass to her lips.

'Don't drink it. Sip it . . . slowly,' he ordered.

The wine in the glass was a light dry Hock, chilled but not icy, and wonderfully refreshing and steadying. After she had taken two or three sips, Justine felt sufficiently recovered to hold the glass for herself, and to say, 'Thank you. I don't know why I felt so groggy suddenly. I'm not usually affected by the heat.'

'Today is exceptionally hot, and you had very little for breakfast,' he reminded her, moving away to replace the tall taper necked amber bottle in its bed of ice.

'So did you,' she said.

'I haven't been working this morning.'

It was then she noticed he had changed the clothes he had been wearing earlier, the casual but unmistakably expensive dark grey linen shirt, with a silk scarf folded inside the collar, and the pale knife-creased slacks. Now, he was dressed in hard wearing *maquis*-proof drill, and a pair of the canvas boots called *pataugas*, the best of all footwear for rough walking in the wilder parts of the hinterland.

This workmanlike outfit so altered his appearance that, had he been wearing it the day before, Justine might well have mistaken him for an islander. Both the shirt and trousers were cheap, mass-produced ones, like those worn by the local fishermen. The shirt had shrunk in the wash, and was tight across his shoulders and chest, drawing attention to the power of his deltoid and pectoral muscles. Noticing this, Justine realised that, however rich and leisured he might be now, there must have been a period in his life when he had had to work with his hands. Only strenuous physical labour—such as hauling in nets—would develop those particular muscles to that degree.

Who is he? she wondered perplexedly, wishing she had thought to question Julien about him when they were down on the beach.

'You had better go back to the villa and rest for an hour,' he said. 'I will explain to your father.'

'Oh, no, I can't do that. Anyway, I'm all right now.'

'You may think you are, but you'll soon feel ill again if you don't take it easy for a while. It isn't wise to work during the hottest part of the day.'

'I've done it ever since we've been here, and I've never felt ill before.'

'Possibly not—but you aren't well today, and you need a rest,' he replied, as if that settled the matter.

71

His tone made Justine bristle. 'I'm not here on holiday, *m'sieur* I have work to do. My father needs me to help him.'

Cassano studied her for a moment. He was standing with his feet apart, and his hands on his narrow hips. The top two buttons of his shirt were undone, and, as he was no longer wearing a scarf, she could see that his throat and chest were as darkly tanned as his face. Somehow, in that attitude and the rough clothes, he looked even more intimidating than he had in the salon the night before.

He said, 'In that case he shouldn't upset you.'

She stiffened. 'What do you mean?'

'There are marks on your cheeks. You've been crying.'

'No, I haven't!' she flared indignantly. 'I—I got some grit in my eyes. I never cry.'

'Never?' he echoed sceptically. 'Then perhaps you should try it. It might release some of the tension.'

Her face flamed. 'I don't know what you're talking about,' she said, in a shaking voice. 'Just because I felt giddy for a minute—'

'Hot climates can be a strain on the toughest people, Miss Field,' he cut in mildly. 'You can't beat the heat—you have to adapt to it.

To rest in the middle of the day isn't weakness, it's common sense.'

'I don't want a rest,' she said mutinously. 'I've told you . . . I'm perfectly all right now.'

She saw his face harden. For an instant he looked so grim that she felt it would not be beyond him to force her to return to the villa. Involuntarily she took a step backwards.

Then he shrugged, and said impassively, 'Very well—but I think you may regret your obstinacy.' And he picked up the basket and the bucket, and strode past her.

He had gone only a little way, and she had begun to follow, when he stopped and turned to face her again. Justine stopped too.

'Tell me, Miss Field, how long is your work on Pisano likely to take?' he asked.

'I'm not sure . . . several months,' she answered uncertainly.

'In that case it would be diplomatic to disguise the antipathy which I seem to arouse in you,' he said dryly, and walked on.

Justine was still puzzling over this cryptic remark when they reached the site. When David Cassano stated his intention to join them for lunch, she expected her father to show as little enthusiasm for his company as she had done.

To her surprise, Professor Field said affably, 'By all means, my dear fellow . . . by all means.'

As well as providing wine, Cassano had supplemented the Fields' usual simple fare with smoked salmon sandwiches, cold roast legs of chicken, grapes and peaches, and three waxed cartons containing tiny, luscious wild strawberries. They were all packed in an insulated bag to protect them from the heat and dust.

'A Lucullan repast!' the Professor exclaimed appreciatively, as they sat on crates under the canvas awning which served as a pottery store. 'Grateful as we are for Madame di Rostini's extremely generous hospitality, I must confess to finding the local cuisine a trifle indigestible.'

'You must do me the honour of dining on board *Kalliste* one night, sir,' the younger man suggested.

To his daughter's dismay, Professor Field said cordially, 'We should be delighted.'

Justine took no part in the conversation during the meal. She could not understand why her father seemed to have taken a liking to the other man. The Professor was not usually forthcoming with strangers, and could be almost offensively brusque to anyone who attempted to engage him in trivial small-talk, or indeed upon any topic which was not related to his all-absorbing life's work.

David Cassano avoided this pitfall by mentioning the cave drawings on the island of Levanzo off Sicily, and asking if there might be similar drawings to be found in the caves of Pisano.

The Fields had not known that there were any caves on Pisano, and, although palaeolithic remains were outside the compass of the Professor's researches, he was interested in the suggestion and agreed it was a possibility deserving investigation.

As soon as they had finished eating, Cassano left them and disappeared over the ridge as he had done the day before.

'Interesting man ... unusually well informed,' the Professor murmured approvingly, watching him go.

'I don't like him,' Justine said abruptly.

Her father frowned at her. 'Indeed? For what reason, may I ask?'

Wishing she had not spoken, she said, 'I don't believe he's really interested in us . . . in our work. I think he's here for some purpose of his own. This morning, when you first met him, did he tell you anything about himself, Father?'

'He appears to be a friend of the family,' the Professor said shortly.

She shook her head. 'I don't think he is . . . I think this is the first time he has been here.'

'Then we must assume the connection is with that young sprig who seems to have made such a favourable impression on you,' her father answered acidly. And with that, he walked away and left her.

When they returned to the villa that evening, Justine learned from Sophia that the excitement of her adored grandson's homecoming had overtaxed Madame's frail strength, and she had not been well enough to get up.

'Monsieur Julien has been with her all day. He is a good boy, that one. Not every young man would exert himself to amuse an old lady,' the housekeeper said fondly. 'He is to have supper with her, and afterwards I will give her a sleeping draught and perhaps tomorrow she will feel stronger.'

'And Monsieur Cassano?' Justine asked.

'He is dining on board his yacht tonight,' Sophia told her. 'No doubt Monsieur Julien will join him later. They do not keep such early hours as we do.'

So Justine and her father had their evening meal alone together, as they had done every night before the arrival yesterday of the sleek white yacht. The only difference was that tonight, instead of discussing the results of their day's work, they ate in a strained silence. As soon as he had drunk his coffee, the Professor retired to his room to work on his notes.

This prolonged estrangement between them made Justine deeply unhappy, but somehow she could not bring herself to go after him and try to heal the breach.

Presently, she poured herself some more coffee and took it across to the balustrade. Resting her forearms on the warm stone, she looked down at the *Kalliste* lying at anchor in the bay below the headland.

She knew that *Kalliste* was the name given to Corsica by the ancient Greeks. It meant "the most beautiful", and it seemed to her typical of Cassano that he should adopt the title for his yacht. Yet, grudgingly, she had to admit that, in the fiery glow of the sunset, the vessel was a lovely sight, the sweeping lines of her hull reflected in the glassy emerald sea, her three tall tapering masts outlined against the damask sky.

How many crew did she carry? Justine wondered. At the moment, she appeared to be deserted—*as idle as a painted ship upon a painted ocean.*

'She is beautiful—yes? I wish she belonged to me,' Julien said enviously, from behind her.

. 'Oh, you startled me!' Justine exclaimed, turning to face him.

'I am sorry,' he apologised, smiling. Then, leaning against the parapet beside her, he looked down at the yacht again. 'But I shall never have the *richesse* to possess a boat like *Kalliste*,' he went on, with a rueful shrug. 'It is for me a dream only. And you, Justine? You also dream of a voyage to far places? *Taiti . . . les iles sous le vent . . . les Lucayes?*'

Justine shook her head. 'I doubt if any of those places are more beautiful than Pisano, and they are probably overrun with tourists.'

He gave her a curious glance. 'You do not like people? You prefer always to be alone?'

'I don't like crowds, and noise, and hideous modern hotels which ruin lovely views,' she replied.

Julien grinned. 'You must tell this to David,' he said, with a gleam of mischief. 'As you know, it is from hotels that he has made much of his fortune.'

'Oh, really?' she said, without expression. 'I wondered what his business was.'

Julien lifted an eyebrow. 'You are saying you have not heard of him? His reputation is unknown to you?'

'I can't remember hearing of him. Should I have done?' she asked casually.

He clapped a palm to his forehead. 'But this is *incroyable*! I think perhaps you are joking with me. In a moment, you tell me you know nothing of Stavros Niarchos.'

She considered the name for a moment. 'Yes, I have heard of him,' she conceded. 'He owns a very fine collection of paintings. I remember reading about them. But what has he to do with Monsieur Cassano?'

'David is also a very rich man—not only from hotels, you understand, but also from many other enterprises,' Julien explained. 'I am astonished you have not heard of him. Everyone knows the name Cassano.'

Justine said drily, 'Well, I'm afraid I'm not as impressed by money as you seem to be. And I know as little about big business as I imagine you do about the Romans.'

He said, on a puzzled note, 'You do not admire a man who is born with nothing and who becomes a great financier?'

'Was he born with nothing?' she asked sceptically.

'You don't believe me? It is true, I assure you. His father was like the men of our village—a fisherman.'

'Where? Not here on Pisano?'

'No, no—on the mainland at Propriano.'

'So he is a Corsican,' she murmured, half to herself. 'I wonder why they christened him David? I thought perhaps—'

'Ah, that was his mother's wish,' Julien cut in. 'She was a foreigner, and it is from her family that he inherits his gift for making money. I did not know of this until Grand'mère told me today. It happened many years ago, and such things were forgotten when the war came. But at the time it was a great sensation, and all Corsica talked of it.'

'Talked of what? I don't understand?' said Justine.

'David's mother was English,' Julien explained. 'She was of a very distinguished family. There was a young brother who was an invalid. He had a weakness here'—he thumped his chest—'which made the English climate dangerous for him. The doctors said he must live in the sun, or he would die. So the family engaged a house not far from Ajaccio and, with his sister and an older person, he came to Corsica. Grand'mère does not know how the sister met Guido Cassano—but it happened, and they fell in love. Naturally, when this was discovered, her father was very angry and ordered her to return to England immediately. But she refused to obey and, when she married Guido, they would not forgive her. They had—how do you say it?—nothing more to say to her.'

'What happened then? Was she happy with Guido?'

Julien shrugged. 'The marriage lasted only three years. There were two children, a boy and a girl. Then Guido was drowned in a storm.'

'Surely her people forgave her then . . . a widow with two babies to support?'

'No, she never saw them again. She stayed in Corsica all her life, and her husband's family helped her to feed the children,' said Julien. 'But it must have been very hard for her.'

'How incredibly cruel . . . to cut her off like that, I mean,' Justine commented indignantly. 'I can see why her family didn't approve of the marriage, but for them to completely turn their backs on her is the most heartless thing I've ever heard. When did she die, poor thing? From what you say, I gather she is dead now.'

'Yes, she died a few years after the war.'

'And the sister? Where is she?'

'That I do not know,' said Julien. 'This is a matter which David had never discussed with me, you understand. Until Grand'mère told me of it, I knew only of his connection with my father. And even that I did not know until he came to my assistance at the casino.'

After this last remark, he flushed and looked rather uncomfortable, as if he had made a *gaffe*.

Then, apparently deciding that, having gone so far, he might as well tell all, he gave her a sheepish grin, and said, 'We met at the tables in Cannes. Grand'mère does not know this, and I beg you will not mention it to her. It would distress her very much. She does not approve of gambling. It was foolish of me to play—this I admit. But, at first, my luck was good, and I thought I might win enough to buy a new car. Then, unhappily, the luck changed, and soon I had lost every-thing—even the money to pay my hotel bill.

'Fortunately, David was also at the tables that night. He recognised my likeness to my father, and asked my name. When he heard of my situation, he lent me the money for my bill, and asked me to be his guest on *Kalliste*. We stayed at Cannes for two weeks—he had some business there—and then he said he would like to visit Pisano and meet Grand'mère.'

'You mean you've only known him for a

fortnight?' Justine asked, taken aback. She could not have explained the feeling, but the discovery that Julien's acquaintance with Cassano was so recent filled her with profound disquiet.

'Yes—and now I am hoping that perhaps he will offer me a place in his organisation,' the young man confided.

'I see. What exactly was his connection with your father?' she asked.

'They were together in the Resistance movement during the war.'

'Oh, but surely they can't have been, Julien,' she objected. 'The war ended twenty years ago. Unless Monsieur Cassano is very much older than he looks, he would have been only a schoolboy then.'

'David is thirty-six. In 1943, the year my father was killed, he was fourteen—old enough to live in hiding in the *maquis*, and to carry messages between the villages,' he assured her.

Justine was silent for some moments. She knew that, of all the European underground movements in operation during the war years, none had been more vigorous or more effective than the one in Corsica. Yet she found it hard to credit that half-grown boys of fourteen had been actively engaged in the

Resistance.

She said, 'How do you know this, Julien? Who told you? Monsieur Cassano . . . or your grandmother.'

'David told me. It is the reason he helped me at Cannes. My father was good to him, and he feels an obligation to our family.'

'And does your grandmother confirm his story?'

Julien looked puzzled. 'Grand'mère was not in the Resistance. She was here on Pisano. The last time she heard from my father was more than one year before his death. He would not have mentioned his *confrères*. I do not understand why you ask this question.'

Justine realised that she was treading on thin ice. She said carefully, 'Last night, after dinner, your grandmother told Monsieur Cassano it was a privilege to have him here. I just wondered what she meant, that's all.'

'But certainly it is a privilege. He is a remarkable man. You don't feel there is something special about him?'

Justine had never learnt to dissemble. She said candidly, 'Perhaps . . . but I like you better.'

Julien watched her finish her coffee. He recognised that there had been no trace of coquetry in her answer, and her honesty amused and intrigued him. In any other circumstances, he would not have interested himself in her. But, as it was impossible to engage in casual relationships with any of the local girls without incurring the wrath of their fathers, this strangely naïve *femme savante* was the only female on the island to whom he could safely give his attention. He had not been lying when he had told her she had a lovely skin, and her figure too, although camouflaged by the ill-fitting khaki shirt and slacks, was not bad—not bad at all! Her trouble was that she didn't know how to arrange herself.

He said, 'There is a *dancing* in the village tonight. Would you like to go?'

Until that moment, she had forgotten her resolve to avoid him as much as possible. But now, remembering the mortifying confrontation with her father before breakfast, she said hurriedly, 'Oh, no, I can't. Thank you—but I can't.'

Julien, seeing the sudden change in her manner, was reminded of a plant—he did not know its name—which, at the slightest touch, instantly folded its leaves and appeared to wilt.

'Why not?' he asked. 'I think you would find it amusing.'

'No, really . . . it's very kind of you, but I would rather not. I—I have some work to do.'

Julien was not used to having his invitations turned down. He felt sure she did not mean her refusal. 'But you have been working all day,' he persisted. 'Now it is time to play a little. Please come, Justine.'

She shook her head. 'I don't know how to dance. I've never learnt.'

'It is not difficult. I will teach you. These village *dancings* are very informal. You have only to put on a skirt. Nothing more is required.'

'What about Monsieur Cassano? Isn't he expecting you to join him on the yacht?'

Julien thought she was weakening. He said, 'David is *affairé* tonight. The yacht has a telephone and each evening he receives reports from his agents in Paris and Marseilles.'

'Where is his home?' she asked. 'Or has he several houses?'

'The *Kalliste* is his home,' said Julien. 'Always he likes to be near the sea. But we have talked enough of David. I want to talk about you.'

Again Justine shook her head. 'I'm sorry, I must go in now. Goodnight, Julien.' And, before he could press her further, she gave him an apologetic smile, and went quickly indoors.

In her room, she undressed and put on her cotton kimono. Then she let down her hair, and went to the window to open the shutters. She had been standing there for some minutes, thoughtfully brushing her hair, when she saw Julien rowing out to the yacht. An involuntary sigh escaped her. It would have been fun to go to the *dancing* with him. She was less naïve than he imagined. She knew why he was being nice to her. But any kind of friendship was better than none.

A great wave of loneliness swept over her and, feeling she could not bear to spend the hours till bedtime alone in the quiet room, she tied her hair back with a ribbon, and went along the corridor to her father's room in another part of the house.

Professor Field responded to her knock, but he did not look up from his writing as she opened and closed the door, and approached the table where he was working.

'Father . . . I—' She stopped short, twisting an end of her sash between nervous fingers, uncertain how to express what she wanted to say. *Please don't be angry any more* sounded so childish.

At last Richard Field laid down his pen,

and looked at her.

'Well?—What is it?' he asked impatiently.

Justine stared at him, shocked. His face had a queer greyish tinge, and there was a film of moisture on his forehead and upper lip.

Instinctively, she took a step closer. 'Are you all right? You don't look well.'

'I am perfectly well, thank you,' he replied repressively.

'Oh, Father, I can *see* you aren't!' she exclaimed, in loving concern. For the sight of his drawn face had instantly dispelled her own troubles. 'You should have gone to see a doctor yesterday.'

'I believe I am the best judge of that. What is it you wished to speak to me about?'

'Nothing important. Father, why don't you go to bed? It's absurd to try to work when you're ill.'

'*I am not ill,*' the Professor said very distinctly, in a tone of intense irritation.

But no sooner had he spoken than his breath hissed between his teeth, and he pressed both hands against his stomach, in unmistakable pain.

Justine flew round the table and dropped on her knees beside him, her grey eyes wide and frightened. As the spasm passed, and his body relaxed, she said, 'This is more than indigestion, Father. I think it's appendicitis. We must get you to Ajaccio at once. Julien has taken the rowing boat, but I can easily swim out to the yacht and get them to help us. Now you *must* lie down on the bed. I'll get you a hot water bottle, if they have one here. The warmth will relieve the pain a bit.'

Her father's colour was even worse now, and his whole face was beaded with sweat. With a visible effort he forced himself to sit up straight, and to speak with his usual authority.

'Nonsense!' he said abruptly. 'I had my appendix removed thirty years ago. This is merely a rather severe attack of colic. Please return to your room, and leave me in peace. I dislike being fussed over—particularly when it is quite unnecessary.'

'Oh, Father, how can you be so stubborn! You're ill. You're as white as a sheet. You must see a doctor—you must!'

'You're being hysterical, Justine. If I continue to feel unwell, I shall certainly take medical advice. But I have no intention of allowing you to make a ridiculous melodrama out of what is very likely nothing more than a temporary digestive disorder. You may fetch me a glass of water and the bottle of tablets by the carafe.'

Justine did as he bade her, and watched him swallow two of the small white pills which probably contained a few grains of magnesium hydroxide.

'Goodnight,' he said coldly, dismissing her.

For a moment she hesitated, torn between the ingrained habit of obedience and the conviction that whatever was the matter with him was something much more serious than colic. Then, with a subdued 'Goodnight,' she turned and left the room.

But she did not go back to her own bedroom. Instead, she went down to the kitchen to find Sophia.

The housekeeper saw at once that she was distraite. She said kindly, 'You look tired, *mademoiselle*. I think perhaps you work too hard. I will make a *tisane* for you. No, no—it is no trouble. I also will take some. It is good for the liver. Please . . . sit down. The water is already hot, and the infusion takes only a few minutes.'

Justine had not come downstairs with the conscious intention of confiding in Sophia. But, as they sat at the long scrubbed deal table and sipped the aromatic lime-blossom tea, the need to share her anxiety overcame her usual reserve.

The old woman listened in silence while Justine unburdened herself. 'Yes, I have noticed that your papa does not seem in such good health as when he arrived here,' she said, at length. 'But surely such a learned man would not be so foolish as to neglect a serious disorder?'

'I don't know,' Justine said distractedly. 'I don't know what to think.'

'Perhaps you should ask Monsieur Cassano to speak to him,' the housekeeper suggested. 'Men do not listen to women as they do to another man.'

'Oh, no, I couldn't do that,' Justine said, taken aback. 'He's the last person . . . I mean we hardly know him. My father would be furious.' And he would be equally annoyed if he knew she was discussing him with Sophia, she realised guiltily.

'It is better for him to be angry than for you to be anxious,' the housekeeper pointed out wisely. 'It is not good to have worries.'

Justine braced her shoulders and mustered a more cheerful expression. 'I'll see how he is in the morning. Perhaps, if he still isn't well, he'll change his mind about seeing a doctor. Thank you for the *tisane*, Sophia. Good-night.'

Next morning, Justine woke up too late to

have time for her usual bathe before breakfast. After she had washed and dressed, she
went along to her father's room, and tapped
on the door. When there was no reply, and no
sound of movement from within, she supposed he must already have gone downstairs.
But something made her open the door and
look in.

Professor Field was still in bed. He was
lying on his side, with his back to her, only the
top of his grizzled head showing above the
bedclothes.

She tiptoed across to the far side of the bed,
and looked down at his unconscious face. She
had never known him to oversleep, and he
was lying so very still that, for one terrifying
moment, she thought he was dead.

When he stirred and made a slight sound,
her relief was so great that she could not help
crouching down and pressing her cheek
against the back of his hand where it lay on
the edge of the bed. It was a gesture she would
not have dared to make had he been awake.
He disapproved of sentimentality, and she felt
it was a weakness in her character that she
had often longed for a more demonstrative relationship with him.

Judging by the rumpled state of the bedclothes, he had passed a restless night before

falling into his present deep sleep. She decided not to wake him, and went downstairs, hoping to finish her breakfast before either Julien or David Cassano put in an appearance.

But Julien was already at the table under the orange tree when she walked out on to the terrace. He was wearing his Turkish beach robe, and his curly dark hair glistened wetly in the morning sun.

'Good morning,' he said with a smile, rising to pull out a chair for her. 'You do not swim today?'

'Good morning. No, not today.'

'Sophia tells me the Professor is not well. Does this mean you will not work today?'

'I don't know. Father isn't up yet.'

'If you do not work, perhaps you would like to come with me to Ajaccio?' Julien suggested. 'I am to meet Diane at the airport. The plane from Nice arrives late in the afternoon, but we could go early and have lunch at *U Fucone*. David has said I may take his motorboat.'

'I didn't know your sister was coming home,' Justine said, in surprise.

'It was arranged last night when I spoke to her on the telephone from the yacht,' he explained. 'You will come with me to meet her?'

93

She shook her head. 'I can't, Julien. Even if Father doesn't work today, he'll want me to get on.'

'But you would enjoy it,' he argued. 'It is amusing to sit in the cafés and watch the people.'

'Yes, I'm sure it is—but I'm afraid I can't spare the time.'

He saw that she was not to be persuaded, and gave a resigned shrug. 'I do not understand this passion for work,' he said wryly. 'One sees that the past is very interesting. But, for me, the present also is exciting. Life is short. Who can say what is in the future? There may be no future for us.'

'People have been saying that for two thousand years,' Justine pointed out. 'The world is still turning.'

Nevertheless, his words stayed in her mind for some time after he had finished his breakfast and gone indoors to see his grandmother.

Presently, she went upstairs to make her bed and tidy her room. She was polishing her sandals when she heard footsteps in the corridor and was surprised to see her father appear in the open doorway.

'I thought you were still asleep. How are you feeling?' she asked.

'I'm quite fit again, thank you. You should

have woken me. We can't afford to waste any time,' the Professor said briskly. 'I take it you've had your breakfast. It won't take me long to have mine. We'll leave in fifteen minutes. Don't forget our lunch today, my dear.'

It was so unusual for him to use an endearment that Justine knew at once he was sorry he had spoken so harshly the night before. It was such a relief to be on good terms with him again that she dared not risk rekindling his annoyance by suggesting that he should spend the morning resting. But surprisingly, considering how ill he had looked a few hours ago, he now showed no sign of being unwell.

It was a happy day, and an eventful one. For, during the afternoon, Richard Field shouted to his daughter to come to the place where he was working. The cause of his excitement was the discovery of a fragment of a wall painting. There was now strong evidence that the building they were laboriously unearthing might prove to be an extremely fine *villa urbana* or Roman country house.

They stayed on the site later than usual, and it was not until they were half way down the cliff path that Justine remembered the arrival of Julien's sister.

When she mentioned it to her father, he

said without interest, 'Oh, really?' and continued to speculate about the ownership of the ruins up on the hillside.

Julien was with Madame and David Cassano when Justine and her father entered the salon together before dinner that night. But Diane had not yet come down. When she did make her entrance, about ten minutes later, Justine thought that, even in London, she had never seen anyone so awesomely beautiful and elegant.

Like a number of Corsicans, Diane St. Aubin had blue eyes. In her stockinged feet, she would have been an inch or two shorter than Justine. But she was wearing high heels and so, as the two girls shook hands, her wonderful long-lashed eyes were on a level with Justine's admiring grey ones.

There was no admiration in Professor Field's scrutiny of the young widow. He saw at once that she epitomised all the vanities he abhorred, and which he had striven to eradicate in his daughter.

Justine did not notice her father's reaction to the newcomer. She was too busy taking in the expensive simplicity of Diane's sleeveless aquamarine silk dress, and the matching hand-made shoes on her pretty narrow feet. But she did see David Cassano's expression in the moment before he bowed over the other girl's hand.

All through dinner, Justine found it hard not to stare at the lovely vital Corsican on the other side of the table. Diane had more than looks in her armoury. She was intelligent and amusing as well. But what really won Justine's heart was that never once did she glance at the shy English girl with the subtle complacency of an exquisitely dressed beauty outshining a dowdy plain Jane. The attention she gave to the two foreigners was as warm and interested as her manner towards David Cassano. Indeed it seemed to Justine that Diane was not very taken with Julien's friend. No doubt, being well off herself—a marquise diamond blazed on her left hand, and she wore a diamond and aquamarine pin on the shoulder of her dress—she was not so impressed by Cassano's affluence as her younger brother seemed to be.

After dinner, as they were returning to the salon, she said to Justine, 'I have some journals in my room . . . *Elle* and *Vogue* and some others. Would you like to look at them?'

Rather startled, Justine said, 'Yes . . . thank you, madame.'

'No, no, not "madame,"' Diane said smilingly. 'May we not be informal? Julien tells me your name is Justine.'

They sat down on the *chaise-longue*, and she went on, 'All the journals speak of Courrèges, but for me Givenchy is the greatest *couturier* since Dior. Do you agree?'

Justine had heard of Dior, but the other names meant nothing to her. The only time she ever saw a fashion magazine was when, in London, she went for a dental check.

She was about to admit her ignorance, when David Cassano said, 'I imagine Miss Field knows more about Roman emperors than French dressmakers.'

His tone held such open mockery that her cheeks burned, and the words she had been about to say shrivelled into mute discomfiture.

It was Diane who answered him. She said pleasantly, 'All women are interested in fashion.' Then, turning to Justine again, 'In England you are so fortunate. You have these charming clothes "off the peg," as you say. I have a friend in Nice whose husband has business in London, and she buys many things there.'

Even if Justine had not already warmed to her, she would have done so then. For although Diane's remarks could hardly be construed as a snub to Cassano, they did confirm that she was not particularly interested in him.

As, judging by the look he had given her when they were introduced, Cassano was extremely interested in the beautiful Madame St. Aubin, Diane's indifference to him afforded Justine considerable satisfaction. It would do him good to be set down, she thought. If someone could puncture his assurance, he might not be so ready to deflate other people.

Julien came over, bringing the two girls their coffee. Smiling down at Justine, he said, 'I missed you today. We would have enjoyed ourselves. Are you sorry now you did not come?'

She felt her colour rising again. 'I'm not on holiday like you are.'

As soon as he had drunk his coffee, her father, who had been talking to Madame di Rostini, asked his hostess's leave to retire.

'Justine!' he said imperatively.

She rose at once, and said goodnight to the others. But, as she followed him from the room, she could not help feeling a prick of resentment at being spoken to in that way— as if she were still a child. He could have said, "Are you coming up, Justine?" The fact that she was glad to get away was not to the point.

It was humiliating to be given no choice.

She wondered what would have happened if she had had the courage to tell him she did not wish to go to bed yet.

Twenty minutes later, she slipped downstairs to have the bathe she had missed that morning. As she tiptoed across the terrace, keeping out of the light from the salon, she saw that Madame was still up. She was in conversation with David Cassano, and Julien had joined his sister on the couch.

By the time she came back from her swim, the salon was in darkness. Justine plucked an orange from one of the trees, and took it upstairs with her. Tired now, she ate the sweet juicy fruit, climbed into bed, and was soon asleep.

*   *   *

In her bedroom, in another part of the house, Diane St. Aubin was pinning up her glossy black hair, and talking to her brother who was sprawled in a chair by the dressing-table.

When he had telephoned at her aged mother-in-law's house in Nice the previous evening, Julien had said he could not explain the matter fully until he saw her, but it was imperative that she should come to Pisano immediately.

At first, when he had disclosed the reason for this urgent summons during the sea crossing to the island, Diane had said crossly that he had brought her on a fool's errand. But, after some argument, he had succeeded in persuading her that his proposition was not as hopeless as it might seem at first thought.

'Well?—What do you say?' he asked her now. 'Can we bring it off? Will the old girl see reason, d'you think?'

Diane shrugged. 'Perhaps . . . but it won't be easy. She's an obstinate old dragon. You may be able to talk her round. You're her pet. She doesn't approve of me. I'm not sure it was a wise move to bring me here. Grand'mère is no fool. She knows I wouldn't come from choice. I detest the wretched place. If she suspects we are up to something, it will make her even more difficult to deal with.'

She finished attending to her hair, and put on a frilly boudoir cap to hide the rollers and clips. 'I hate sleeping like this,' she said petulantly. 'What a nuisance it is to be so far from a hairdresser.'

Julien helped himself to a cigarette from the cylindrical gold case which lay on the table at his elbow. Both the case and the lighter beside it bore the initial "D" in emerald chips.

'These must have cost you a packet!' he remarked with a covetous expression.

'I don't like cheap things,' she said carelessly.

'Neither do I. But you're lucky—you can indulge your expensive tastes.'

Diane had begun to cream her delicate hands. She gave him a sparkling glance, and said coldly, 'Luck had nothing to do with it. I earned every sou.'

Julien grinned. 'I agree that Mathieu wasn't much to look at, but you didn't have to put up with him for long, did you?'

'He was a pig!' she retorted fiercely. 'A gross disgusting pig. You do not know what I endured. You cannot imagine it. And even now I am not free. I'm saddled with his querulous old mother, and if I choose to marry again I shall lose all the money to his nephew.'

'If what we plan is successful, it will not matter,' he reminded her. 'We shall both have plenty of money.'

'*If* it is successful,' she responded. 'To be frank, when you telephoned I thought you were going to tell me Grand'mère was dead. If she were, we would have no problems,' she added unemotionally.

Julien looked shocked. 'How can you be so callous?' he exclaimed. 'Surely you must have some affection for her? Myself, I hope she will live for many years yet.'

'If I were her age, and had her heart condition, I would not want to go on living,' his sister replied. 'What is the point of it? What is there left in life for her?'

'What a cold-blooded creature you are!' he said, frowning at her. 'I don't believe you have an ounce of feeling for anyone but yourself.'

'But you, of course, are a paragon of all the virtues,' Diane answered tartly.

He flushed slightly. 'I'm no saint—I admit it. But I wouldn't wish someone dead—not for a million!'

Diane rested her elbows on the dressing-table and contemplated her reflection in the mirror. Even with her make-up removed, and a sheen of night-cream on her skin, she was beautiful.

'Why should I care for anyone?' she said, on a bitter note. 'No one has ever cared for me. Juliette ran off and left us. Grand'mère doesn't like me because I have Juliette's looks. Sophia was never kind to me as she was to you. I was always being punished, and told I would go to Hell. Mathieu was so jealous, he set the servants to spy on me. Who has ever loved or been kind to me?'

'Andria loved you,' Julien reminded her.

Her eyebrows lifted. 'Andria?' she repeated interrogatively. Then she threw her head back and laughed. 'Oh, yes . . . poor besotted Andria. I'd forgotten him. Surely you don't suggest I should have married a fisherman? That would have been considered even more disgraceful than my marriage to Mathieu.'

'Perhaps, but you might have been happier,' said her brother.

'What?—living in a hovel in the village, and eating bean soup every day? You must be out of your mind.'

'Maria seems to like it.'

'Maria? Who is Maria?'

'Maria Angeletto . . . old Tomaso's eldest daughter. She's Maria Sebastiani now. Andria married her six months ago. It won't be long before she presents him with a son and heir.'

'Oh, really?' Diane said off-handedly. 'Well, I can't say I'm very much interested in village doings. I have more important things to think about. Go away, Julien. I'm tired, and I want to go to bed now.'

But, after he had said goodnight and left her, she went to the window and stood gazing out into the night, the slight breeze stirring the ruffles on her negligée.

It was not true that she had forgotten Andria Sebastiani. It was several years since she had seen him, and no doubt he had changed a good deal and would no longer attract her now. But as a boy, in his middle teens, he had been as handsome as a young god and, like every other girl on the island, Diane had fallen in love with him. Julien knew about her relationship with Andria because one night he had caught her creeping out of the villa to meet the young fisherman. She had been nineteen that year, and Andria twenty. Nearly every night for several months they had met by moonlight up on the clifftop.

What Julien did not know was that if, then, Andria had asked her to marry him, Diane would have said "yes" eagerly. But he had not asked her, and when, sacrificing all pride, she had taken the initiative herself, he had told her it could never be. No matter how passionately they wanted each other, the difference in their backgrounds made marriage an impossibility.

Diane had tried every way she knew to make him change his mind. She had coaxed him. She had stormed at him. She had even threatened to go to her grandmother and accuse him of seducing her so that he would be forced into marrying her. But, as Andria had pointed out, she was not one of the village girls and it was much more likely that, if she did try such a trick, Madame would prefer to send her away in disgrace rather than permit a mésalliance.

In the end, after the final and most bitter of all their quarrels, it was he who had left Pisano. He had gone to Marseilles to work in the docks as a stevedore, and by the time he returned to the island Diane was married to a man old enough to be her father.

And now Andria is married to the plainest girl in the village; the girl who, so everyone said, would never get a husband at all, Diane thought, with a grimace. *I wonder why he picked her? Is it possible that he still cares? Well, what if he does? It makes no difference. It's too late now . . . years too late. And he was right—it would never have worked. I would have tired of him in six months.*

Nevertheless, remembering Andria as he had been that long-ago summer, she could not help feeling a faint pang of regret for what might have been. To dispel the mood, she turned away from the window and began pacing the room, concentrating her mind on the problem of how Julien might best approach their grandmother with the project which had caused him to send for her. Her brother had little finesse. Left to himself, he would probably blurt it out in a way which would antagonise Madame di Rostini from the outset.

Presently, she returned to the window to look down at the yacht in the bay. From the little Julien had told her about the owner of the *Kalliste*, she had been prepared to meet someone of much the same stamp as her late husband. It had been an agreeable surprise to discover that David Cassano was personable as well as rich.

Her coolness towards him had been deliberate. She knew that, if a man was attractive to women and was aware of it—as Cassano obviously was—nothing tantalised him more than feminine indifference.

After she had climbed into bed, Diane took two sleeping pills, and turned down the wick of the oil lamp on the bedside table. Then she lay back on the thyme-scented pillows and watched the moonlight slanting through the window. Just before the pills took effect, it occurred to her that, if Julien's scheme failed, there might be another way for her to use the visit to Pisano to her advantage.

*　　　*　　　*

The following evening, everyone at the villa, including Madame di Rostini, dined on board the *Kalliste*. Justine was surprised when she learned Madame was to accompany them, for she had assumed that the old lady would not be able to manage the crossing to the yacht. However, David Cassano had arranged for a brawny member of his crew to carry Madame down the steep flight of steps to the jetty below the villa, and there to put her into the cushioned rear seat of the motor boat. The three women were ferried to the yacht first, leaving Julien and the Professor to be fetched a few minutes later.

The dinner party took place on the main deck, which was sheltered by a blue and white canopy, and furnished with bamboo chairs and couches with buttoned blue linen squabs. An oval table with a glass top was laid with exquisite Madeira lace mats, fine china and silver, and long-stemmed cut crystal goblets. The centrepiece was a Meissen bowl filled with dark crimson carnations which must have come from Ajaccio, or perhaps from Nice.

The meal was served by three white-jacketed stewards. In reply to a question from the Professor, their host said that *Kalliste* carried a complement of twenty.

'Most of whom are related to me by blood or marriage,' he added. 'Guido is my sister's youngest brother-in-law'—this with a gesture indicating the steward who was filling Diane's wineglass.

Hearing his name, the youth, who was about sixteen, looked swiftly to the head of the table. Evidently he did not understand English, as Cassano repeated in French what he had said about him.

The lad beamed, and gave a slight bow. Justine had the impression that he was very proud of the relationship.

She found it puzzling that Cassano should surround himself with family connections, for he did not strike her as a man who would be swayed by sentiment. Perhaps the answer was that it was cheaper for him to employ his in-laws.

After dinner, he took Madame and Professor Field to see some paintings in the main saloon. Diane went with them but, when Justine would have followed, Julien caught her wrist and detained her.

'I wish to talk to you,' he said, tucking her hand through his arm, and leading her towards the starboard rails.

'What about?' she asked, with an uneasy glance over her shoulder. But the others had already disappeared down a stairway leading below decks.

'About you,' he said, smiling.

She tried to free her hand, but he pressed his arm against his side, and would not let her go.

'Why are you afraid to be alone with me?' he asked, amused.

'I'm not . . . don't be silly. It's just that I want to see the pictures.'

'You can see them later. There's no hurry. Why don't you like us to be alone? You think I will make love to you, perhaps?'

'Of course not!' she protested, trying to laugh in an unconcerned way.

'Why do you laugh?' he asked seriously. 'You don't enjoy to be kissed? I am not attractive to you? You are very attractive to me, *chérie.*'

She began to think he must have had too much wine at dinner.

'We scarcely know each other, Julien,' she said, managing to free her hand, and moving a little distance away from him.

This proved to be a tactical error, for he promptly followed and put his arm round her waist.

'It is not important how long one knows a person. I have wanted to kiss you from the moment I saw you,' he said softly.

Justine didn't know what to do. She had no experience of situations like this.

'I think now you're laughing,' she murmured, in helpless confusion. 'Look, doesn't the villa look lovely from here? It makes me wish I could paint. I wonder if I could? I'm not bad at drawing. I do all the drawings for our excavation reports.'

'It is you who should be painted,' he answered, his lips very close to her cheek. And then, in French, 'You are like a flower which has not yet blossomed . . . a white rosebud waiting to bloom.'

In her secret dreams, Justine had often imagined that some day, somewhere, she would meet someone who would say sweet, tender things to her. But never, in her wildest fantasies, had she dreamed of being called a white rosebud. The smile struck her as so singularly inappropriate that, instead of being overwhelmed, she had a strong urge to burst out laughing. She did not do so, for she had had her own feelings bruised too often to wittingly hurt anyone else's. And, before she could think of any reply, someone else

111

damped Julien's ardour.

'Won't you join us in the saloon, Miss Field?' said David Cassano, from behind them.

Both Justine and Julien jumped, and turned quickly round. From where he stood, about a dozen paces away, it seemed unlikely that their host had overheard Julien's words. But he had seen his arm round Justine's waist and that, alone, made her blush a mortified scarlet.

'W-we're just coming,' she stammered.

Except for its silk-curtained portholes and rather low ceiling, the main saloon might have been a drawing-room in a luxurious house in Paris, London or New York. The walls were panelled with silver-grey wood, the fitted carpet was also a silvery colour, and the chairs and sofas were covered with lustrous Thai silk in two subtle shades of green. But even if *Kalliste* had been cruising in grey northern waters, this décor would not have seemed cold or too subdued. For it had been chosen as a foil for the rich colours in the paintings on the walls. There were five of them. An unmistakable Gauguin, a Van Gogh, a Rouault, and two others which Justine did not recognise.

'Ah, there you are, Justine,' said her father,

in a tone of tacit reproof, and with a steely glance at Julien.

'Miss Field has been admiring the view of the villa from here,' David Cassano explained sardonically.

Justine bit her lip, and was grateful when Diane distracted their attention by asking a question about one of the pictures.

Some time later, the older girl took Justine with her when she went to powder her nose. A steward showed them the way to a guest cabin with an adjoining bathroom.

Justine had never seen such a bathroom. It was all mirror-glass and mosaic, with gold-plated swan taps, and Baccarat *flaçons* containing oils and coloured bath crystals.

In the bedroom, decorated in lilac, Diane settled herself at the dressing-table and repainted her mouth with a fine sable brush. Catching Justine's fascinated eyes on her, she said, 'You never use cosmetics?'

The younger girl shook her head. 'I don't think they would suit me. I—I'm not beautiful like you are,' she added impulsively.

Diane smiled. 'Thank you.'

Usually she had no time for other women. If they could not compete with her in looks, they were jealous and resentful. This ingenuous admiration amused and pleased her. Up to a point, she felt sorry for the English girl. Yet, at the same time, she thought Justine's obvious unhappiness was largely of her own making. If she would not assert herself, she must expect to be downtrodden. Had Diane been in her shoes, she would soon have put that desiccated old despot in his place.

Aloud, she said, 'A touch of lipstick improves everyone. Why don't you try it? Come, I will show you how it is done.' And she shifted her place on the dressing-stool, and beckoned the younger girl to sit beside her.

Hesitantly, Justine did so. Diane took her chin in one of her cool soft hands, and carefully outlined her lips.

'There . . . you see? At once you are changed,' she said, leaning back to survey the effect of her work.

Justine turned her face to the looking-glass, and was astonished to see how the vivid colour on her mouth altered her appearance. Her lips looked softer and fuller, her eyes seemed brighter, even the shape of her face had become more interesting.

'You do not agree? You don't think you look better so?' the older girl prompted.

'Oh—yes. Yes, I do.'

'That colour is perhaps a little too strong for you,' Diane said critically. 'I have another which would be better. I will give it to you later, when we return to the house. You may keep it. It is one I do not use now.'

'It's very kind of you, but I wouldn't be able to use it,' Justine said uncomfortably. 'You see, my father doesn't like cosmetics.'

'You mean he forbids them?' Diane exclaimed incredulously. *Mais c'est incroyable!* You are not a little girl. You are a woman.'

'He's never actually forbidden them. It's just that I know he wouldn't like it,' Justine answered defensively.

Diane's generous mood became tinged with exasperation. What a doormat the little fool was, she thought impatiently. She unscrewed a spiral mascara brush, and began to touch up her eyelashes.

'Don't wait for me,' she said carelessly. 'You go back to the others. I will join you when I am ready.'

Justine sensed a certain change in her manner, but she could not be sure if Diane was offended because she had refused the offered lipstick, or if it was simply that the Frenchwoman wished to be alone for a few minutes.

'Yes . . . all right,' she agreed, and went out into the passage, closing the door quietly

115

behind her.

On her way back to the saloon, she passed the open doorway of what appeared to be a small library. The walls were lined with closely packed shelves of books, and the only pieces of furniture were two or three deep leather chairs, and a table strewn with periodicals and French newspapers.

To Justine, books were like a flame to a moth. The open door, the lamp left alight on the table, the rows of coloured bindings were a lure she could not resist. Stepping across the threshold, she began to walk round the shelves, reading the titles. Presently, unable to decipher the faded gold lettering on one volume, she took it from its place and opened it.

It was a calf-bound edition of Chamfort's *Maximes et Pensées*. As she turned the pages, scanning a line here and there, she came upon a sentence which made her pause and murmur the words aloud.

'*La plus perdue de toutes les journées est celle où l'on n'a pas ri.*'

'The most wasted of days is that on which one has not laughed,' someone translated, from behind her.

Turning with a start, for there had been no sound to warn her of his approach, she saw

David Cassano watching her from the door-way.

'I—I hope you don't mind my coming in here,' she said awkwardly. 'The door was open and I saw all these books, and I couldn't resist having a look at them.'

'Why should I mind?' he asked pleasantly.

'Well . . . perhaps it wasn't very polite of me.'

'On the contrary, I am glad to find you here. I want to talk to you,' he answered.

This statement was daunting enough. When he followed it by firmly shutting the door, she felt even more apprehensive.

'Oh? What about?' she asked nervously.

Instead of enlightening her, he came across and looked over her shoulder at the book she was holding. 'Ah, Chamfort. Do you agree with that particular maxim?' he asked, watching her with that peculiarly intent expression which made her feel like a specimen under a microscope.

'I suppose there is some truth in it,' she said.

'I'm sure Julien would agree with it.'

Justine slid the book back into its place on the shelf behind her and pretended to be looking at its companions. 'Yes, I expect he would.'

'You like him, don't you?' he said lazily.

She stiffened. 'I like all the di Rostinis. Madame has been very kind to us.'

'You are not obtuse, Miss Field. I think you know what I mean.'

'Yes, I like Julien. Is there any reason why I shouldn't?' she enquired distantly, still with her face to the bookshelves.

'Not as long as you appreciate his weaknesses. He's a selfish young cub.'

She turned at that, her grey eyes angry and scornful. 'Don't you think that's rather an unpleasant thing to say about someone behind their back? Julien admires *you* enormously,' she added, with a thrust of sarcasm.

Her disdain seemed only to amuse him. 'He envies me,' he agreed cynically. 'I doubt if he has given much thought to my personal qualities.'

'Perhaps that's just as well,' she retorted caustically.

The sardonic lift of his eyebrow made her flush and bite her lip. 'I beg your pardon. That was rude. I'm sorry,' she said, in a goaded voice.

'There's no need to apologise. You are probably right,' he said carelessly. 'But it is not my character which is at issue.'

'I think I'm capable of making my own

118

judgments about people, thank you, *m'sieur*,' she answered stiffly.

'You are certainly very acute in your judgment of me,' he said dryly. 'But unfortunately it is not from me that you stand in danger, Miss Field.'

It was Justine's turn to raise her eyebrows. 'Danger?' she echoed, with what she hoped was a look of faintly amused incredulity.

'The danger of being hurt—badly hurt.'

She willed herself not to show any change of expression. 'I must be very dense,' she said airily. 'I'm afraid I don't know what you're talking about.'

A flicker of impatience showed in his hard eyes. 'I'm talking about a hot-blooded and self-indulgent boy, and an impressionable and totally inexperienced girl,' he told her, with a trace of sharpness. 'It's a dangerous combination, and one which could do great harm—to the girl in question.'

Justine flinched as if he had struck her. For some moments she couldn't speak, she was so outraged.

And then, to her own astonishment, instead of angrily telling him to mind his own business, she found herself saying, with acid politeness, 'You forget . . . I am what is known in England as a blue-stocking, *m'sieur.* I am much too busy helping my father to have time for flirtations. Women like me are not interested in men—except to prove our superior intellect. As you warned Julien yourself, he will have no luck in this quarter.'

It seemed he had forgotten his remarks about her that first evening on the terrace. He frowned, and looked momentarily puzzled. Then his eyes narrowed, and Justine had the satisfaction of seeing a gleam of annoyance in them.

But her advantage was short-lived. Even as she was congratulating herself on taking the wind out of his sails, his mouth began to quirk at the corners.

'So that's why you dislike me so much,' he said provokingly. 'Well, I'm sorry if I hurt your pride, my dear. But you must know the saying about eavesdroppers never hearing good of themselves.'

'I wasn't eavesdropping!' she flared. 'You were sitting directly under my window, and your voices woke me up from a nap. I couldn't avoid overhearing.'

'In that case I may count myself fortunate that I wasn't the victim of an unfortunate "accident,"' he said mockingly. 'You have such a fiery temper that I'm surprised you were able to restrain yourself from emptying your water jug over me.'

It was on the tip of her tongue to say childishly, 'It would have served you right if I had!' but she set her teeth and said nothing.

'Oh, come now—' he went on disarmingly, 'you are too intelligent to bear a grudge. I admit I was entirely wrong. You are not at all like the popular image of a learned English female. Be magnanimous, Miss Field. Accept my most humble apologies'—and he held out his hand to her.

For a moment he looked so genuinely contrite that Justine was almost placated. But then a lurking glint of amusement in his eyes made her ignore his offered hand.

'Very well,' she replied, with chilly politeness.

'That doesn't sound very friendly,' he commented dryly.

Before Justine could answer, there was an urgent tattoo on the door, and one of the stewards came in, speaking to his employer in rapid Corsican.

Cassano answered with what sounded like a terse instruction. Then he turned to Justine, his dark brows drawn together. She knew before he spoke what he would say.

'Your father has been taken ill.'

CHAPTER THREE

WHEN they reached the saloon, Professor Field was lying on the floor, unconscious. Another of the stewards was in the act of slipping a cushion under his head. Julien and his sister were standing helplessly by—the front of Diane's dress all stained and spattered with brandy from an overturned glass. Madame di Rostini, shocked but composed, was directing the steward to loosen the Englishman's collar and tie.

'*Father!*' Justine flew across the room, and fell on her knees beside him. 'What happened . . . did he faint? What happened?' she demanded of the steward.

The man scrambled to his feet, clearly very much relieved that his employer had come to take charge of the situation.

He said, in French, 'I think it must be a heart attack, *patron*. The old man was in great pain before he collapsed.'

Cassano knelt and felt the Professor's pulse. As he did so, the sick man groaned and began to come round.

'It isn't his heart. It's his stomach. He had an attack the other night,' Justine said distractedly. 'Please—we must get him to a hospital. Your motor-boat—'

'No,' he cut in abruptly.

She gasped. 'But you must help—you must! By the time a doctor gets here, it could be too late. It's urgent! He's seriously ill. You must help me to take him to Ajaccio.'

'Of course . . . but not in the launch.' He rose to his feet, and began to give calm, concise commands.

Within minutes, the Professor had been lifted on to a couch, the others were being taken back to the island, and the crew were under orders to get the yacht to Ajaccio as fast as possible.

For Justine, the voyage was a nightmare. Her father, although no longer unconscious, was in such excruciating pain that he could not speak, but lay with closed eyes, groaning and writhing as the spasms seemed to increase in intensity.

There was nothing she could do but crouch beside him, bearing his grip on her hand in white-faced silence, and praying that the doctors at the hospital would be able to ease his agony.

David Cassano stayed with them, sponging her father's beaded forehead from time to time. But the only time he spoke to her was after a steward had brought him a message.

Then he said quietly, 'We have contacted the port authorities. There will be an ambulance waiting on the quay for us. We'll be there in about ten minutes.'

As soon as they berthed, two ambulance men came on board and transferred Professor Field to a stretcher. With Justine and Cassano accompanying him, he was driven to the Hospice Civil Ste. Eugénie. There, Justine answered questions put to her by a young doctor, and then her father was wheeled away on a trolley and she was shown to a waiting-room.

The following forty minutes were an even worse ordeal than the crossing from Pisano. Cassano glanced through some dog-eared magazines. Justine sat staring at the door, tensing each time footsteps approached in the corridor.

She was thankful he did not attempt to comfort her. She could not have borne any conventional expressions of sympathy and optimism. Yet she was glad of his presence, for it forced her to control her emotions. If she had been alone, it would have been harder not to cry.

After they had been waiting for half an hour, he went outside for a few minutes, and

124

came back with two cups of strong black coffee.

'Thank you,' she said huskily. 'I'm sorry we've put you to all this trouble. You've been very kind.'

At last the door opened, and the young doctor reappeared. As Justine sprang up, he said, 'I'm sorry to have kept you waiting so long, *mademoiselle*. Naturally you are very anxious. However, you will be relieved to hear that your father is more comfortable now.'

'What's wrong with him? Do you know?'

'We cannot say with certainty, but his condition suggests an obstruction of the intestine. It will be necessary to perform an exploratory operation.'

'You mean now?—Tonight?'

'No, probably tomorrow morning. There are various tests to be completed before we can operate.'

'I s-see,' she said unsteadily. 'May I see him for a few minutes?'

'It would be better not to disturb him at present. If you come back in the morning—I suggest about eight o'clock—you will be able to see him before he goes to the theatre. You must try not to worry too much,' he added kindly. 'You may be sure he will have every attention.'

125

'Yes . . . thank you,' she answered hollowly.

The doctor excused himself and went away. Cassano took Justine's arm, and led her along the corridor. She submitted to his touch like someone dazed, and it was not until they were outside the building that she pulled herself together, and said, 'Monsieur Cassano, I haven't any money with me. If you could lend me a little, I will pay it back tomorrow.'

'You are shivering. Put this on.' He took off his coat and held it out for her to slide her arms into the sleeves.

It was much too big for her. But the silk lining was warm from his body, and she was in no state to care for appearances. As if she were a child, he fastened the buttons and turned the sleeves back at her wrists.

'You had better call me David,' he said. 'Now, why do you need money?'

'For a hotel. I must stay near Father. I can't go back to Pisano with you.'

'I'm not going back tonight. You can sleep on board *Kalliste*. This is no time for you to be alone. Anyway, the hotels are usually full at this season.' And with this he put her into the taxi which had drawn up alongside them.

'But I can't possibly impose on you like

that. There must be a vacant room some-where,' she objected, as he climbed in beside her.

'If there is, we aren't going to search for it,' he answered decisively. 'I have already arranged for some night gear to be obtained for you. What you need is a stiff brandy, a hot bath and bed.'

Two hours ago, that authoritative tone would have annoyed her. But now she had no spirit for argument. All her feelings were focused on her father.

'Very well . . . if you're sure,' she agreed wearily.

It was only a few minutes' drive back to the waterfront. A deckhand was on watch near *Kalliste's* gangway. He was lounging on a bol-lard when the taxi drew up, but he jumped to his feet when he recognised the car's occu-pants, and hurried forward to open the door for them.

As Justine stepped from the gangway on to the deck, an elderly steward appeared.

David said, 'Battista will show you to your cabin. Ask him for anything you need. He is a grandfather. You need not be shy of him.' Then he walked away along the deck, leaving Justine to follow the steward below.

If she had been familiar with the layout of

five-hundred-ton private yachts, Justine would have guessed that the "cabin" to which she was conducted was the stateroom designed for the owner's wife. Dominated by a huge seven-foot-wide double bed, it was even more spacious and luxurious than the lilac bedroom where, earlier, Diane had repaired her make-up.

While Justine gazed in wonder at the rose velvet curtains draped from a gilded corona above the head of the bed, the old man called Battista went through a communicating door. A moment later she heard water running, and realised that he was preparing a bath for her.

The bed had already been turned down and, on it, lay a white chiffon nightdress and a pale blue dressing-gown. A pair of pretty brocade slippers had been placed neatly together on the carpet near the pleated silk valance.

'Your bath is ready, *mademoiselle*,' the steward told her, when he returned. 'If there is anything you require, you have only to send for me.' He indicated one of several push-buttons on the base of the white bedside telephone.

When he had gone away, she ventured into the bathroom. The water in the sunken pink bath gave off a faint pine fragrance.

Everything she would need had been set out for her—a new toothbrush, paste, a face flannel, talcum powder, a bath cap, even a brand new bristle hairbrush and tortoiseshell comb.

When she had bathed, and dried herself on one of the thick soft towels from the heated rail, Justine padded barefoot into the bedroom and put on the filmy white nightdress. She had never worn a nightdress before, and this one was fit for a trousseau. The dressing-gown, too, was obviously very expensive. She wondered where they had come from: Surely the shops must have closed hours ago? But no doubt, if one was very rich, anything was obtainable, no matter what the time of day or night.

After she had brushed her hair, tidied the bathroom, and folded her own cheap clothes, Justine wandered restlessly round the bedroom, worrying about her father.

He had always been so fit and active that she never thought of him as an old man. With his thick grey hair and upright figure, he looked years younger than his age. And, as they never celebrated his birthdays—or hers either—it was easy to forget that he was now only two years short of seventy.

A major operation at sixty-eight . . . the thought made her shiver suddenly. Even when the patient was young, there must always be a degree of risk. How much greater was the risk for her father?

There was a tap at the door. 'Come in,' she called, expecting Battista.

But it was not the steward. It was David. He was carrying a silver salver with two cut-glass tumblers on it. When he had closed the door, he crossed the room and set the salver on a low table between two chintz-covered chairs.

'This is an anxious time for you. It might be a good idea to talk for a while. I daresay you won't find it too easy to sleep tonight,' he said, as he straightened. 'Are you comfortable here? Have you everything you need?'

'Oh, yes—yes, thank you.' She realised he was waiting for her to sit down, and followed him across the room, the long skirts of the blue silk robe swishing softly on the velvety pile of the white carpet. 'About this—' she said, awkwardly, indicating the robe. 'You must let me know what all these things cost.'

His shoulders lifted slightly. 'Don't worry about that now. Come and drink this cognac. You may not like it, but it will do you good.'

'I do hope all this hasn't made poor Madame ill,' said Justine, as he handed her one of the glasses. 'It must have been a fearful shock to her. Diane will be upset too. Her dress was ruined—not to mention the stain on your carpet. Oh dear, what a disastrous evening.'

'I don't think you need concern yourself on Madame's account. She is physically frail, but her nerves are very sound,' he said easily. 'The carpet is a trifle. It can be dealt with. As for Diane's dress, I've no doubt she has a dozen others. Tell me, is there anyone in England who should be notified of your father's illness?—Anyone you would like to send for?'

She shook her head. 'No . . . no, I don't think so, thank you.'

'You have no relations?' he enquired, with a raised eyebrow.

'Father has one sister . . . Aunt Helen. But they aren't very close. He wouldn't want me to send for her.'

'What about you? Wouldn't you like to have her with you?'

Again Justine shook her head. 'She couldn't come at the moment. Her daughter is expecting a baby any time now. My aunt will be busy looking after the other two children for her. I'll write to her, of course—but not until all this is over. There's no point in worrying her unnecessarily. Anyway, I can manage. We have funds at the Banque de

France here. If Father signs an authority, I can draw what money I need.'

'Are you insured against this kind of contingency?' he asked.

She nodded. 'Yes, I shan't have to worry about the hospital bills. We're covered for illness and accidents.'

He said, 'There is something I don't understand. Surely it's very unusual for an archaeologist to work alone as your father does? He has you to help him, of course, but I was under the impression that any major excavations were the work of a team of specialists nowadays.'

'Well, yes, that's true in most cases,' Justine agreed. 'Some of the big sponsored expeditions do have a very large staff. There's usually a deputy director, and supervisors and foremen, and a photographer and a field chemist. Very often they have an epigraphist and a numismatist as well. It depends where the site is, and what they expect to find. Father doesn't like working on that kind of project. There's so much administration and supervision that the director has hardly any time for practical work.'

She drank some cognac, and coughed as its warmth coursed down her throat.

'But surely it's rather a waste of time and

effort for you to do the preliminary digging yourselves?' he said, crossing his long legs. 'Isn't it customary to use students for the un-skilled work?'

'Yes, a lot of directors do. Father prefers local labour.'

'Why is that?'

'Well, for one thing, not many students are used to hard manual work, and they haven't the stamina for it. They're better at semi-skilled jobs like marking the small finds and pottery washing. But even then they tend to waste time chatting, and fooling about.'

'I see,' he said dryly.

Justine flushed. She had not meant to sound priggish, but she felt sure that that was what he thought her. She said, 'I expect you think we're mad anyway . . . spending our lives grubbing for broken pots.'

'Not at all,' he responded mildly. 'But I be-lieve it's possible to become too immersed in one's métier. I can understand your father's dedication. I think you're rather young to be equally committed.'

Her colour deepened. 'I'm twenty-three—that's not so very young. I—' She stopped short, blinking. Suddenly, for a second or two, everything had gone out of focus and a queer clouded feeling had come

133

over her. 'I like being committed,' she finished.

He did not seem to notice her pause, nor did he pursue the subject. For not far away, perhaps on one of the fishing boats moored further along the quayside, a man had begun to sing.

Justine had first heard Corsican folk music when, one evening on Pisano, an old man straddling a mule laden with brushwood had ridden past the dig. His sonorous voice, and the strange sad air he had been singing, had made a deep impression on her. Next day, in the village, she had heard two fishermen singing a *chiame e risponde* as they mended their nets. Sophia, too, often sang as she went about her work. It was she who had told Justine about the *voceri*—the songs of grief and revenge chanted by mourners after a *vendetta* killing. Fortunately these bitter blood-feuds no longer overshadowed Corsican life. But the women of remote villages continued to improvise *ballate* at funerals and, on the island, it was still the custom for young men to serenade their girls.

The song drifting through the open portholes sounded like a lament, and the strong true tenor of the singer made it more haunting than any she had heard before. Justine leaned her head against the wing of the chair and closed her eyes. As she did so, a wave of lassitude swept over her, and the misty sensation returned. She felt as if she were floating far out to sea, with the song and the strumming of the guitar gradually fading in the distance.

As the last note died away, she was dimly aware that something in her hand had been taken away. With an effort, she opened her eyes and saw David bending over her. But whatever it was he said to her was in a foreign tongue which she could not understand. Then, like an image in still water when a ripple disturbs the glassy surface, his dark face blurred and was gone.

★   ★   ★

When Justine awoke the next morning, she was lying in the huge ornate bed, and the ceiling above her was patterned with golden reflections from the sunlit sea outside the ports. She was not alone. Battista was standing by the bed, smiling and bidding her good morning. He was holding a wickerwork tray with short legs at either end of it.

In some confusion, for she had been dreaming when his voice roused her, Justine sat up and piled the pillows behind her. Then the steward placed the tray across her lap, and bowed and went away.

It was not until she had unfolded the napkin, spread it over the crêpe-de-chine sheet, and drunk the delicious chilled orange juice in the tall glass, that she realised she had no recollection of getting into bed the night before. With a puzzled frown, she broke and buttered a roll, and sliced the top off the egg in the silver cup.

As she dipped a spoon into the yolk, she remembered that she had to be at the hospital at eight, and was momentarily alarmed in case she had overslept. But a glance at the little enamelled clock on the bedside table reassured her. It was early—only a few minutes past seven.

When she had finished breakfast, she slid out of bed and went to the bathroom, where she decided it would be a good idea to have a cool shower—if she could discover how to operate it. At first she turned the dial the wrong way, and a fierce downpour of almost scalding water burst from the rose above the bath. But she quickly reversed the controls, and eventually achieved a more gentle stream of tepid water.

As she was drying herself, she discovered

that her clothes had disappeared from the stool where she had left them. But, as she was on the point of ringing for Battista, she noticed that the door of one of the cupboards in the bedroom had been left open. Her blouse and skirt were inside the cupboard, on hangers, and her underclothes were on a sliding shelf. During the night they had been spirited away and beautifully laundered.

By the time she had dressed and done her hair, it was a quarter to eight. She left the stateroom and, wondering where her host would be at this hour, found her way back to the deck.

Justine had never seen the famous Bay of Naples, but she was inclined to doubt that its beauty could surpass that of the Golfe d'Ajaccio. From where *Kalliste* was berthed, the mouth of the gulf was out of sight, and the city appeared to lie on the northern shore of a mountain-encircled lake.

As she stood at the rails, shading her eyes from the dazzling morning light and admiring this splendid panorama, she heard David's voice, and turned to see him coming along the deck. He was accompanied by a stocky middle-aged man in a white uniform. As they approached her, the man gave Justine a dignified salute before taking off his gold-braided cap and revealing a head of close-cropped greying ginger hair.

David introduced him as Angus Stirling, the yacht's master. Captain Stirling shook hands, made some civil remarks, and then excused himself.

'I didn't realise you had a captain,' said Justine, when he was out of earshot. 'I thought you commanded *Kalliste* yourself.'

David looked amused. 'Did you indeed? You have a higher opinion of my qualities than you care to admit,' he said quizzically. Then his mouth took on a wry twist. 'But I'm afraid the truth is that you have very little idea of what is involved in handling a vessel of this size. Stirling is a remarkable man. I'm lucky to have his services. The reason you did not meet him at dinner last night is that he does not care for social occasions. But make no mistake about his position. It is he who commands *Kalliste*. I am merely the owner. Come, it's time we were on our way to the hospital. I've ordered a taxi.'

At the foot of the gangway, she said, 'It really isn't necessary for you to come with me. I'm sure you must have more important things to do.'

'Don't be foolish—of course I am coming with you,' he said, rather abruptly.

At the hospital, they did not see the sympathetic young casualty officer who had admitted Professor Field the night before. Another doctor, an older man with a somewhat severe manner, came to talk to them. He told Justine that her father was due to go to the operating theatre at ten. The operation would take about three hours, and it was unlikely that the Professor would come round before early evening. If she telephoned about seven, they would give her news of his condition. But she would not be able to see him until the following day.

'May I see him now?' she asked diffidently.

The doctor replied that a short visit was permissible, providing the patient was not excited. Then, before she could ask any of the questions which were worrying her, he summoned a nurse to take her to the surgical ward, and hurried on his way.

'But I still don't know what's *wrong* with Father,' she exclaimed in dismay, turning to look up at David.

He was eyeing the departing doctor with a rather grim expression on his face.

'Don't worry—I'll find out for you,' he said reassuringly, his look of annoyance softening as he met her anxious eyes. He gestured for her to follow the waiting nurse. 'Off

139

you go.'

Justine found her father lying in a high white bed, looking so grey-skinned and haggard that it took all her will-power to hide the alarm she felt, and to say with a semblance of cheerfulness, 'Hello, Father. How are you feeling?'

'Damned uncomfortable,' Richard Field said irritably. 'I suppose you've been told they're going to open me up? I only hope the fellow who does it knows his job, and isn't an incompetent butcher.'

'I'm sure they have very good surgeons here,' said Justine, sitting down by the bed.

'I wanted to speak to you last night, but they told me you had gone. Where did you spend the night? I take it you didn't go back to Pisano?'

'No, I slept on the yacht. Monsieur Cassano has been very kind. He brought me here this morning. I expect he'll go back to the island after lunch. I must find a room somewhere near. Father, I don't want to bother you, but could you give me a note to take to the bank? I need some money for the hotel, and meals and so on.'

'I can't see why it's necessary for you to put up in Ajaccio. You may as well go back with Cassano, and get on with some work,' said the

Professor. 'There's no point in us both being idle.'

'But I want to be near you,' she protested. 'I can't go back while you're in hospital.'

'Nonsense!' he retorted testily. 'There is nothing you can usefully do here, and a great deal to be done at Pisano.'

Justine braced her shoulders. 'Well, it will just have to wait,' she replied, with unwonted resolution. 'I can't possibly concentrate on work while you are in here, especially when the island is so cut off. I'm sure you wouldn't leave me, if I were ill. I must stay, Father—at least until you're convalescent.'

It was the first time she had ever asserted herself and, as soon as she had spoken, she expected to have her head bitten off. But, to her surprise, after glowering for a moment, her father said grumblingly, 'Oh, very well . . . very well. But only for a few days.' And he summoned a passing nurse to ask for a pen and paper.

Justine stayed with him for about twenty minutes, until a Sister came to give him an injection, and she had to leave. As she rose to go, she was seized by the agonising thought that something might go wrong during the operation, and she would never see him again.

Somehow she managed not to show how

afraid for him she was and, at the door, she turned to smile and wave. But as soon as she was outside, in the empty corridor, her knees went weak. She leaned against the wall and closed her eyes.

Dear God, please don't let him die, she prayed, in terror.

David was waiting when she returned to the main entrance hall. As he heard her footsteps on the polished floor, and turned towards her, she had an extraordinary desire to put out her hand and have them taken in his strong cool grip.

'How is he?' he asked.

'He seems fairly comfortable, but he looks very ill. Were you able to find out anything?'

He nodded. 'Yes—I'll explain it to you as we go.'

'Go?' she echoed blankly. 'Go where?'

'You can't spend the day biting your nails in that depressing waiting-room. The time will pass more quickly if we go for a drive.'

'Oh, no, I must stay. I may be needed. I can't go out while Father is in the theatre.'

'Yes, you can—and you will,' he said firmly. 'There is nothing you can do for him at present. Come along.' And he took her by the arm, and propelled her out of the building.

The taxi which had brought them to the hospital was still there. David gave a brief instruction to the driver.

To Justine, he said, 'Try not to worry so much. It isn't necessary. Your father is going to be all right. If he had consulted a doctor some time ago, this operation wouldn't have become necessary. But the damage can still be repaired. In three months from now, he'll be as fit as he ever was.'

She clasped her hands in her lap, and looked out of the window. 'What did they tell you was wrong with him?'

'It's a thing called diverticulitis . . . an inflammation of the colon. Usually it responds to conservative treatment. Your father must have been in considerable pain for weeks for it to have reached this stage.'

She said unsteadily, 'It's all my fault. I knew he wasn't well. He was in pain in his room the other night. I should have made him listen to me. I should have made him see a doctor.'

'My dear girl, you can't blame yourself. If your father wouldn't take your advice, the fault is entirely his own,' he informed her bluntly.

'But why wouldn't he *admit* he was ill? What possessed him to try to hide it?' she

143

exclaimed bewilderedly.

'I imagine he thought it was something incurable, and was afraid of having his suspicions confirmed.'

'Afraid?—Father? Oh, no, that can't have been the reason.'

'Why not?'

She turned to look at him. 'Well, because it doesn't make sense. He isn't that sort of person. He wouldn't be afraid. He'd want to know the truth.'

David studied her for a moment, his grey eyes narrowed and enigmatic. 'Don't you think it's time you realised he isn't infallible?' he said dryly. 'The most brilliant men have some human failings, you know.'

She flushed, and bit her lip. 'I suppose you think it's peculiar of me to—to admire him,' she said, in a low voice. 'I know it isn't fashionable. The smart thing seems to be for children to despise their parents.'

'And that shocks you, I suppose?'

'Yes, it does. I don't understand it. I would rather be old-fashioned,' she said stiffly.

David did not pursue the subject, and there was an interval of silence until he said suddenly, 'How did you sleep last night? Did the noises of the harbour disturb you?'

'No, I slept like a log until Battista came in

with my breakfast.' She wrinkled her forehead. 'It's very odd ... I can't remember going to bed.'

'No, you wouldn't. I put a powder in your brandy, and you went to sleep in the chair,' he said casually.

Justine gaped at him. 'You mean y-you drugged me?' she stammered, dumbfounded.

His mouth twitched. 'There's no need to look so scandalised. My intentions were entirely honourable. I didn't want you to lie awake half the night, worrying.'

'Well, I think you might have told me,' she said, in confusion.

'If I had, you would probably have refused to take the stuff.' He lit a cheroot, and eyed her with a gleam of mockery. 'If you're wondering how you got into bed, I carried you there.'

It was precisely what she had been wondering, and the answer made her blush a fiery red. For, if he had put her to bed, he must also have taken off her robe, and seen her in that flimsy nightdress. Her face burned, and she felt a queer tightness in her throat.

They did not speak again until, about twenty minutes later, the driver halted the car on a winding and lonely stretch of road. As far as she could judge, they were now about ten kilometres from Ajaccio and, as there was no village in sight, it seemed a peculiar place to stop. David climbed out and, as soon as Justine had followed suit, the taxi moved off and left them alone on the roadway.

'We'll walk the rest of the way. It will give us an appetite for lunch,' he said. 'There's a chestnut forest about half a mile ahead, but in the meantime you had better wear these or the light may give you a headache.' And he handed her his own expensive smoked glasses.

For some time, after they set out, they could still hear the drone of the taxi's engine, and the warning blare of the horn at the frequent blind bends. But presently these sounds faded in the distance, and the stillness of the hot summer morning was broken only by the fluting note of a bird, and the chirping of crickets in the underbrush.

David set an energetic pace and, although she was accustomed to brisk walking, Justine had her work cut out to keep up with his long loose-legged stride. They had gone about a quarter of a mile when they met a huddle of ewes in the charge of a small peasant boy. Justine, somewhat out of breath, was glad to stand still for a space while the sheep ambled leisurely by. David said something to the boy which made him grin and nod his tousled head.

As the child and his flock went on their way, he stood watching them for some moments, an expression on his face which she found it hard to interpret.

He caught her eye, and said—rather ironically, she thought—'Myself, twenty-five years ago.' Then he turned and began to walk on.

As she followed, a pace or two behind, Justine found it difficult to relate this tall man, with his innate air of authority and sophistication, with the kind of ragamuffin youngster they had just passed. Although she had supposed that there must be an essence of truth in it, she had never quite believed Julien's story about David's background. But now, suddenly, she knew that she did believe it, because there was something in him which made any attainment possible.

It was cool in the chestnut forest. The air had a damp, mossy smell. On either side of the track, a sea of tall bracken receded into the shadows. Occasionally, the great trees opened out into sunny glades where butterflies fluttered among the ferns and wild honeysuckle.

For nearly an hour they walked through this peaceful green world. The dim light, and the arching branches overhead, gave the forest something of the atmosphere of an ancient cathedral. Justine, thinking of her father, found herself soothed and comforted, and was grateful to David for bringing her here.

They came out of the forest not far from an underground spring gushing from a crevice in an outcrop of granite.

'If you're thirsty, try a drink from the stream. The water is quite safe,' said David.

She was thirsty. Kneeling by a small cascade, she drank from her cupped palms. The water, ice-cold from its source deep in the hillside, was delicious; as different from adulterated English tap-water as champagne from flat lemonade.

When she sat back on her heels, she saw that David was lounging on a stretch of turf with his back against a boulder.

'The village where we're going to have lunch is down the valley, behind that ridge over there,' he told her. 'But we aren't expected till one, so we may as well stay here for half an hour. It's a pleasant spot, don't you think?'

'Lovely,' she said, looking round. 'It's a lovely country, Corsica.'

He lit another cheroot, and eased his shoulders against the rock which was cushioned with mosses and lichens. 'You haven't seen the best of it yet. In February, we have what we call "the white spring." It's when the orchards come into blossom, and the white heath in the *maquis*, and the mimosa trees. That's the best time of year for hard walking. Now it's too hot to go far, although it's cooler up in the alpine regions, of course.'

Justine turned her head to look at the distant mountains. Even at this season, the highest peaks still had snow on them.

'Come over here and be comfortable,' David suggested, from behind her. When she glanced over her shoulder, he crooked his forefinger and indicated the place beside him.

'I'm quite comfortable here, thanks,' she said, looking quickly away again.

'You're not still nervous of me, are you?' His voice was lazy and amused.

'I never was,' she said untruthfully. 'It's—it's just that I'm not used to meeting people.'

'You didn't seem to have any trouble establishing a rapport with young Julien.'

'He's different,' she said unguardedly.

'Ah, yes, he didn't commit the unforgivable sin of calling you a blue-stocking . . . and that still rankles, I fancy?'

She gave an unwilling laugh. 'No, I'd
149

forgotten about it. Anyway, it's true, I suppose.'

'What would you like to be? An ornamental creature like Madame St. Aubin?'

His shrewdness was always disconcerting, but this time it was also curiously painful. 'I should think everyone would like to be as lovely as Diane,' she answered lightly. 'She's the most beautiful-looking person I've ever met.'

David made no comment and, after a moment, she could not resist glancing at him, and saying, 'Don't you think she's lovely?'

'Oh, certainly,' he said negligently. 'But I don't think you would really enjoy having those looks. You may think you would, but you haven't considered the consequences.'

'What consequences?' she asked, puzzled.

He raised one knee and rested his forearm on it, the cheroot held lightly between his first and second fingers. 'If you were as beautiful as you would like to be, I might not be able to resist making love to you—and I'm sure you wouldn't like that at all,' he said derisively.

For the second time that morning, Justine felt her face growing hot. She said, with a tartness which surprised her, 'Well, at least I have had that distinction. From what I heard you saying to Julien, I gather it's usually the

150

other way about—though I can't say I've noticed Diane "presuming an interest when it doesn't exist,"' she added, quoting his own words.

For an instant, she thought she had at last succeeded in getting through his guard. Under his dark skin, the muscles at his jaw hardened slightly.

Then he laughed, and said without rancour, 'I seem to have ruffled your feathers on several counts. But I'm afraid you must acquit me of vanity. If I suffer from a superfluity of feminine attention, it's not inspired by my personal attributes. It's the depth of my pocket, not the charm of my character, which makes me popular.'

Justine felt something tickling her wrist, and blew away a small insect. She said, 'You're very cynical. I suppose, if one has money, one is bound to come across some sycophants. But most people aren't like that. And it's not as if you—' She stopped short, and fiddled with her watch strap, wishing she could learn to discipline her impetuous tongue.

'Go on . . . it isn't as if I what?' he prompted intently.

She knew it was futile to prevaricate. He would guess she was quibbling, and probe until he forced her to finish what she had meant to say.

'Well, it isn't as if you were an—an objectionable person,' she said awkwardly.

'Really? I had the impression you found me exceedingly objectionable,' he remarked provokingly.

'You know that isn't true,' she said, in a low voice. 'How could it be when you've been so kind to us?'

'My dear child, bringing your father off Pisano wasn't such a notable service that you need feel obliged to like me,' David said dryly, as he got to his feet.

He held out his hand to help her up. Unexpectedly, when she was standing, he took hold of her chin, and tilted her face so that she was forced to look up into his eyes.

'You underestimate yourself, you know,' he said carelessly. 'If you wished, you could be very attractive. Not in the same class as Madame St. Aubin—but engaging enough, in your own way.' And, with a casual pat on the cheek, he let her go, and began to lead the way down the hillside.

It was a half hour's walk to the village further along the valley, and Justine was still fuming when they arrived in the cobbled square in front of the church. Their taxi was

152

parked under some trees, but the driver had disappeared, probably into the nearby bar.

David spoke to some old men who were sitting on a bench, chewing *anise*. Then he turned up a steep narrow alley where the ground floor windows of the buildings were all barred by stout grilles.

It was a rather dingy street, with a good deal of litter underfoot, and paint flaking off the walls and shutters. Justine was surprised when he stopped at the foot of a flight of worn stone steps, and gestured for her to precede him. At the top, outside a massive iron-studded door, he pulled an old-fashioned bell rope.

The woman who answered the bell gave a cry of pleasure when she saw who had rung it. Judging by the warmth of their greetings, it seemed that she and David were old friends. Her name was Maria Bussaglia and, after he had introduced them, she took Justine to a bathroom where she could wash before lunch.

In spite of its unprepossessing exterior, the inside of the house was spotless. Left to herself, Justine washed her hands and face, and did what she could to tidy her hair without a comb. When she had finished, she did not at once leave the room, but leaned against the rim of the basin, frowning at her reflection in the mirror clipped to the wall.

What David had said by the stream—and, more particularly, the way he had touched her—had made her feel like a half-grown girl of sixteen. The more she thought about it, the more her chagrin intensified.

'I'm *not* a girl—I'm a woman!' she exclaimed aloud.

And, suddenly, in a flash of comprehension as stunning as a physical shock, she knew why she felt so fiercely angry and resentful. For the very first time in her life, she was in the grip of a compelling physical attraction. Trembling, her heart thudding, she sank down on the edge of the bath and buried her face in her hands.

'Justine? Are you all right?'

The knock on the door, and the sound of David's voice, made her start and draw in her breath.

'Y-yes . . . I'm just coming,' she stammered.

Opening the door and confronting him was one of the hardest things she had ever had to do. 'I'm sorry—have I kept you waiting?' she murmured, avoiding his eyes as she joined him in the stone-flagged passage.

'Well, for a girl who doesn't use make-up, twenty minutes seems a longish time to take

154

to freshen up. You're not feeling groggy, are you? The walk hasn't knocked you out?'

'No, of course not. I was just . . . thinking. I didn't realise I'd been in there so long.'

'Look, I understand that you can't help worrying about your father,' he said quietly. 'But the operation must be nearly over by now. There's a telephone here. After lunch, we'll call the hospital. Even though he won't regain consciousness for several hours, they'll be able to give you some news.'

Justine paled, stricken with guilt and shame. The last time she had thought of her father had been while they were in the forest. Since then, on the hillside, and walking to the village, she had not given him a thought. Incredibly, she had forgotten him.

They had lunch in a cool room at the back of the house. Afterwards, Justine had only the vaguest recollections of the meal. Presumably she had behaved fairly normally, or David would have made some remark. But, inwardly, she was so appalled by her own callousness that she would not have noticed if the food set before her had been uneatable.

While they were having coffee, David said, 'Shall I ring the hospital for you, or would you rather speak to them yourself?'

'Would you do it for me, please?'

155

'Certainly.' He pushed back his chair, and left the room.

He was gone about eight minutes, but it seemed much longer. Justine waited in mounting tension. She was thankful Maria did not come in to talk to her. She could not have borne the effort of thinking in another language just then.

At last, David came back. 'Good news,' he told her briskly. 'The operation finished a few minutes before I rang up. Your father came through it very well. As you've already been told, you won't be able to see him until tomorrow, but you needn't worry any more. The worst is over. Now all he needs is rest and good nursing.'

Justine felt her mouth beginning to quiver, and pressed her lips tightly together. After some seconds, she was able to say fairly steadily, 'Thank you . . . thank you very much.'

'Have some more coffee.' He refilled her cup, and his own. 'What would you like to do this afternoon? Another walk? There's a mediaeval baptistery not far from here which might interest you.'

'Could we go back to Ajaccio, please? Father gave me a note for the bank, and I must find somewhere to stay.'

'That isn't a problem. You'll continue to be

my guest on board *Kalliste*.'

'But you have to go back to the island. The di Rostinis will be wondering what's happened to you.'

'They already know,' he told her. 'I sent a message to Pisano this morning, explaining about your father, and also about my own change of plans. Certain circumstances have arisen which make it necessary for me to stay in Ajaccio for a few days. That being so, there's no point in your looking for a hotel room. I'm sure your father would prefer you to be with someone he knows—even though our acquaintance is of only a short duration. You have no objections, have you?'

Justine had the strongest possible objection, but it was not one she could express.

She said lamely, 'But I've been so much trouble already. Really, I'd be perfectly all right in a hotel. They can't all be full up. Of course I'm very grateful for your offer, but—'

'That's settled, then,' he cut in firmly. 'We will drive back to Ajaccio. You will rest for an hour or two, while I attend to some business matters. This evening, after we've been in touch with the hospital again, I'll take you to a café to watch the *passeggiata*.'

So, fifteen minutes later, after they had thanked and taken leave of Maria, and found the driver of the taxi, they began the run back to the city.

To Justine's relief, David did not talk on the return journey. After they had gone a little way, she closed her eyes and tried to make her mind a blank. Emotionally, she had had as much as she could take in one day, and she longed to be alone for a while.

When they got back to the yacht, the man on watch said something which made David frown and look annoyed.

'Is anything wrong?' Justine asked.

He shrugged. 'Julien is here to see you. I would have preferred you to spend the rest of the afternoon sleeping.'

They found Julien relaxing with an iced lager under the awning on the main deck. But he was not alone. His sister had come with him—and David did not look at all put out at seeing her, Justine noticed.

After she and her brother had heard the news about Professor Field, Diane said, 'I have come to stay with you, Justine. It is not proper for you to be alone at this time. Grand'mère has been most anxious for you. I should have come with you last night, but everything happened so quickly there was no time to consider what was best.' She glanced at David. 'I am sure Monsieur Cassano has shown every kindness, but when a woman is distressed she needs another woman with her.'

Before Justine could answer, Julien put in, 'Yes, Diane is right, *petite*. It is bad for you to be alone. You must let her remain with you until your father is better. Where do you stay? At the Grand, or the Impérial?'

It was David who answered him. He said, 'Justine is staying on board for the present. You know what the hotels are like at this season. Everywhere is fully booked.'

Diane's smooth forehead puckered. '*Ah, oui*—one forgets it is the season. The city is crowded with tourists. I had overlooked that difficulty.' She fingered the pearls at her throat for a moment. '*Néanmoins*, I do not think it is *convenable* for Justine to stay here.' She looked up at David, her blue eyes grave and faintly troubled. 'Forgive me, *m'sieur*, but perhaps you have not considered what may be said. Of course it is very foolish—but people are so malicious. They love to gossip, to make *un scandale*.'

'A scandal?' Justine said blankly.

'What Madame means is that people who do not know the facts are likely to misinterpret our relationship,' David explained

159

sardonically. 'I must confess it's not a contingency which had occurred to me, but I daresay she is right.'

Her face grew hot. 'Oh, that's ridiculous. How could anyone think that—' She broke off, biting her lip.

'What else should they think?' said Julien. 'If one sees a girl on a yacht such as *Kalliste*, one will naturally conclude—'

'The point is taken, Julien. We aren't obtuse,' David cut in, rather curtly. He turned to Diane. 'The problem is easily resolved if you are willing to act as Justine's chaperon, *madame*.'

The Corsican girl hesitated. Evidently, so simple a solution had not occurred to her.

'*Oui, certainement*,' she agreed, after a moment's thought. 'That is an excellent suggestion. As you say, it is most unlikely that we can find two suitable rooms at this time of the year.'

'Well, now that's settled, you can have your nap, Justine,' said David. 'Off you go.'

Down in her stateroom, Justine took off her clothes, and decided to have a shower. Afterwards, cooled and refreshed, she drew the curtains across the ports, and climbed into the wide luxurious bed. The sheets in which she had slept the night before had been changed for a pair of palest eau-de-nil ones. It seemed to her very extravagant to have clean sheets every day, although she could not deny that it was a pleasant sensation to feel their smooth silky texture against her bare skin. She wondered, a little scornfully, if David also slept on crêpe-de-chine.

David—the thought of him made her groan and shut her eyes. What did one do when one found oneself violently attracted to a man? Perhaps, being a purely physical reaction, it would eventually pass off—like measles. In the meantime, the only palliative seemed to be to try not to think about it. But that was easier said than done, when circumstances had thrown them into such close contact, and also deprived her of the distraction of hard work.

Even here, in this room, she could not shut him out of her mind. Remembering how, last night, he had brought her the doctored brandy, she turned her face into the pillow, her nails digging into her palms. When he had told her about it, she had thought she was angry at being tricked. Now she realised that what she had really felt was disappointment at having been in his arms without knowing anything about it. It was not an experience which was likely to come her way again. He would never want to hold her close. If he knew the effect he had on her, he would probably grin and dismiss it as a schoolgirl crush. Never mind that she was twenty-three. As far as he was concerned, she was still a half-fledged kid. It was obvious from the way he teased her that he didn't think of her as an adult, with an adult's emotions and responses. He would no more consider making love to her than he would think of old Sophia in that way. And even if it did dawn on him that she was a woman, it would make no difference to his attitude. To attract a man like David, one had to have poise and allure.

Restlessly, she changed her position. If only, just once, he would look at her as she had seen him look at Diane. But of course he never would, and to indulge in such wishful thinking would only prolong her unhappiness.

* * *

At dinner that night, Diane wore narrow silver trousers, and a sapphire silk mandarin jacket with wide sleeves and intricately frogged fastenings. It was the kind of outfit only the most leisured of women would possess, and therefore entirely appropriate to her present surroundings. She looked like an exotic butterfly—and made Justine feel like the drabbest of grey-and-white moths.

The news from the hospital was that Professor Field had come round shortly before six, and was resting comfortably. Justine would be able to see him—but only for a few minutes—the following morning. His condition was satisfactory, but he would be very weak for several days, and must have complete rest and quiet.

A few minutes before dinner was served, they were joined by Captain Stirling.

'Will you be going home as soon as your father is well enough to travel, Miss Field?' he asked Justine, as he took his place beside her at the table. 'I imagine it will be some time before he's fit enough to resume his work.'

'Yes, I should think it will,' she agreed. 'But I doubt if he'll want to go back to England. We haven't a house there. I don't know what's going to happen.' She unfolded her napkin, and smoothed it across her lap. 'I'm afraid it may be difficult to make him convalesce as long as he should. He's always been so active. As soon as he begins to feel better, he'll be itching to get back to Pisano. We were just beginning to uncover some really interesting finds.'

To Julien's ill-concealed annoyance, the Captain engaged her attention for the greater part of the meal. There were intervals of general conversation but, for the most part, David talked with Diane, and Julien was obliged to listen to the interchange between the other two. Nor did he get a chance for a tête-à-tête with Justine after dinner, for no sooner had they left the table than David said it was time for him to return to Pisano in the *vedette*.

'Would you care to take a walk before you retire, Miss Field?' Captain Stirling suggested, after Julien's rather summary dismissal. 'I usually have a short constitutional at this time of day.'

Before she could reply, David said, 'A good idea, Angus. She'll sleep better after a turn along the quay. Off you go, *ma fille*.'

It had been Justine's intention to accept the Captain's invitation, but she could not help resenting the way David had taken the decision out of her hands. Nor did she like being called "my girl" in that patronising tone.

As they went down the gangway, and the watch sprang to attention and saluted, she wondered if the Scotsman was really in the habit of taking an evening stroll, or if he was acting on David's instructions.

'Have you been with *Kalliste* long, Captain?' she asked, as they turned in the direction of the Citadel and the old, Genoese part of the city.

'Aye, ever since she was launched, ten years ago,' he said, with a note of pride in his voice. 'She was built for an Australian. He died in '63, and Mr. Cassano bought her and gave me command of her. I'd been first mate up to then. Captain Wallace, her previous master, was near retiring age when she was sold, and he didn't take too kindly to the idea of a Corsican crew. He was a fine seaman, but a wee bit set in his ideas.'

'Don't you find it rather strange?' she asked curiously.

'No, I like the Corsicans verra well. No doubt you'll have heard the saying—"If you're going into danger you should take a Corsican as your friend, and if you want a good wife you'll not do better than to marry a Corsican girl"? It's sound advice, in my opinion—at least as far as the first part goes. Being a bachelor, I couldn't say if the second part is true or not. I daresay it may well be.'

They walked in silence for some minutes. Justine remembered that, if Diane hadn't turned up, David would have taken her to see the *passeggiata*—whatever that might be. She asked the Captain if he knew.

'It's their name for the evening parade in the main streets,' he explained. 'The lassies dress up in their best clothes and walk about the city, and the laddies sit in the cafés and watch them.'

When they returned to the yacht, about half an hour later, a steward informed them that Monsieur and Madame had gone ashore. Monsieur had left instructions that the young lady was to go to bed early, and to have a glass of hot milk before she did so.

'I will prepare it at once, and bring it to you, *mademoiselle*,' the man said, smiling.

Even the crew treated her like a child, she thought vexedly. It was surprising that David hadn't ordered that someone should read a bedtime story to her.

*   *   *

She was already dressed when, next morning, Battista brought her breakfast tray.

'As you are up, no doubt you would prefer to have breakfast on deck, *mademoiselle*,' he suggested.

Justine agreed, but wished she had not when she found David at the table.

166

'Good morning,' he said, rising. 'Did you sleep well?'

'Yes, thank you,' she answered stiffly.

If he noticed her reserve, he made no comment. 'I expect Diane is still asleep. We were out rather late last night,' he remarked. 'But she will be called in time to go to the hospital with you.'

'If you don't mind, I'd prefer to go by myself today. Afterwards I'll go to the bank and do some shopping.'

For a moment, she thought he was going to insist that Diane accompanied her. Then he shrugged, and said, 'Just as you wish. Lunch is at one o'clock.' He selected a peach from the fruit basket, and began to peel the downy golden skin with a sharp-bladed silver dessert knife. 'I expect Julien will be here when you get back,' he added, without expression.

Professor Field was dozing when Justine visited him, and the Sister told her that it would be best not to rouse him.

'I'll tell him you've been,' she promised. 'And if, later, he wishes to see you, we know where you can be reached. But it's unlikely that we shall call you. It's usual in such cases for the patient to be very drowsy for the first day or two, and it's better so. Presently there will be considerable discomfort from the wound.'

After she had been to the bank, and drawn thirty pounds, Justine set out to buy an inexpensive cotton frock. It was impossible to go on wearing her white blouse and grey skirt every day, and even her father would not expect her to wear her khaki working kit on board *Kalliste*.

The first dress shop she passed was an elegant little boutique, showing a cocktail dress and a hat made of organdie roses. The price tickets made her gasp and quickly move on. In London, she would have made for a branch of Marks & Spencer, but Ajaccio did not seem to have an equivalent store.

She had been walking the streets for some time, and was beginning to feel rather hopeless, when she came to a shop where an attractive grey-haired woman was leaning through the curtains behind the window to rearrange the display. The beach clothes in the window were not cheap, but neither were they astronomically expensive, and the woman had such a pleasant face that Justine felt she would not mind being asked where there was a cheaper shop.

As she opened the glass door, the woman withdrew from the window, and smiled and said in French, 'Good morning, *mademoi-selle*. May I help you?'

Her accent, though good, was not that of a native of France. Nor, when seen at close quarters, did she look like a Frenchwoman. Something about her reminded Justine of her Aunt Helen.

On impulse, she said, 'Excuse me, *madame*, but are you by any chance English?'

The woman laughed and nodded. 'Yes, I am. Are you? I wouldn't have guessed it. You have such a nice even tan. Usually one can recognise English people by their red faces and peeling noses. They will overdo their sun-bathing, poor dears. You've obviously been sensible and browned yourself slowly.'

'Well, I'm not on holiday. I've been here all summer,' Justine explained. 'I'm afraid I didn't come in to buy anything,' she went on diffidently. 'I wondered if you could direct me to somewhere where they sell very cheap clothes.'

'Oh, dear, that's rather a problem,' the woman answered, looking thoughtful. 'Unfortunately Ajaccio is rather on the expensive side where ready-mades are concerned. If one has to economise, it's best to find a dressmaker. There are some cheap shops, of course, but I doubt if their stuff would suit you. What exactly did you want, my dear?'

'A cotton frock—but I can't afford to spend more than three or four pounds.'

The woman's face brightened. 'Oh, well, I can help you there. I've several little dresses at that price. To be frank, they aren't very well finished, but the styles and colours are good. I'll show you. What size? A forty, I should think, by the look of you. That's an English ten. You're tall, but you're very slender. I shan't be a minute. Do sit down.'

She waved at a spindly gilt chair, and disappeared through a bead curtain. Presently Justine heard the shuttle of metal hangers along a rail.

While the proprietress was in the back premises, she could not resist having a look at the clothes in the front part of the shop. They were all so attractive that, if she had been able to afford them, it would have been hard to decide which she liked best. Then she came upon one dress which appealed to her so much that she ventured to take it down from the rail and look at it more closely. It was a white dress, with a sleeveless crochet bodice and a slightly flared matt crêpe skirt—the perfect dress to wear for lunch or dinner on *Kalliste*.

'Ah, yes, that's one of my favourites,' said the Englishwoman, reappearing. 'It would

170

look wonderful with your tan. But I'm afraid it's above your limit. It's a hundred and twelve francs—that's about eight pounds in English money.'

The dresses she had brought from her stockroom were precisely what Justine had had in mind, and from them she chose a lemon tunic which cost only forty-five francs.

To her surprise, when the proprietress had folded it and put it in a paper carrier, she asked Justine if she would care to have coffee with her.

'Come up to my flat,' she invited, when Justine had accepted this offer. 'I shall hear the doorbell if there are any other customers, but the late afternoon is usually my busiest time.'

In a small but delightfully decorated sitting-room above the shop, she told Justine that her name was Laura Marnier. She was the widow of a Frenchman who had come to Corsica for his health.

'Jules died last year and, as I didn't want to go back to Paris or to England, I had to find some way of making a living here,' she explained. 'I've always loved clothes, and when this shop came up for sale—it used to sell rather horrid souvenirs—I had just enough money to set up in business. Now I'm doing quite well. Do tell me, what are you doing in Corsica?'

Justine explained about her father's work on Pisano, and how he was now in hospital.

'Oh, my poor child, how dreadfully worrying for you. Have you found somewhere decent to stay? If not, I could put you up here. I've a minute guestroom on the top floor. You'd be very welcome to it if you're stuck in some third-rate hotel without a soul to talk to.'

'It's very kind of you,' Justine said gratefully. 'But at the moment I'm staying on a boat in the harbour.'

'Well, if you should need help at any time, you have only to ask,' said the older woman. 'As a matter of fact, it's a treat for me to talk to another English person. I love this country and the Corsicans. They seem a bit dour sometimes, but when you get to know them they're wonderfully kind and hospitable. Nevertheless, it's nice to slip back into one's own language occasionally. In spite of being married to a Frenchman for ten years, I still think in English, I'm afraid.'

Presently, when the conversation had returned to the subject of clothes, she said, 'Look, you're going to think me frightfully impertinent, but I simply must tell you something. The way you wear your hair in that bun . . . it doesn't suit you a bit. Haven't you ever considered having it cut? It would make all the difference. You've got a lovely figure and gorgeous eyes, but your hair spoils the effect. It makes you look prim and governessy.'

Justine stared at her. 'A lovely figure—me? But I'm all arms and legs.'

Laura Marnier smiled. 'You aren't, you know. With a different hair-do, and some make-up, and a bit more confidence in yourself, you could be a knock-out. I spotted your potential the minute you walked into the shop. Lots of girls are like you. They could look marvellous, but they just don't know how to go about it.'

Justine remembered how, that morning when he had caught her swimming in the nude, Julien had also remarked that a chignon was too severe for her. She remembered, too, what a difference it had made to her face when Diane had painted her mouth with lipstick. Even David had told her she could be more attractive, if she wished.

'I'm sorry, I'm afraid I've offended you,' Laura Marnier said contritely.

'No, no, you haven't,' Justine assured her.

'Actually, I've always wanted to have my hair cut, but—but I couldn't pluck up the courage.' She paused, a queer tingle of excitement running through her. 'I'll have it done now—this morning. Where can I go? Is there a hairdresser near here?'

Mrs. Marnier seemed slightly taken aback by this instant acceptance of her suggestion. 'Yes, there are several, but I don't know if they could take you right away. I could ring up the place I go to, and ask them, if you like?'

Half an hour later, with her plait irreparably severed, and her remaining hair hanging in a ragged bob, Justine began to regret her impetuosity.

The hairdresser, a suave young man in an Italian suit, saw the dismay in her eyes, and said reassuringly, 'Don't worry, *mademoiselle*. You won't look like this when I have finished.' He dropped the cut braid on to her lap. 'If you wish, with this we can make you a *postiche* for evening wear.'

In spite of his encouraging comments about the silky texture of her hair, and its tendency to wave, which would become more pronounced now that it was no longer pulled straight by its own weight, Justine found the following ninety minutes decidedly nerve-racking.

174

When she was released from the dryer, the stylist suggested that she should close her eyes until he had completed the brush out. Justine obeyed, secretly dreading the moment when he would tell her to open them. She had no idea what sort of style would result from the arrangement of plastic rollers and clips, and was wretchedly afraid that it might be one which would not suit her at all.

At last, after a seemingly interminable interval of brushing and combing, she heard the hiss of a lacquer spray and knew that he had completed his handiwork.

'There—it is done. Does it please you?' he asked, tapping her shoulder.

She opened her eyes and, for nearly a minute, gazed at her reflection in silence.

'You don't like it so?' he asked, frowning.

'I—I can't believe it,' she whispered, in a wondering voice. 'I look . . . so different.'

He stood behind her and with the blunt end of a hairpin made a fractional adjustment to the placing of one soft shining curl. Then he whisked off the protective nylon smock, brushed down her neck and shoulders, and waited to pull back the chair for her. 'It should be cut often to keep the shape, *mademoiselle*,' he said, well pleased with her reaction.

Not very coherently, Justine thanked him, and—as Mrs. Marnier had told her to—slipped a generous tip into his pocket. As she paid the bill at the reception desk, she still found it hard to believe that the girl looking back at her from the mirror behind the desk was herself.

'I feel like a doll which has had a new head put on,' she said dazedly, to the receptionist.

The girl laughed. 'Perhaps a new lipstick to go with the new *coiffure*?' she suggested.

It was noon, and the shops were closing and would not re-open until two or even three o'clock, when Justine hurried back to Laura Marnier's premises, to show her her transformation, and pick up the lemon dress.

Mrs. Marnier saw her coming, and came out to meet her. 'There, what did I tell you? You look lovely,' she exclaimed delightedly.

In the shop, Justine said, 'I think I've gone a little mad. I've bought a lipstick, and mascara, and some scent—and now I'm going to buy that white dress. It is my size, isn't it?' She went to the rail, and took it down, and held it against herself. 'I don't care what it costs. I must have it. I want to wear it for lunch today. Oh, dear, what about shoes? These sandals won't do, and now the shops have all closed.'

'Monsieur Césari, just down the street, sells shoes. He'll open up for you, if I come and explain the situation,' said Mrs. Marnier. 'But are you sure you can stand all this extravagance, my dear? I thought you were rather hard up? You mustn't let yourself get too carried away, you know.'

Justine turned and looked at her and, for a moment, the sparkle went out of her eyes. 'The last time I had anything pretty was when I was twelve, and my aunt sent me one of my cousin's dresses,' she said quietly. 'I think I deserve a little extravagance.' Then she laughed, and the glow returned. 'Don't worry, Mrs. Marnier. I won't go completely overboard.'

It was exactly one o'clock when, wearing the white dress and her first pair of high-heeled shoes, she climbed into a taxi and waved goodbye to her new friend. As well as the two dresses and the shoes, she had also bought nylons, a French suspender belt patterned with cornflowers and butterflies, and a strapless bra to wear under the crochet bodice. In all, she had spent nearly three hundred francs, or about twenty-one pounds.

As the taxi approached the harbour, her excitement mounted to such a pitch that her hands began to tremble. She locked them tightly together, and took several slow deep breaths.

How surprised they would be when they saw her. What would they say? What would *he* say?

When *Kalliste* came into view, she saw that Julien was talking to the seaman on gangway watch. As the taxi came to a halt a few yards away from them, he hurried towards the nearside.

'Justine! Where have you been? You're late. We've been worried about you,' he said, a shade crossly, as he opened the rear door.

Justine, who had been sitting on the far side of the back seat, slid across it and stepped out into the sunlight.

'I'm sorry,' she said, smiling at him.

The young man's jaw dropped, and he took an involuntary step backwards.

'*Diable!* What have you done? I would not have known you. You are—*dazzling!*' he blurted, stupefied.

A thrill of exaltation went through her. Would David also be dazzled? She turned to retrieve her parcels, and to pay and thank the taxi-driver.

At the head of the gangway, she said, 'I'll just take these down to my cabin. Where are the others?'

'They are having drinks in the saloon. David has some guests for lunch today. They are, I think, business associates,' Julien said, still looking stunned.

A few hours ago, she would have been daunted. Now she felt equal to anything. 'Oh, I see . . . well, don't wait for me. I'll join you there in a minute or two. And, Julien, don't say anything, will you? I want to surprise the others too.'

In her stateroom, she cast her parcels on to a chair, and rushed to wash her hands. Her heart was pounding against her ribs, and she felt slightly giddy, as if she had drunk too much wine. Careful not to spot her skirt, she dried her hands and hurried back to the bedroom for a final look at herself in the glass-panelled doors of the wardrobe.

The mirrors reflected a dream which she had thought could never come true—a tall, graceful, fashionable girl with shining grey eyes and short, loosely curling hair brushed up from the nape of her neck and coaxed into airy tendrils across her forehead.

'Oh, please, *please* make him like me,' she whispered aloud.

The door of the saloon was open, and Julien was hovering nearby as she paused on the threshold. There were four strangers present; two men, who were talking to David, and two women, conversing with Diane.

One of the men was the first person, other than Julien, to notice Justine's arrival. He touched his host's arm, and murmured something to him.

As David rose and came towards her, Justine's heart seemed to stop. It took him about three seconds to cross the room, and to appraise every detail of her appearance. If he was astonished, he did not show it. She could not tell what he felt.

'I'm sorry I'm a little late,' she murmured huskily, as he reached her.

For a moment longer, his expression remained unreadable. Then, slowly, he arched one black eyebrow.

'Well, well . . . your little white rosebud has burst into bloom,' he said, with a brief glance at Julien.

He looked down at Justine again. But what she saw in his face was not what she wanted to see. The curl of his mouth was more like a sneer than a smile, and his eyes were cold and indifferent.

In an undertone the others would not hear, he added sarcastically, 'I realise you have been at pains to make a dramatic entrance, Justine, but it would have been

180

equally effective, and certainly more courteous, had you also contrived to be punctual.'

CHAPTER FOUR

THE luncheon party went on till after three o'clock, the meal being served in a formal, air-conditioned dining-room with high-backed antique Spanish chairs surrounding a dark green marble table.

When at last David escorted his guests on deck, leaving the three younger people alone in the saloon, Diane smothered a yawn.

'What boring people! I thought they would never leave.'

'Yes—typical provincials,' Julien agreed, with a grimace.

Justine said nothing. She had liked the short stocky men, and their ample, tightly corseted wives. Although they had been smartly dressed in black—each with a diamond clip, a large and expensive bag, and a fussy hat—the two Corsican matrons had had an engagingly homely quality. She sensed that they had not always been of the bourgeoisie, and that they were proud of their humbler origins. Naturally they enjoyed the fruits of their husbands' rise to prosperity—who would not?—but they were both much too sensible to assume any artificial airs. And if their homes and families were their principal interests in life, why should they pretend otherwise? But, even if she had not liked them, she would have felt it was a breach of good manners to criticise fellow guests.

Julien left the chair in which he had been lounging, and came over to join her on the sofa. 'There is a *plage* across the bay where the tourists do not go. You will come with me to swim there?' he asked, smiling.

'Not today, Julien. Father was sleeping when I went to the hospital this morning, so I haven't seen him yet. There's a chance I may have to look in later. They promised to let me know if he wakes and asks for me.'

'But we will come back for dinner,' he persisted. 'Surely, if it is necessary, you can visit the hospital this evening? It will be good for you to relax for an hour or two, *chérie*.'

Justine shook her head. 'I wouldn't feel comfortable, going off to enjoy myself so soon after the operation. Perhaps another day, when Father is beginning to get better.' She glanced at his sister. 'If you'll excuse me, I'll go to my room now. I want to write to my aunt in England.'

Diane crushed out her cigarette. 'I'll come with you, Justine.' She pressed her fingers to her temples. 'I have a slight headache. I think I'll rest for an hour.'

However, before retiring to her quarters, she asked if she might see where the younger girl was sleeping.

'Yes, certainly,' Justine said politely, though she was longing to be alone.

Diane had been put in the lilac stateroom where the two girls had washed their hands on the night of Professor Field's collapse. When she saw the even greater opulence of the English girl's accommodation, her delicate eyebrows lifted.

'*Charmant!*' she commented, strolling into the centre of the room, and looking about her at the furniture and other appointments. Her gaze came to rest on the wide bed with its velvet draperies and rose silk *capitonné* headboard. 'I wonder who was the last person to sleep there?' she said dryly. 'Someone very different from yourself, one imagines.'

She saw that Justine did not understand what she meant, and a slight smile touched her beautiful mouth. 'You think because David is not married there are no women in his life?' she asked cynically. 'You are very innocent, *petite*. This room is part of his private suite. There is your bathroom—yes? And that other door is to his dressing-room.'

Justine had noticed the second door, but had taken it for a cupboard, probably a linen closet. She watched Diane walk towards it and turn the cut-glass knob. The door was locked.

'Tell me, is it for David or for my brother that you have had your hair cut and bought this new dress?' Diane asked, coming back and seating herself in the chair where David had sat the night before last.

The question caught Justine off guard. 'I—I don't understand. I did it for myself. Why should they have anything to do with it?'

Diane said gently, 'When a woman changes her hair and buys new clothes, it is always for a man, *ma chère*. If it is Julien you wish to please . . . *eh bien*, you are of an age, it is natural and very suitable. But if it is David—' She frowned, and shook her head.

'Well, it isn't,' Justine answered shortly. 'I may be naïve, but I'm not a complete fool.'

'Forgive me—I did not mean to offend you,' the older girl said soothingly. 'It is merely that I would not like you to be hurt. What will your father say when he sees how you have changed yourself? He will be angry with you?'

'I expect so,' Justine said flatly. For the

moment, she didn't care how angry the Professor was likely to be. That was something she would have to face later. Now, all she wanted was to be left alone.

At last Diane went away. Justine closed the door, slipped off the high-heeled sandals, and went to sit on the cushioned windowseat below the central port. It was nearly four o'clock, but it did not seem like three hours since that humiliating moment when David had rebuked her for being late. The hurt was still as raw as if it had happened only a few moments ago.

It might have been a little more bearable if she had felt the reproof was deserved. But, at breakfast, he hadn't mentioned that he was expecting guests—and anyway she had been only a little late. It was not as if they had all been kept waiting for her. It had been at least another twenty minutes before the chief steward had announced luncheon. Come to that, she was a guest herself, and surely it wasn't usual to reprimand guests, however unpunctual they were? No, the more she thought about it, the more she was convinced that it was not her lateness which had made him speak to her so crushingly. He had had some other reason. But what? He couldn't have been angry about her dress and her hair. It

186

didn't make sense. He had said himself that she could be more attractive if she wished. So why should he be annoyed when she did try to improve herself?

At five, Battista brought her tea and sandwiches. Feeling that she couldn't face dining on deck with the others, Justine asked him if he would tell Monsieur and Madame that she was very tired and was going to have an early night.

'Certainly, *mademoiselle*. I will bring your dinner on a tray,' the old man replied.

'Oh, no, please don't bother. We had such an excellent lunch that I can't really manage another meal. Just some fruit and a glass of milk will do. I don't want to make a lot of extra work.'

When he had gone, she changed her white dress for the inexpensive yellow one, and took a cup of tea to the writing desk. But, after she had written *Dear Aunt Helen* on a sheet of the expensive die-stamped paper in the shagreen blotter, she sat back and gazed at the picture on the wall in front of her. It was a Monet; an exquisite painting of a river in the early morning sun, with the banks still shadowed by the blue-green reflections of willows. She was still gazing at it, fascinated by the pearly transparency of the dawn sky, and the subtle play of light on the quiet water, when there was a knock on the door.

Justine started and tensed, for there was only one person on board who would rap in that imperative way. But, before she could think of an excuse to refuse him admission, David opened the door and walked in on her.

'Battista tells me you don't wish to dine with us,' he said briskly. 'Aren't you feeling well?'

'I'm perfectly well, thank you. I—I thought it would be a good idea to go to bed early, that's all,' she answered evenly. 'You don't mind, do you?'

'Not in the least—if that's your real reason,' he said, on a sceptical note.

Justine averted her face. 'Well, of course it is. What other reason could there be?'

'Hurt feelings,' he suggested.

Her fingers tightened on the pen she was holding. 'Hurt feelings? I don't understand?'

'I fancy I was a little hard on you before lunch. I spoiled your big moment. Not unnaturally, you're piqued.' He strolled across the room to where she was sitting, and she felt him touch one of the short curls at the nape of her neck. 'I'm sorry, little one. I didn't mean to take the wind out of your sails.'

The audible amusement in his voice, and

the casual familiarity of his touch, made her want to throw something at him.

'You didn't,' she retorted lightly. 'I suppose you might have done if I'd bought that dress and had my hair done especially for your benefit.' She stood up and faced him, forcing herself to smile straight into his eyes. 'Julien told me I looked "dazzling,"' she added cheerfully.

It was the first time in her life that she had ever put on an act, and it surprised her to find how easily it could be done.

David's left eyebrow shot up, and she had the satisfaction of seeing that he was equally surprised.

'I see,' he said dryly. 'Did you believe him?'

She shrugged, and moved away. 'Oh, no, I knew he was exaggerating. But he obviously thought I looked nice. Actually, it was he who suggested this.' She indicated her hair.

'So you are not as indifferent to him as you would have had me believe,' he said keenly.

'I never said I was indifferent. I said I wasn't likely to lose my head over him.'

His lean face hardened suddenly. 'You won't get the chance, my girl,' he informed her dampingly.

'What do you mean?'

'If I see any signs of it happening, I shall

189

put a stop to it,' he said incisively.

'I don't really see what you can do about it,' she answered airily. 'I am over twenty-one, you know.'

'Physically—yes. Emotionally, you're still in your teens.' He walked towards her until they were only a yard apart. 'Let me give you a piece of advice. It takes more than high heels and lipstick to change a girl into a woman. Even if you were more mature, you'd be a fool to engage in any sort of relationship with Julien. You aren't the type to take love lightly, and your common sense must tell you that anything else is out of the question.'

Justine's chin lifted, and a sparkle lit her clear grey eyes. 'Diane doesn't agree with you,' she said coolly. 'She thinks my friendship with Julien is very suitable. In fact, she's just been warning me not to lose my heart to you.'

This was more than she had meant to say and, as soon as the words were out, she could have bitten off her tongue.

What David felt, it was impossible to tell. The expression on his face was the one she could never interpret, the one she had come to think of as his "masked" look.

His tone, when he spoke, was equally ambiguous. 'Has she indeed? And what did you say

190

to that suggestion?'

Under his enigmatic scrutiny, Justine felt her aplomb beginning to slip a little.

'I told her what I've told you—that I'm not in danger of losing it to anyone. I can't think why you should both suppose that I am. I haven't suddenly changed my whole personality, you know.'

'In that case, it's a little difficult to see why you've been at such pains to change your appearance,' he said, with a quizzical gleam. 'One doesn't usually bait a hook if one has no intention of fishing.'

Her colour deepened, but she managed not to look away. 'Yes, Diane said that too,' she answered evenly. 'But—' She stopped, interrupted by another knock at the door. 'Yes, come in.'

One of the stewards appeared, and spoke to his employer in their own language.

David listened, nodded, and turned to Justine. 'I'm sorry, I'm wanted by Marseilles. We'll have to pursue this most interesting discussion another time.' He gave her a rather Machiavellian smile. 'Enjoy your early night.'

And then he was gone.

*   *   *

On the way to the hospital next morning, Justine bought a cotton kerchief to hide her shorn head from her father. It was not cowardice which drove her to this deceit. She knew he was bound to be furious when he found out what she had done, and how much money she had spent and, from her own point of view, she would have preferred to face up to his anger as soon as possible. But, clearly, any agitation, so soon after the operation, would be very bad for him, and somehow she must try to postpone the inevitable row until he was stronger.

When she arrived at the hospital, she found that he had been moved from the public ward to a side ward. The Sister told her that he was still very weak, but that already he was demanding to know when he would be discharged, and worrying about his work on Pisano.

'Perhaps you can convince him that he must not worry, *mademoiselle*,' she said earnestly. 'To fret will only delay his recovery. Please do what you can to set his mind at rest.'

'I'll try,' Justine said dubiously. 'But if he won't listen to you and the doctors, I doubt if I can influence him. How long do you think it will be before he is fit to leave?'

The Sister said it would probably be three weeks before the Professor could be discharged, and at least a further eight before he was fit enough to resume an active life.

'You haven't told *him*, have you?' Justine asked anxiously.

'No, we have not committed ourselves.'

'Thank goodness for that! If he realises he's going to be convalescent for the best part of three months, he'll worry more than ever,' Justine said wryly. 'Oh, dear, what a difficult situation. Thank you, Sister. I'll do my best.'

She found her father looking so alarmingly pinched and frail that most people in his condition would have been content to surrender their cares.

But, as soon as he saw her, Richard Field said querulously, 'Now look here, Justine, I want you to find out exactly how long I've got to be laid up in here. These confounded hospital people are behaving as if I were *non compos mentis*. I won't stand for it. If they refuse to give me a straight answer, then it's up to you to get it out of them.'

Justine sat down on the chair provided for visitors. 'I've already asked them, Father. I don't think they can say with any certainty. It all depends on you yourself. You simply must rest and relax. It's the only way to get well quickly.'

'You can spare me the soothing platitudes. I've heard them all before,' he growled impatiently. 'How can I be expected to rest when I'm treated as if I were senile? I want a definite prognosis. In fact, I insist upon it.'

'Oh, Father, you mustn't!' she exclaimed, as he made a feeble effort to raise himself.

But, even as she reached out to restrain him, the Professor slumped on his pillows with a stifled groan of pain and exasperation.

'Damned officious bureaucrats,' he muttered weakly. 'Even the little chits of nurses treat me like a doddering old fool. It's quite intolerable!'

For several minutes, Justine listened to his complaints in troubled silence. Then, suddenly, her patience snapped.

To her astonishment, she said severely, 'Oh, do stop grumbling, Father. You're wearing yourself out, and it doesn't do a bit of good. If you hadn't been so foolish in the first place, you wouldn't have needed an operation. And if you keep carrying on like this, you'll take twice as long to get better.'

The instant the words were out, she expected to have her head bitten off. But, for some seconds, her father was too astounded to speak and, before he had recovered from the

194

shock, she went on hurriedly, 'I don't mean to be unkind, but you are being rather silly, you know.'

'Silly! *Silly!*' he expostulated. 'What the devil do you mean? I think you forget yourself, Justine. Don't imagine that you can start badgering me.'

"He's flustered," she thought. "It's the first time I've ever stood up to him, and he doesn't know how to deal with it."

'I'm not badgering you, Father,' she said quietly. 'I'm simply telling you the truth. Getting so worked up is bad for you. You've had a major operation. You can't expect to get over it in a matter of days. If you rest, and do as you're told, you could be out of here in three weeks. I'm sure they don't want to keep you in longer than necessary. They must need the bed for other patients.'

'So they did tell you something?' he said sharply. 'Why didn't you say so before? Who said it would be three weeks?'

'The Sister,' Justine answered. 'But I'm not supposed to have told you, so if you don't want to get me in hot water, you'd better not mention it. But it will be much more than three weeks if you won't do as you're told and rest properly.'

'Oh, very well . . . very well,' he said irritably.

At this point, a nurse came in to give him an injection, and Justine had to leave.

'Shall I ask if I can come again this evening, Father?' she suggested.

'If you wish,' he replied, without enthusiasm.

Strangely, his coldness did not hurt her. Instead, she felt a kind of pity for him. He looked old and exhausted, and she could guess how much he must detest submitting to the ministrations of a girl even younger than herself.

'Goodbye,' she said gently, and put her hand on his for a moment.

Down in the main entrance hall, she went to the women's cloakroom where she took off her headscarf and shook out her hair. It still felt strange to have no weight on the nape of her neck. As she applied a light touch of lipstick, she knew that it was only because her father was ill that he had accepted her strictures so mildly. Would she have the courage to stand up to him when he was better? Or would this tenuous new confidence wilt at his first slashing sarcasm?

Before leaving the yacht—she had breakfasted in her room, and had not seen David or

Diane—she had told Battista that, after visiting the hospital, she was going to spend the rest of the morning at the Musée Fesch.

But, as she walked out of the building into the sunlight, a hand grasped her elbow, and she found David beside her.

'Oh, you startled me! What are you doing here?' she asked, conscious that her heart was beating much faster than it would have done had anyone else accosted her unexpectedly.

'I'm going to have lunch with my sister. I thought you might like to come,' he said, steering her towards a small open car with the name of a hire firm painted on the boot.

'Where's Diane? Isn't she coming?' Justine asked, as he put her into the passenger seat.

He walked round the bonnet and settled himself behind the wheel. 'Unfortunately she has an appointment to have her hair done.' He took the ignition key out of his pocket, but paused before inserting it in the lock. 'Of course if you object to being seen with me without a chaperone—' he said, with an amused glance.

Justine tugged at her skirt, which had ridden high above her knees. 'You know I don't,' she said shortly.

He laughed, switched on the engine, and slid the gear lever into reverse. As he twisted round and laid his arm along the top of her seat to back out of the parking space, his fingers brushed her shoulder for an instant. She knew it was only an accidental contact, but it sent a slow tingle through her.

'How is your father?' he asked. 'I gather they only allowed you to stay a few minutes.'

'Yes, but I can look in again tonight, the Sister says. He's not being a very good patient, I'm afraid. I managed to calm him down a little by saying that he should be discharged in three weeks. But it'll be much longer than that before he can work again. I don't know what to do for the best. I daren't tell him the whole truth until he's stronger, but on the other hand there's no point in my going on with the dig single-handed. I can't possibly finish it alone before he comes out of hospital and, when he does, I think we shall have to go back to England.'

'How long would it take you to complete the dig if you had a team of helpers?' David asked. 'Supposing you had a dozen men working for you—could you get it done in a month?'

'I don't know,' she said doubtfully. 'It would depend how intelligent they were. I suppose it might be possible. But where would I get a dozen men? All the men on Pisano are busy fishing. Anyway, it would cost too much to employ a team.'

'Not necessarily. I could put twelve men at your disposal, and it wouldn't cost you anything,' he said casually.

Justine gaped at him, dumbfounded. 'B-but why?' she stammered, after a moment. 'Why should you help us? I mean, you aren't specially interested in archaeology. I don't understand.'

He was concentrating on the traffic ahead, and did not look at her. 'Yes, I suppose it must seem rather a suspect proposition,' he said sardonically. 'You're too shrewd a judge of character to credit me with the capacity for an act of disinterested philanthropy.'

Justine flushed and bit her lip. 'You know that isn't true,' she said, in a low voice. 'I didn't mean that at all. I think you're a very kind person. You rescued Julien when he lost all his money in Cannes. You've looked after me. If you were a . . . a hard man, you wouldn't have bothered with either of us.'

'Oh, so he told you about that, did he?' David said, mildly surprised. 'I should have thought he'd have preferred to forget it—reckless young fool. Well, I can assure you I wouldn't have helped him if he hadn't been Pietro di Rostini's son. In fact I think I'd have

199

done better to leave him to extricate himself. He could do with a few hard knocks.'

The road was clear now, and he slanted a mocking smile at her. 'No indignant protests? I thought you had a soft spot for him.'

'I like him—yes. Perhaps I don't expect as much of people as you do. Though even you probably did some foolish things when you were his age.'

'When I was his age, I was running my first hotel up at Calvi.'

She said, 'That's what I don't understand about this offer you've made. You're a business man. How can you afford to put twelve of your men to work on the dig? You won't be here much longer, will you? I thought you were always on the move, supervising your hotels.'

'Normally, yes—but it so happens that I'm staying here until the end of the season this year.'

Her heart gave a queer little lurch. Until that moment, she had not realised that, subconsciously, she had been dreading the day when his business in the city would be finished, and he would cruise out of her life, and she would never see him again.

'I don't know what to say,' she answered uncertainly. 'It's extraordinarily generous of you.'

'Well, think it over. Discuss it with your father, and let me know in a day or two. Personally, I think it would do you good to have a complete rest for a few weeks, but that's up to you.'

'I don't need a rest,' she said, puzzled. 'Why do you say that?'

He shrugged. 'Everyone needs a holiday from time to time. When did you last have nothing to do but enjoy yourself?'

'We enjoy ourselves differently from most people.'

'Do you?' he said dryly. 'Your father may, but I doubt if you do. By the way, what did he say about this?' He took his right hand off the wheel and touched her breeze-ruffled hair.

'He didn't see it. I wore this scarf over my head. I didn't want to upset him.'

She expected him to say something derisive, but although his eyebrow lifted slightly, he made no comment.

The drive to his sister's home took the best part of two hours, for the road up into the mountains was so narrow and circuitous that it was impossible to travel at more than forty kilometres an hour, and very often their speed was considerably less.

'My sister is married to a schoolmaster,'

David said, when they were nearing their destination. 'They have four obstreperous youngsters, and pets all over the place. You aren't nervous of dogs, are you?'

Justine shook her head. 'I like animals. Do they know you're bringing a stranger with you?'

'Yes, I telephoned them this morning.' His mouth quirked up at the corner. 'I told them you were a very learned female archaeologist, so they had better be on their best behaviour.'

She smiled, wondering what, if anything, he had really said about her. They were coming to another blind bend and, as he changed down and touched the horn, she wondered if his sister would be like him. Covertly studying his profile, she found it impossible to visualise a feminine edition of his face. His features were too uncompromisingly masculine. Reduce the big high-bridged nose, soften the angular jaw and square jutting chin, and the essence of his looks would be lost.

"He is like Madame di Rostini," she thought. "Even when he is old, and lined, and grizzled, women will still admire him, and wish they had known him as he is now."

The village where his sister lived was perched on a shoulder of mountainside not far below a great forest of *lariccio* pines, the giant trees which the Romans had used as masts for their galleys. The village itself was surrounded by terraces of cultivated land, and dominated by a tall campanile, and a church with a domed roof. The school and the schoolmaster's home stood a little way apart from the other houses, and had been built in recent years.

As David stopped the car, a woman came hurrying out to meet them. She was small and slight, with fair hair and hazel eyes. Justine's supposition had been right. She was not in the least like her brother.

'David! How lovely to see you again,' she said, in English, embracing him. 'It's ages since you last came up. I wish you would come more often. Never mind, you're here now. How are you? You look very fit.'

'I'm always fit,' he said, smiling, his arm round her shoulders. 'Mary, this is Justine Field. Justine, my sister, Madame Ghilardo.'

'How do you do, Miss Field. Welcome to our home.' With a friendliness which put Justine instantly at ease with her, Mary Ghilardo came forward to shake hands.

'I'm sure you are longing for a cold drink, aren't you?' she asked. 'It's such a long, hot, bumpy drive from Ajaccio. Come in where it's cool, and relax. The children are all out playing somewhere, and won't be back till lunch, so we can talk in peace for half an hour.' Leaving David to get something out of the boot, she led the way through the house to a large tile-floored living-room where a wide modern window framed a magnificent view across the valley.

'What a happy room,' Justine said impulsively, when she was seated in a deep comfortable chair, and her hostess had brought her a glass of chilled orange juice.

Perhaps "happy" was a curious adjective to use, but she could think of no other which described her reaction more accurately. The room was not strikingly decorated. It contained no fine furniture or ornaments. By some people's standards, it might have seemed shabby and untidy. The loose covers were faded and mended, the rugs had threadbare patches, and there were books and toys scattered about. But it was a room which, to Justine's eyes, immediately gave the impression of being the heart and hub of a large, busy, loving family. She liked the way childishly crude crayon drawings were given a place on a wall hung with prints and old engravings. The half-finished jigsaw puzzle left on a table, the mending basket with a man's grey sock spilling out of it, and the collection of pipes stuck in a mug on the window ledge reminded her of her Aunt Helen's house. This was how she would like to live herself, if she ever had a home of her own.

Mary Ghilardo glanced round her living-room and laughed. 'It's very different from David's elegant drawing-room,' she said cheerfully, as her brother came in with his arms full of parcels.

'Some things for the children, and a belated birthday present for you,' he said, dropping all but one of them on to the sofa.

While he helped himself to orange juice, his sister opened her present and, from a nest of white tissue, lifted out a creamy cashmere jacket, lined and faced with pale blue silk.

'Oh, David, it's charming!' she exclaimed. 'Let me try it on.' She jumped up and went to a mirror to see how she looked in it. 'You'd be surprised how chilly it can be in the evenings at this altitude,' she said, over her shoulder, to Justine. 'Isn't this nice? I love the feel of cashmere.' And, to David, 'Thank you, my dear.'

As they smiled at each other, Justine sensed that, although they bore so little resemblance, there was a very strong bond of affection between them.

David glanced out of the window, and saw

his brother-in-law coming along the road from the village. He said he would go to meet him.

When he had left the room, Mary laid the jacket back in its box. 'I wonder what he's brought for the children?' she said, glancing at his other gifts. 'I didn't tell them he was coming. When they see the car, they'll guess who's here and rush in like a pack of hounds.' She gave the kitten-soft cashmere a final stroke before putting the lid on the box. 'He's such a considerate person. Most men in his shoes would give cheques, or possibly jewellery. David never does. He really takes trouble over his presents. He always picks them out himself, and gets the size and the colour right. This is just what I'd have chosen myself. He doesn't spoil the children either. He adores them, and he could spend the earth on them. But he knows it's much better for them if he buys quite cheap, ordinary things.' The lines round her hazel eyes crinkled. 'I'm sure he'd love to smarten up this house for us. But we're perfectly happy as we are, and my husband would hate feeling under an obligation to him.'

Nicolo Ghilardo, whom Justine met a few minutes later, was a short, thickset man in his middle forties, with kind dark eyes, and flecks of grey above his ears. He greeted her as warmly as his wife had done, and then went off to help Mary in the kitchen.

Justine asked if she could wash her hands before lunch, and David showed her the way to the bathroom. While she was there, she heard the children and dogs coming in.

The babel of barking and high, excited voices had subsided when she returned to the living-room, and the four young Ghilardos were opening their presents. The smallest, a little boy of five, was perched on David's lap. He alone had inherited a likeness to his mother. The other three were black-haired and olive-skinned, and showed no trace of the English strain in them.

With reluctant politeness, they stood up to bow or bob as their uncle presented them. The eldest lad, Donat, was about twelve. Nicoletta, the only girl, came next. Carlo was probably six or seven, and the baby of the family was called Francesco. They all wore striped tee-shirts, and shorts, and rope-soled scarlet espadrilles.

'English today, please,' said David when, after the introductions, they began to chatter again. The children obediently changed from their own language to Justine's.

As their mother had surmised, their

presents were not the extravagantly expensive toys with which David could have indulged them, had he wished. Francesco had a plastic building kit, Carlo a kite, and the two eldest children books.

Presently, David shooed them off to wash, going with them to supervise Francesco's ablutions. His easy way with them surprised Justine. His own way of life was so remote from this domestic atmosphere that she would have expected him to pay only the most casual attention to them. Instead, he seemed genuinely to enjoy their company.

Lunch was a simple wholesome meal of soup, salad, cheese and fruit.

Afterwards, Justine volunteered to help Mary with the washing up, and the men went outside with the children.

'I gather David has told you about our parents,' Mary said, giving her guest an apron to protect her dress from splashes. 'It's odd how I take after my mother, and he after our father. Usually, it's the other way about, as it is with little Francesco.'

'No, your brother has never mentioned your parents. Someone else told me the story,' Justine answered.

Mary looked surprised. 'Really?—Who?' Then, when Justine had explained how she had had it from Julien, and he from his grandmother, 'Oh, I see. Yes, she would remember, of course. It caused quite a sensation at the time. All Corsica was agog. The newspapers picked it up, and made a big splash with it. Then some other nine days' wonder happened, and most people forgot all about it. It's strange David didn't tell you. If you hadn't known, you'd have been astonished when you met me. No one would ever take us for brother and sister.'

'I suppose he assumed that I knew about it,' said Justine.

Mary put on a pair of rubber gloves. 'Poor David,' she said, with a sigh. 'I'm afraid he is still very bitter about the way my mother's people treated her. She was never bitter herself. She was a wonderful person. She used to say that she had had more happiness with my father in their few years together than most people have in a whole lifetime. But her life was terribly hard after he was drowned. David adored her. He couldn't bear to see her struggling to make ends meet. The Cassanos were very good to us, but they were all desperately poor themselves. Mother wore black, like all Corsican widows, and she looked years older than she was. Even when he was quite a small boy, David's burning ambition was to

209

make a lot of money for her. The irony of it is that it's from the people he hates so intensely that he's inherited his financial genius.'

She began to wash the dishes. 'I think if she had lived, and he could have given her a lovely house and every comfort, it would have exorcised his hatred. But unfortunately she died before he was really on his feet, and ever since there's been this core of hardness in him. It's hard to explain what I mean. When he's here with us, he doesn't show that side of his nature. Probably he hasn't shown it with you either. But I know that, in his own world, he's different—cynical, even rather ruthless. As you know, most of the crew of *Kalliste* are related to us, so things filter back that he wouldn't tell us himself.'

Justine was a little startled that Mary should confide in her like this, and she felt sure that David would be furious if he knew his sister was discussing him with her.

She said, 'Well, to be honest, I didn't like him much when I first met him. But he's been incredibly kind to us.'

Mary smiled at her. 'I'm glad he's taken you under his wing. It's good for him to be with someone like you—someone young and unspoilt and sincere. Most of the women he meets are frightful creatures—ravishing to look at, of course, but completely amoral, and out for all they can get. I've met some of them, and they make me shudder. What is this Madame St. Aubin like? David mentioned that she was on board, but he didn't say much about her. She isn't after him, is she?'

'Oh, no!' Justine said positively. 'She's chaperoning me.' She coloured slightly. 'Not that it's at all necessary.'

Mary laughed. 'I'm afraid it is,' she said ruefully. 'David has a scandalous reputation. According to the gossips, he's a satyr of the deepest dye.' Her mouth took on a wry twist. 'I'm afraid there's an element of truth in it. But what can you expect when a man has a great deal of money, and is attractive too? Women simply fling themselves at him. He would have to be super-human to resist them all.' She put the last of the plates on the draining board, and gave Justine a look of rather amused curiosity. 'Don't you find him attractive?'

Justine felt herself blushing. 'He's very good-looking,' she said awkwardly.

'He isn't really, you know,' his sister replied dispassionately. 'He has a fine physique, but he isn't handsome. Actually, he's rather an ugly man, if you study him detachedly. I don't know what it is about him that makes most women so susceptible. There were several much better-looking boys in the village where we grew up, but it was always David the girls used to want to catch. Tell me more about Madame St. Aubin. She's a widow, I believe. Why are you so sure she isn't chasing him? She's a *rara avis* if she isn't. Is she pretty?'

'She's beautiful,' Justine said sincerely. 'And I think she must be quite rich herself. She has lovely clothes and jewellery. She's very nice, too. I like her.'

'Beautiful, rich and likeable . . . she sounds a paragon,' Mary said thoughtfully. 'You've whetted my curiosity. Perhaps I'll come to Ajaccio one day next week and take a look at her. I might stay overnight. Nico can cope with things here for forty-eight hours.'

Her brother put his head through the window. 'Have you two nearly finished? We're going for a tramp. Will you come, or would you rather stay here?'

'We'll only be a few more minutes. You go on, and we'll catch you up,' said Mary. 'I was just saying to Justine that I may come down to shop and spend a night with you some time next week.'

'You know you're always welcome, *ma mie*. Bring the kids, if you like.' He glanced at Justine, his shrewd eyes narrowing slightly, and his mouth curling in the way that always made her tense, and feel a faint tremor.

'An apron becomes you, little one,' he said, on a teasing note. 'I fancy this is your true métier.' He made a gesture encompassing the pleasant kitchen.

'Perhaps it is,' Justine said equably.

David laughed, and withdrew from the window, and disappeared. And it was then, as the sound of his footsteps died away round the corner, that she knew that what she felt for him was more, much more, than a purely physical attraction. She knew she had fallen in love with him.

The others were still in sight when she and Mary left the house. Francesco was riding on his father's shoulders, and Nicoletta had her hand in David's. Seeing the two women coming after them, the men stopped and waited for them to catch up.

'I took Justine to have lunch at Maria Bussaglia's place the other day,' David said to his sister.

'Oh, how is she?' Mary took her daughter's other hand, and the three of them moved off together, with the two older boys scampering ahead, and Justine and Nicolo bringing up

213

the rear.

'How many children are there in your school, Monsieur Ghilardo?' Justine asked, forcing herself not to watch the tall figure a few yards in front of her.

She and her host engaged in a separate conversation all the way to the fringe of the forest. There, his father set Francesco down to run among the trees with the other children, while the grown-ups followed more leisurely. The objective of the walk was a waterfall, which they could hear for some time before they reached it. As soon as they arrived at the place, the children tugged off their shirts and shorts and jumped into the pool below the fall.

'What a heavenly spot,' said Justine, watching the sparkling torrent pour down from the rocks above the clearing which surrounded the pool. 'I wish I had brought my swimsuit. I'd go in with them.'

'You'd find it very cold compared with the sea,' David told her, settling himself beside her on a boulder out of range of the haze of spray.

'The children aren't allowed to come here by themselves,' said his sister. 'The pool isn't deep, and they can all swim well, except Francesco, but we think it's best to keep it out of bounds until they're a little older.' She moved away to keep an eye on her youngest son, and her husband also strolled off to stretch out on the turf some distance away, and enjoy a pipe of tobacco.

If Justine had foreseen this, she would not have sat down. But, having done so, she felt she could not get up again without David guessing that she did not want to be alone with him. And, although they were not far from the others, they were virtually alone because the sound of the rushing water and the delighted shrieks of the children made their conversation inaudible to anyone more than a few steps away.

'What would do you good is a couple of weeks up here with Mary and her brood,' he remarked, after watching the antics of his nephews and niece for several minutes.

His avuncular tone was more than she could bear just then. 'I wish you wouldn't always treat me as if I were Nicoletta's age,' she said, with some heat.

To her confusion, he responded to this cross retort by slipping a hand under her chin and turning her face towards him.

'If any other girl said that to me, I should take it as a challenge,' he said dryly. 'Perhaps it is. Perhaps I've been underestimating you.'

His touch made her pulses race, and her face flame. 'I don't know what you mean,' she said huskily.

Perhap it was a trick of the sunlight, but it seemed to her a glint of anger lit his eyes. Then he dropped his hand, and shrugged, and looked away.

'No, I daresay you don't,' he said off-handedly. 'Anyway, I'll give you the benefit of the doubt.' And he eased his tall frame off the boulder, and went off to join his brother-in-law.

Perversely, as soon as he had left her, Justine wished he would come back. Although it had not been calculated, she saw now that what she had said *had* been a challenge. But why should that make him angry? Or had she only imagined a momentary flash of fierceness in the heavy-lidded grey eyes which were always so unnervingly perceptive, and usually so unrevealing of his own emotions?

Watching him, as he sat down beside Nicolo and lit a cigar, she felt the kind of terrified helplessness that poor swimmers must feel when swept out of their depth by an unsuspected undertow. Until today, she had been able to comfort herself that what she felt was no more than a simple infatuation, which would eventually pass and be forgotten. But now, all at once, she knew with a terrible certainty that the whole course of her life had changed direction on that stiflingly hot afternoon when a stranger had stopped by the dig and said, "I am David Cassano."

"Why him—why him, of all people? The last man on earth who could ever love me," she thought achingly.

And yet, even though she knew it was the grossest folly to hope for a miracle to happen—and it would be a miracle for someone like David to love her—there was still, deep down inside her, a crazy conviction that, if only the miracle would happen, she could give him much more than the women who had gone before her.

What could you give him? Beauty? Elegance? Wit?

No, but he's known women who've had all those attributes, and he hasn't fallen in love with any of them.

Perhaps he doesn't wish to marry. Why should he? He doesn't need someone to cook for him. He has a French chef. He doesn't have to darn his own socks, and wash his own shirts. He has a manservant to attend to his clothes. What does his life lack that marriage would supply?

He must want children . . . a son to inherit

*his name, and his money and possessions.
Every man wants a son.*

*Any number of women could give him a
son. What could you, Justine Field, give him
that no one else can?*

*I love him for himself. I don't care about
his money. If he lost every cent tomorrow, it
wouldn't bother me. I wish he were a poor
man.*

'We mustn't stay too long, or you will be
late for your visit to the hospital this evening,'
said Mary Ghilardo, touching her arm, and
ascribing her frowning abstraction to concern
about her father.

Startled out of a mental duologue between
mind and heart, Justine feared for a moment
that she must have been talking aloud. Then
what Mary had said to her registered, and she
hastily masked her consternation, and said
with artificial brightness, 'Goodness, it's four
o'clock. I had no idea it was so late. I was
miles away.'

'Yes, I guessed you were thinking about
your father,' Mary said sympathetically. 'You
must be very close.'

'Yes . . . yes, I suppose we are.'

'He'll miss you very much when you marry.
I should think that, however unpossessive
parents try to be, it must always be a wrench

when children leave home—and particularly hard for widows and widowers,' said Mary. 'But of course your father has his work, so he won't be too lost without you.'

Justine took off one sandal, and shook out a fragment of grit. 'I may never marry,' she said casually. But even to her own ears, her voice had a brittle ring which made her regret the remark.

Mary gave her a curious glance. 'Don't you want to?' she asked.

Justine buckled her sandal, and stood up. 'I haven't given it much thought.'

'Well, I suppose, if you have a career, you don't—until you fall in love. It was different for me. I never had a vocation for anything interesting. I'm a natural home-bird,' said Mary contentedly. She called the children out of the water.

By five o'clock David and Justine were on the road again. Turning in her seat for a last glimpse of the village before it was lost to view, Justine felt a pang of envy for the people who lived there, and especially for Mary Ghilardo.

'It's been a lovely day,' she said to David. 'Thank you for bringing me with you.'

'I'm glad you've enjoyed it,' he answered, without glancing at her.

It was the only time he spoke during the whole long drive back to the city and, after the first half an hour, Justine felt that his silence must be deliberate.

Outside the hospital, he said, 'I won't wait, if you don't mind. Get a cab to bring you back to the harbour. Have you some money on you?'

She nodded, and he reached across to open the nearside door for her. 'Give my regards to your father.'

Justine swung her legs to the ground, then paused and looked over her shoulder at him. 'David, I'm sorry. Please don't be angry,' she said contritely.

His eyebrow lifted. 'Angry? Why should I be angry?' He had not switched off the engine, and his hand was on the brake, ready to release it the moment she was out of the car.

'When you said it would be good for me to have a holiday up in the mountains, I didn't mean to sound . . . ungracious,' she murmured, her throat tight.

'Good God! Is that what you've been brooding about for the past couple of hours? I gathered you had something on your mind.' He depressed the clutch and moved the gear out of neutral and into first. 'You're too introspective, my girl. I'm not angry. Why on earth should I be? I'd forgotten about it.' The engine revved, and he drummed his fingers on the wheel. 'Off you go. I'll see you later.'

She stood up, and closed the door. The lock didn't catch, and she had to shut it more forcefully. As the car rolled forward, he gave her a casual wave.

But, as she watched him drive away, she was not convinced. He *was* angry . . . she was sure of it.

*   *   *

While Justine was entering the hospital, Diane was pacing the lilac carpet in her stateroom, smoking a cigarette, her sixth in the past hour.

She had returned from the beauty salon at three o'clock, and had been surprised and annoyed when one of the crew had informed her that Monsieur and the young lady from England were spending the day inland, and it was not known when they would return.

She was on the point of ringing for a steward to fetch her an apéritif, when she heard a car being driven fast along the quay. Hurrying to the port, she was just in time to see David slam on the brakes, and bring it to a halt at the foot of the gangway. Judging by his expression, as he climbed out and strode on board, he was in a savage temper.

Diane smiled to herself, her own crossness instantly dispelled. Clearly, he had had an excruciatingly boring day, and would be all the more responsive to her. So far, she had kept her manner cool, verging on indifference. Now the moment had come for a change of strategy.

She was too well versed in masculine psychology to confront him while he was still at boiling point. Let him take the edge off his mood with a shower, and a glass of *pastis*, and then what was left of his temper would not be a hazard, but an advantage to her.

She was glancing through *Paris Match* when, half an hour later, he appeared on deck, his dark head still damp from the shower.

'Good evening,' she said, smiling. 'Have you had a pleasant day?'

She said this in French as, although he spoke such faultless English, she fancied that French was the language of his private thoughts. It would certainly be the one he used in making love, she reflected, with a flicker of excitement.

He bowed, and sat down beside her. 'It was necessary to visit my sister. I've left Justine at the hospital.' His eyes glinted appreciatively. 'You are looking particularly charming to-night, *madame*.'

'Thank you.'

'Perhaps you would like to dine on shore again?'

'Yes, by all means, if you prefer it. Is Justine to accompany us?'

'I think not. She is tired, and will prefer to go to bed early.'

He pressed a bell and, when a steward appeared, gave instructions for a table to be reserved at a new restaurant in the hills above the city. It was a place which, according to Julien, who was always well informed on such matters, catered exclusively for intimate dinners *à deux*.

After they had had a drink, Diane went below to change her silk shirt and pants for a Marucelli dress of finely pleated black and white georgette, which she had already laid out on her bed in anticipation. In case she felt chilly driving back later, she also put on a black silk theatre coat, with a cowl which would protect her hair from being blown about by the slipstream from the car's windshield.

As David escorted her down the gangway, neither of them noticed a figure dodge quickly behind a palm tree a little way along the quay.

When the car had driven off, Justine stepped out of hiding and walked the hundred yards which had saved her from meeting them face to face.

'A fine evening, *mam'selle*,' the man on watch said politely.

She nodded and managed to smile. A few moments later, she was in the sanctuary of her stateroom. Through the portholes, the western sky was ablaze with sunset colours. The sea shimmered like amethyst lamé shot with crimson. The moon and some stars were already out. She had noticed them on her way back from the hospital, and remembered Longfellow's lines—*Silently, one by one, in the infinite meadows of heaven, blossomed the lovely stars* . . .

But now, the beauty of the evening, the scent of the *maquis*, and the gentle lapping of water, seemed only to intensify her misery. For when, from her place of concealment, she had watched David hand his companion into the car, everything which had puzzled her had suddenly become clear. It should have been clear that first night when Diane had come into the *salon* of the di Rostini villa on Pisano.

Mary had asked if Diane was after David.

In fact, it was the other way round. David was after Diane.

"That's why he insisted on my staying here," Justine thought, sickened by her own guilelessness. "He knew very well that Madame would think it improper, and send Diane to chaperone me. And that's why he's offered to provide a team for the dig. It gives him a perfect pretext to anchor off the island again, and pursue Diane at his leisure. He wasn't being kind. He doesn't give a damn for me. He's just using me as a stalking horse."

CHAPTER FIVE

IT was almost midnight when Diane and David left the restaurant on the Route du Salario, high above the moonlit gulf. They had dined at a candlelit table in a secluded alcove, with a violinist playing in the background to enhance the romantic atmosphere.

As she retouched her make-up in the powder room, Diane wondered how the evening would end. Would he make love to her, or not?

With any other man, she would not have had to speculate. With David, she could not be sure. She had no doubt that he wanted to make love to her; she could tell by the way he looked at her. But that did not mean he would do so—at least not tonight, not so soon. He was not a lecherous old fool like Mathieu, or young and importunate like Julien.

'He isn't sure of me either,' she said, to her reflection in the mirror. And she laughed, well pleased with her skill in leading him on, but only to a point from which she could still, if she chose, repulse any further advance.

No doubt, with most women, the possibility of a rebuff would never occur to him. Why

should it, indeed, when he was such an outstanding *parti*? But she was different from
most women. Firstly, she was confident that
her allure, though it might have been equal-
led, had certainly never been surpassed by
that of his previous quarries. Secondly, he
knew that her late husband had left her an exceedingly handsome independence.

So he would not suspect her of being
swayed by mercenary considerations. Therefore it was possible that she might rebuff him
and, when men were accustomed to easy conquest, they did not relish being snubbed, however gracefully.

'I wonder?' she murmured aloud. 'We are
well matched, he and I.'

David was not in the foyer, and the obse-
quious proprietor (he was French—a Corsican would have been too proud to fawn)
informed her that Monsieur Cassano was
waiting for her outside. Diane cut him short
as he started to express the hope that she and
M'sieur would honour his establishment
again. She strolled outside into the forecourt.

David was standing near the car, his arms
folded across his chest, looking down on the
spangled skeins of light which were the streets
of Ajaccio by night. She started towards him,
then stopped, her eyes dilating, her hand

going up to her mouth.

He had heard her high heels on the flag-stones, and he turned, and moved round the car to open the door for her. Diane relaxed, and her arm fell back to her side.

It had been only a trick of the moonlight but, for one unnerving instant, she had thought he was someone else . . . someone she had not seen for more than eight years. Like that, with arms crossed, Andria had stood on the cliffs on Pisano, waiting for her to keep a clandestine rendezvous.

Angry with herself for allowing such a fool-ish illusion to disconcert her, even momen-tarily, Diane readjusted her composure and took her place in the car.

When, some distance along the road, David pulled up at another vantage point—one less public than the restaurant's forecourt—she repressed a smile, her speculation resolved.

Naturally, he had too much finesse to take her in his arms the moment he had switched off the engine and the headlamps. She would have been disappointed if he had. They both knew what was going to happen presently, but it was more amusing and exciting to post-pone the moment for a little. He offered her a cigarette, and lit a *petit corona* for himself. It would take him about fifteen minutes to smoke it, and then he would toss it way, and turn towards her.

She controlled a slight shiver, and was annoyed by the quickening of her pulses. It was vital not to let emotion impair her judgment.

'Do you mind if I adjust the seat? This car is rather cramped for me,' said David.

He reached down for the lever beneath it, and shunted the bench seat backwards. As he eased his long legs, Diane saw that he was smiling slightly. The blue-black sheen of his hair, and the way the moonlight accentuated his high cheekbones, reminded her of Andria Sebastiani again. But this time the memory of the young fisherman had no effect on her, except that it suddenly made her understand the secret of David's magnetism.

She had tried to define it before, but it had eluded her. Now, in a flash of enlightenment, she saw that what made him so dangerously attractive was the mixture of patrician and peasant in him. His bearing and manners were those of a shrewd and sophisticated man of the world. But physically, apart from his shapely hands and strange grey eyes, he was a big, tough, virile Corsican *marin*.

229

'It seems we have both been lecturing Justine on the hazards of her sudden emancipation,' he said casually. 'I've been warning her not to take your young brother too seriously, but I gather you feel she stands in more peril from me.' His tone was lazy and amused. 'You don't seriously suppose I would take advantage of such an *ingénue*, do you?'

Diane laughed, but inwardly she was not too pleased to learn that the English girl had told him what she had said to her.

'No, of course not,' she answered, matching his tone. 'Justine must have misunderstood me. Naturally, I assumed that she had her hair done, and bought some clothes, to please someone. I was afraid she might be developing an adolescent penchant for you. She is very immature, poor girl. It's not her fault, of course. It's her father who's to blame. But, as you know, young girls are often attracted to older men, and I would not like her to be hurt, or for her to embarrass you.'

'What did she say when you spoke to her about it?'

'She denied that her transformation had anything to do with you or Julien.'

'Did you believe her?'

'I think I was wrong in suspecting that it

230

was you she wished to please. Why do you disapprove of a love affair with Julien? Surely it's what she needs to give her confidence in herself?'

'Possibly, but I am not at all sure that your brother is a suitable person to initiate her,' he replied. 'She has no experience at all, and Julien might not go gently with her.'

Diane watched the end of his cigar glow as he drew on it. "Like a lighted fuse slowly burning its way to the charge," she thought, and passed the tip of her tongue over her lips.

Aloud, she said, 'I don't think you need worry that he'll seduce her. He's not always wise, but he isn't as foolish as that.'

'I'm not concerned about that,' he answered, with a trace of curtness. 'I doubt if he'd succeed if he tried. But I do think she might fall seriously in love with him.'

'Perhaps he'll fall in love with her,' Diane suggested.

'And marry her?' David asked sceptically.

She shrugged. 'It's possible. She is rather charming now that she's begun to arrange herself.'

'It would never work,' he answered crisply. 'She's too intelligent for him. Besides, she's English. She would never tolerate his liaisons. However, enough of Justine.' Unexpectedly,

231

he flipped the half-smoked cigar into the bushes. 'You aren't cold, I hope? It's cooler up here than in the harbour.' He slid his arm behind her, along the backrest, and his hand closed on her shoulder.

She turned her face up to his. The glitter in his eyes sent a stab of wild excitement through her.

'But it's late, and you're tired,' he said blandly, withdrawing his arm.

And, five seconds later, the headlamps were blazing, and the car was in motion again.

* * *

As she walked to the hospital next morning, Justine wished she had not already told her father about David's offer to expedite the completion of the dig. If she had not mentioned it last night, she might have been able to persuade him that the rest of the work would have to be postponed until the following season. But unfortunately she had told him, and he had accepted the idea with enthusiasm.

'When is Cassano proposing to return to the island?' he asked, as soon as he saw her.

'I don't know. I haven't seen him since he

dropped me here yesterday evening,' she said. 'Not until next week, I should think. His sister is coming to spend a night with him.'

Today he was more alert, and as she sat down, he noticed the yellow dress.

'How much did you spend on that?'

Justine told him.

'The colour doesn't suit you, and the skirt is too short,' he said, frowning. 'Surely you could have found something more practical.'

For a moment, she was tempted to flash back an angry retort, even to snatch off her scarf and show him her hair. But she choked the defiant words back, and said only, 'Clothes are expensive here. This was cheap, and it will wash well. How are you feeling today, Father? Did you have a fairly comfortable night?'

'No, I did not,' he said fretfully.

As the Sister had told her he had slept well, Justine could not help feeling rather exasperated with him. She realised that his wound must be painful, and that the injections he was being given, though designed to speed his recovery, did not ease his present discomfort. Nevertheless, he was bearing his illness with a good deal less fortitude than he would have expected of her, had their positions been reversed.

As she listened to his list of grievances, she remembered the maxim she had read in David's library, shortly before her father's collapse, "The most wasted of days is that on which one has not laughed."

It occurred to her suddenly that, even when he was well, she could not remember her father ever laughing. Not once had she seen him throw back his head and guffaw, or even grin and chuckle.

"How strange," she thought, staring at him, 'It's not only that he has no sense of humour—he has no gaiety at all. He's like someone who's tone-deaf, or colour-blind. He can't help it. It's not his fault. He was born without any fun in him. Why haven't I noticed it before? Am I like that, too?'

And the thought that she might be was so unnerving that, involuntarily, she got up and moved to the window, and stood there, twisting the cord of the green holland sun-blind.

'Must you fidget?' her father said irritably. 'Do sit down and be still, girl.'

'I'm sorry,' she said automatically.

I'm sorry . . . Yes, Father . . . No, Father . . . I'm sorry . . . I'm sorry . . . How many times had she said those two words to him?

She did not stay long. 'When I come this evening, I'll bring you something to read,' she said, before she left.

'Ask Cassano if he can spare the time to look in for a few minutes. I'd like to talk to him.'

'Very well, but they may not allow you to have two visitors yet. I'll have to speak to the Sister about it.'

'In that case, I'd prefer to see him.'

There was a café near the hospital, a café with a gaily striped awning and window-boxes, and red wicker chairs and tables set outside on the pavement. Justine saw a vacant table, and sat down. Corsican women and girls did not sit alone in cafés and, even in pairs, went only to the most fashionable establishments. However, the Corsicans did not expect foreigners to conform with their own rather strict codes of behaviour, and there were no raised eyebrows or disapproving glances from the other patrons as she ordered coffee and the cheesecake called *fiadone*.

Even if there had been, she would not have noticed. As she sat in the sun, waiting for the coffee to drip through the aluminium filter on top of the cup, she was wholly absorbed in the change that had suddenly come over her between entering and leaving the hospital.

"I'm free!" she thought, with a wonderful sense of release. "I'm not afraid of him any more. If he snaps, I'll snap back. If he's sarcastic, I'll smile and shrug. I'm never going to say *I'm sorry* again—at least not out of habit and cowardice."

And, at last, she understood that, for years, she had not loved Richard Field. But she had gone on enduring his coldness and his captiousness because she had felt it was wicked and abnormal for a daughter not to love her father, and because it had been easier to bottle up her increasing sense of injustice and resentment than to admit that she was guilty of hating him.

"But I wouldn't have hated him if he'd let me go, if he hadn't tried to possess me," she thought. "And now that I'm free, I don't hate him any more. It's gone . . . that tense, bitter feeling which I tried so hard to suppress!"

She paid the bill, and walked round to the bank, and asked if she could see the manager. She wanted to know the exact extent of the funds her father had transferred from England. She had no difficulty in obtaining this information and, as their resources were considerably higher than she had anticipated, she drew out some more money to buy a swimsuit and some coloured pants and shirts to replace her shapeless khaki ones.

"I've been a fool," she thought wryly. "I

work much harder than most directors' assistants. I'm entitled to a reasonable salary, not a schoolgirl's pocket-money."

At Laura Marnier's shop she had some more coffee and a chat, and then chose a sleek white nylon swimsuit, and two trim but feminine working outfits, and another dress for her leisure hours.

When she returned to the yacht, she was told that Madame St. Aubin was ashore, and Monsieur was in his study. Justine asked where this was and, after she had left her parcels in her stateroom, she made her way there.

There was a curt *'Entrez'* in response to her knock and, opening the door, she found herself in a small, austerely furnished cabin with a battery of filing cabinets along one wall and a blown-up map of the Mediterranean on another. There were no pictures, ornaments or flowers.

David was sitting behind a flat-topped desk, studying some documents, and holding the microphone of a dictaphone.

'Oui?' He did not look up to see who had come in.

'I'll come back later. I don't want to disturb you.' She turned to go out.

'Oh, it's you. You needn't run away.' He rose, and switched off the machine, and came

237

round the desk. 'I'm not doing anything urgent. Come and sit down.' He shut the door and gestured her to the chair in front of the desk. 'What can I do for you?'

'My father wondered if it would be possible for you to visit him this evening, or whenever you can spare half an hour.'

'By all means—I'll go tonight.'

'Thank you. He isn't allowed more than one visitor at a time yet, so in that case I think I'll go over to see Madame di Rostini this afternoon. I can hire a boat from that place along the quay.'

'There's no need for that. I'll arrange for one of the crew to take you in our *vedette*. I'm sure Madame will be delighted to see you— and no doubt Julien will too,' he added dryly.

Obviously he thought it was Julien, not his grandmother, whom she really wanted to see.

'I shan't stay long at the villa. I want to go up to our site, and do a little work,' she said stiffly. 'My father's very grateful for your offer. I expect that's why he wants to see you—to thank you in person.' She opened her bag. 'I haven't forgotten that I owe you the cost of those night things you got for me. If you'll tell me how much they were, I'll pay you now.'

He resumed his seat behind the desk. 'I've

no idea,' he replied, with a slight shrug.

'Well, can't you find out?' she said awkwardly.

'I could—but is it really necessary?' His eyes were narrowed and unreadable.

"He's deliberately baiting me," she thought. "It amuses him to watch me squirm."

Aloud, she said, 'They're expensive things. I can't possibly let you give them to me.'

'No? I don't see why not.'

Her hands tightened on the arm of the chair. 'It—it just isn't done. You know that.'

'What is "done" or "not done" has never greatly concerned me.' A gleam of humour lit his eyes. 'I owe my existence to a breach of convention.'

He took up a horn-handled paper-knife, and held it in his lean brown hands, flexing the supple blade. 'Tell me something. If Julien gave you a present—let's say a scarf— would you refuse to accept it?'

'That would be entirely different. Besides, the robe and the nightdress weren't presents. You had to get them because I had nothing of my own to wear.'

He did not reply for a moment, and suddenly, during the pause, the narrow blade snapped in half.

'Careless of me.' He tossed the pieces into a waste box. 'Even tempered steel has a breaking point.'

Something in his tone made Justine suspect the remark had a hidden significance, but she could not think what it might be.

David glanced at his watch. 'Almost lunch time. Will you make my excuses to Madame St. Aubin? I shall not be joining you today.' He rose, and stood looking down at her. 'As for this matter of the night gear, which seems to concern you so much, I suggest we compromise. I won't accept payment. But, if wearing the things offends your sense of propriety, give them to Battista. He can put them away, and perhaps they may be of use in some similar contingency one day.'

He walked to the door and held it open. As she followed, he said unkindly, 'Disabuse yourself of the idea that I have any dark designs, my dear Miss Field. I assure you it is quite unfounded. I may have the reputation of having few morals or scruples, but I have some discrimination.'

She opened her mouth to protest, but he went on smoothly, 'I'm glad you seem to have developed a proper awareness of your not inconsiderable charms, but don't go to the other extreme. Don't overrate yourself, *mam'selle*. I believe I can resist the temptation to inflict unwelcome attentions on you.'

A buzzer on his desk began to bleep. 'Excuse me,' he said, with a slight bow, and went to answer it.

For a moment, Justine stood frozen by shocked disbelief. Then, slamming the door behind her, she fled down the corridor, nearly blundering into a startled steward as she turned the corner which led to her stateroom.

There, she flung herself on the bed, her whole body shaking with outrage and humiliation. She clenched her fists, not feeling the pain of her nails digging into her palms.

"I'm free!" she had said to herself, less than two hours ago.

Now she saw that all she had done was to exchange one bondage for another. She was free from Richard Field's domination. But when, like a fool, she had fallen in love with David, she had made herself vulnerable to a man who could hurt her far more than her father had ever done.

★　　　★　　　★

When Diane heard that David was not having lunch with them, she felt a blend of vexation and amusement. She guessed his absence from the table was not really due to any sudden pressure of work. It was a gambit in the game they were playing.

"So that's your technique, *mon brave*," she thought, her blue eyes glinting. "First you advance a little . . . then you retreat, and hope that I will make a move. You'll be disappointed, I'm afraid. When the stake is high, I can be very patient. You won't catch me out as easily as that."

During the first course, she was preoccupied. But presently, she noticed that Justine had scarcely touched the *caneton aux cérises*, and appeared to be under some strain.

'You have a headache?' she asked. 'You don't look very well today.'

Justine sipped her wine. 'Don't I? I feel all right. I'm going over to Pisano this afternoon.'

Diane did not want to spend the afternoon in her room, nor did she wish to sit about on deck where David might see her and think she was lying in wait for him.

'I'll come with you,' she said. 'I'm surprised we haven't seen Julien since the day before yesterday. Perhaps Grand'mère is not well, and he doesn't like to leave her.'

"Or perhaps he has told her about the deal,

and she's being difficult. Well, if he's botched it—too bad! It's his misfortune, not mine. I have my own fish to fry," she thought unsympathetically.

Before they set out for the island in the yacht's motor-boat, Justine put on one of her new working outfits—an Italian-pink cotton shirt, and a pair of sky-blue tapered pants with braided side seams.

'*Très chic*,' said Diane, with a nod of approval, when she saw them.

Rather surprisingly, she had changed the sun-dress she had worn at lunch for an elegant white piqué suit, with navy silk revers and cuffs. It struck Justine as being more suitable for a wedding than for a trip to a place like Pisano.

Normally, the sea crossing, with the bows cleaving white wings of foam as the boat soared over the calm and shining water, would have exhilarated her. But today everything was spoiled by the persistent echo of David's scaling sarcasm.

Why had he snubbed her so brutally? What had she done to provoke it? Surely there was no offence in wanting to discharge some part of her obligation to him? It was all very well for him to deride her for conventionality, but the fact remained that it was not *comme il faut* for a girl to let a man buy clothes for her. Even Aunt Helen and Uncle Charles, the most broad-minded of people, would not approve of it, especially when it was barely a fortnight since she had first met him. But what was most unjust and incomprehensible was his taunt about her overrating herself.

Julien must have heard the motor long before the *vedette* was in sight, as he was waiting on the jetty to meet them when the boat swept round the promontory.

'Justine!' He helped her to jump ashore, and kissed her hands, first one and then the other. 'It seems so long since I have seen you, *chérie*. Each time we meet you are more enchanting.'

His extravagance made her smile, but nevertheless it salved her raw pride a little to receive such an eager welcome.

The seaman who had brought them over helped Diane to land. If the ladies had no objection, he said, he would take the boat round to the village and come back for them later. What time did they wish him to return?

'You must stay for dinner,' said Julien. 'If you hadn't come to Pisano, I would have come to see you.' He asked the man to come back at nine o'clock.

As Justine started to climb the steps up to

the terrace, she heard him say, in an undertone, to his sister, 'I have spoken to
Grand'mère, but she hasn't yet made up her
mind, and I don't think it wise to press her.'

It seemed to Justine that, in the short time
she had been away from the island, Madame
di Rostini had become thinner and less erect.
As they shook hands, the old lady's fingers felt
cold and fragile.

'I am so relieved to hear that your father is
making good progress, my dear child,' she
said kindly. Even her voice seemed fainter.

"She is sinking," Justine thought, with a
pang. "Something has happened. She's lost
that extraordinary vitality."

And, as they talked, she became more and
more oppressed by the conviction that
Madame was dying; not because of any
sudden deterioration in her heart condition,
but because she had at last surrendered the
strength of will which, in spite of age and
infirmity, had made her such a great lady
still.

"She has given up," Justine thought,
deeply shocked and perplexed. "She is letting
herself fade away."

She could not understand it, because
Madame had seemed the kind of person who
would never willingly relinquish her hold on

life.

Later, she went to the kitchen to see Sophia. Madame di Rostini had made no remark about Justine's changed appearance, but the housekeeper threw up her hands, and declared that she scarcely recognised her.

'Such a pity to have cut off your lovely hair, *mademoiselle*,' she said, clicking her tongue. 'There are so few women with a fine head of hair these days.'

Presently Justine said cautiously, 'Madame doesn't look very well today, Sophia.'

'Ah, you have noticed it too.' The housekeeper sat down at the kitchen table, and sighed, and shook her head. 'M'sieur Julien tells me I am foolish. He says he can see no change in her. But I have served her for twenty years, since my good man passed over, God rest him, and I know there is something amiss. Last night, when I put her to bed, she held M'sieur Pietro's portrait, as she does every night before she sleeps. "Oh, my son, if only God had spared you," she said, and she wept, *mademoiselle*. She thought I did not see, but there were tears on her cheeks. She has always grieved for him, but it is many years since I have seen her weep, poor soul. There is something troubling her. I do not know what it can be, but she is not at peace here.' She put one hand over her heart, and sorrowfully shook her head again.

At this point, Julien came into the kitchen and said that, if Justine was going up to the dig, he would accompany her.

Seeing him reminded Justine of his low-voiced aside to his sister on the jetty. Was he responsible for his grandmother's unrest? As they left the villa and climbed the path to the clifftop, she was tempted to ask him what it was that he had spoken to Madame about, and upon which she had not yet made up her mind. Then she decided that her warm regard for the old lady was no justification for intruding in a private family matter, and held her tongue.

Professor Field had been worried that, during their absence from the island, the village children might have interfered with the dig. But it was just as they had left it.

'What will you do with all these things when you have finished here?' Julien asked, examining a tray of small finds with an expression which betrayed his opinion that only eccentrics would spend their lives grubbing for bits of broken pottery and lumps of iron slag. 'You will take them to England for one of your *musées*?'

Justine shook her head. 'We may have dug

them up, but that doesn't mean they belong to us. Anyway, we're only just getting to the interesting levels. Those things there are quite commonplace. The museums are full of them already. Normally, if we find something of special interest, it has to be handed over to the government of the country where we're working. I'm not quite sure what the position is here. Although your grandmother owns Pisano, I imagine the Corsican government could probably claim any really outstanding antiquities. We certainly couldn't make off with them, the way Lord Elgin did with the Marbles.'

'Lord Elgin . . . who is he?' Julien asked.

Justine explained how, in 1812, the then Earl of Elgin had brought to England a collection of friezes and pediments taken from the Parthenon at Athens.

'He sold them to the British Museum for £35,000, and they're known as the Elgin Marbles,' she said. 'Not surprisingly, the Greeks have been agitating to have them back—and so they should too, I think. Not that Lord Elgin was the only one to go round pilfering other people's national treasures. It was common practice years ago.'

Julien was not much interested in Lord Elgin, but he did seem interested in what the deeper levels of the site might reveal.

'This *villa urbana* . . . it would be possible to rebuild it as it was when the Romans were here?' he asked presently, when she had shown him the fragments of wall painting, and mentioned the likelihood of a fine mosaic floor being found.

Justine looked doubtful. 'It depends how much of the fabric has survived. Complete restorations have been done, of course, but not on sites like this. It would cost a great deal of money.'

'Yes, but it would attract many visitors,' he said thoughtfully.

'But you don't get tourists. There are no facilities for them,' she said, rather puzzled. 'If you're thinking of day-trippers, I doubt if many would come all the way over here to look at one Roman villa. Most people aren't all that interested in antiquities. Those who are go to Rome or Athens.'

'Perhaps you are right.' He dropped the subject, and said it was too hot on the hillside, and suggested a bathe.

'I can't. I haven't brought my bathing suit,' said Justine.

He gave her a mischievous glance. 'I thought you preferred to swim without one?'

Not long ago, the remark would have made

her blush and stammer. Now, she smiled, and said, 'Yes, but only when I'm by myself. Let's walk over to the other side of the island. I've never been there.'

* * *

While her brother was following Justine along a track through the maquis, and admiring her slim back view in the well-cut blue pants, Diane was strolling down the village. By the time she reached it, she was beginning to regret giving way to her curiosity, for her high-heeled, thin-soled navy shoes had not been designed for walking on rough country paths. But, when Justine had said she was coming to Pisano, Diane had suddenly felt an irresistible urge to see what the years had done to Andria Sebastiani.

If they had not heard of her return from Sophia, the villagers would not have recognised her. She had never mixed with them much, and, the last time they had seen her, she had not had paint on her face, and long lacquered nails, and city clothes.

They stared at her from their doorways. Those whom she recognised, and spoke to, acknowledged her greetings with their customary politeness. But there was disapproval in their eyes as they watched her on her way. By the time she arrived at the quay, which was also the main square, a dozen children were sidling along behind her, gawking as if she were a being from another planet.

Andria was not among the fishermen mending their nets and gossiping by the low quay wall. One of them noticed her and discreetly passed the word along and, within seconds, they were all covertly eyeing her.

'Ignorant peasants!' she muttered, under her breath. She turned away, only to find herself the cynosure of another group of men, drinking *pastis* outside the café-bar.

Diane was not easily discomfited, but she was hot and her feet were aching, and she had the unnerving feeling that, instead of being impressed by her fashionably coiffured hair and *haute couture* suit, the villagers were poking fun at her—not only those she could see, but others who peered from shadowed doorways, or through the slats of shuttered windows.

As she turned to leave the square, one of her heels caught in the cobbles, and she jarred her ankle and drew in a gasp of pain. For a moment, recovering her balance, she expected to hear a concerted burst of mocking laughter. But there was no sound. The square was as quiet as if it were deserted.

Furiously, sensing the sly grins they were exchanging, she hobbled up a narrow side street leading to the church, and leaned against the wall to rub her ankle.

As she was cursing her folly in ever setting foot in the place, a nearby door opened and a young woman came out. Like all the women on the island, she was dressed in black, with a black scarf covering her hair. In many parts of Corsica, the younger people had begun to put off this sombre garb, and to wear colours and modern styles. But, on Pisano, it was still the custom to observe five years of mourning for a close relative, and two for more distant connections. This meant that most adults were more or less permanently in mourning, and did not bother to change their dress even when it would have been permissible to do so.

If the girl had not addressed her, Diane would not have given her a second glance. But when she smiled and said a pleasant good day, she realised with a shock that this was Maria Angeletto, or Maria Sebastiani as she was now.

'You have hurt yourself, *madame*?' the girl enquired.

'It's nothing . . . just a slightly twisted ankle.'

'Won't you come into the house and rest for a moment?' Maria offered.

Diane hesitated. A moment ago, she had wanted to leave the village with all speed. But now this chance encounter with the wife of the man she had come to see revived her curiosity.

'Very well . . . just for a moment. Thank you.' She followed Maria through the door.

There was no one else at home. Maria invited Diane to take a chair beside the old-fashioned smoke-stained stone hearth, and asked if her guest would care for a cup of *verveine*.

'You have heard that I am married to Andria Sebastiani?' she asked, seating herself on a bench by the table.

'Yes, someone did mention it.' Diane crossed her legs, and lit a cigarette. She was beginning to enjoy the situation.

'As you see, we are soon to have a child,' Maria said, with a note of pride in her voice. 'My husband has made this cradle. Isn't it a fine one? He is so clever with his hands, my Andria.'

Scarcely able to hide her amusement, Diane agreed that the cradle was a very handsome one. "Poor Maria—little does she know that 'her' Andria would never have looked at

253

her if it had not been for me," she thought. "Surely she can't believe that he really cares for her? She was always plain, but at least she had a passable figure. Now she's lost even that. What a bore it must be to have to waddle about like an over-stuffed sack for months. And look at her hands, all swollen from washing and scrubbing."

'Where is your husband today?' she asked, when Maria had made the *verveine*, an infusion of verbena leaves.

'He has only gone up the street. He should be back in a few minutes.' Maria paused. 'I expect it was to see him that you came to the village, *madame*?'

Diane stiffened. What a strange remark— what did the girl mean? She couldn't possibly *know*—or could she? No, no, of course not.

But it seemed that Maria did know. Smiling, she said placidly, 'It must amuse you to recall that once you wanted to live like this, *madame*.' She made a gesture encompassing the clean but sparsely furnished room. 'No doubt you often laugh when you think of it.'

Diane could hardly believe her ears. That Maria knew was shock enough. But that she should admit her knowledge so casually and good-humouredly . . . Diane set her teeth, her whole body stiff with outrage. The girl had

254

the insolence to speak as if what had happened, years ago, had been nothing more important than a harmless youthful calf-love.

'Ah, here comes Andria now,' Maria said eagerly, as they heard the outer door open.

With an unsteady hand, Diane set aside her cup, and waited for him to come into the room and see her.

She had been so sure he would have changed. She had wanted him to be changed. Then she could have forgotten about him.

Instead, he was so little altered that it was she who felt suddenly aged.

'Diane!' His surprise was no more than that of anyone finding an unexpected guest in their home. 'I heard you had come back. How are you?' He offered his hand.

She took it, forcing her mouth to put on a smile. His palm felt rougher, more calloused, than it had eight years ago. But his waist was still narrow, his jaw still clearly defined. If anything, he was more handsome now than as a youth.

Maria explained to her husband how Diane had turned her ankle and come in to rest for a few minutes. 'Will you take some *verveine*?' Her face glowed when she looked at him.

He shook his head, frowning slightly. 'I told you to rest, *mon coeur*. Where were you

255

going when you met her outside?'

'Only to the *épicerie*. I am quite well now,' she assured him.

'You were not well this morning. You should rest. I can fetch whatever you want.' He laid his hand on her shoulder, and turned to Diane again. 'It's a good walk back to the Villa di Rostini. If your ankle is still painful, perhaps you would like to ride home. I'm sure Joseph Santone would be happy to lend you his mule.'

'No, that won't be necessary, thank you,' Diane said, tossing her cigarette into the hearth. 'I must go. They will be wondering where I am. Thank you for your hospitality, Madame Sebastiani.'

They did not press her to stay longer, but they went with her to the door, and watched her walk up the street to the Place d'Eglise.

Outside the village, Diane sat down on a rock. Twice before in her life, she had experienced despair—once, after her last quarrel with Andria, and again in the early hours of the morning after her wedding to Mathieu St. Aubin. Now, for the third time, she was overcome by a feeling that there was no point in going on.

"If only I had waited for him to come back from Marseilles," she thought. "If only I had not sold myself to Mathieu!"

And she wished passionately that she had never come back to Pisano. For now, just as she had never quite forgotten the meetings on the moonlit cliffs, she would never be able to forget the indifference in Andria's eyes this afternoon. She meant no more to him now than the women he had probably consorted with during his time in Marseilles. Incredible as it might be, he really did love his plain wife.

Remembering how tenderly he had reproved Maria for attempting to slip out in his absence, Diane pressed her hands over her eyes. Although she tried never to think of it, she knew that, one day, her looks would fade, and she would no longer be desirable. When that happened, the whole meaning and purpose of her life would be lost. But for Andria and Maria, life had a different meaning, and a different purpose. For them, middle-age was not something to be feared and fought against. Time, and their children, would strengthen the bond between them.

When Maria was forty, the hardest part of her life would be over, Diane thought bitterly. But for herself, and women like her, the ordeal by mirror, the fight against age with face-lifts, and massage, and rigorous dieting, would just be beginning.

And as she contemplated her future—ten, perhaps fifteen years of being beautiful, and spoiled, and envied, before the dreaded point of no return was reached—she knew that it was Maria who was truly the lucky one.

*　　　　*　　　　*

Next day, the *Kalliste* left her berth in the harbour at Ajaccio, and returned to the bay below the villa. If Julien had not suggested the probable reason why David wanted to see the Fields' work completed, Diane would have been secretly furious at having to go back to the island. She did not care for swimming, which was the only pastime Pisano offered, and much preferred to be near the shops and cafés of the capital. She had counted on them staying in the harbour until Justine's father came out of hospital.

However, as her brother said, David wouldn't put half his men to work on the dig unless there was something in it for him. And the move did not mean she would have to suffer the relative discomfort of life at the villa. David thought it best for the two girls to continue to stay on board the yacht in order to spare Sophia too much work.

Justine found that the members of the crew

who were put at her disposal quickly mastered the tasks she set them. Every morning at eight, she and her team set to work on the hot, dusty hillside. And every evening she was taken to Ajaccio to see her father and report on the day's advance.

In the week that followed the yacht's return to Pisano, she saw almost nothing of David. But one afternoon, he and Captain Stirling came up to the site to see how things were progressing. Julien was lending a hand that day, and it so happened that, just as the two men came in sight, he was trying to flirt with Justine.

Ordinarily, she would have said, 'Oh, Julien, not now,' and urged him to get on with the job she had given him. His ardent glances, and exaggerated compliments, embarrassed her in front of the crew.

However, when, out of the corner of her eye, she caught sight of David approaching, she did not disengage her hand, but let Julien hold it, and gave him such a dazzling smile that he promptly bent his handsome head and kissed her.

This was more, much more, than she had bargained for, and her sun-browned face became suffused with rosy colour.

'Look out—here comes David,' she muttered.

Still holding her hand, Julien turned to call an unabashed greeting to the newcomers.

Captain Stirling's blue eyes were twinkling as he came towards the young couple, but David's grey ones were icy. With the stiffest of nods, he walked past them to have a word with some of the crew. Fifteen minutes later, without speaking to Justine or Julien, he went back the way he had come.

*   *   *

On the day Mary Ghilardo came down to Ajaccio for a shopping spree, they all dined at an open-air restaurant on the coast road between the city and the Iles Sanguinaires, a group of rocky islets at the northern extremity of the Golfe d'Ajaccio.

The party from *Kalliste* (which included Captain Stirling, to make the numbers even) crossed from Pisano in the yacht's big eight-seater launch. Then, having collected Mary from the beauty parlour where she had had her hair done and changed into evening clothes, they drove out of the city and along the beautiful Route des Sanguinaires, bordered by oleander hedges, and orange groves, and the gardens of luxury villas. David drove the leading car, accompanied by Diane and her brother, and Captain Stirling chauffeured Mary and Justine.

The restaurant stood between the sea and an idyllic garden, made even more enchanting by garlands of coloured lights festooned between the pine trees.

Justine, who was wearing the white dress she had bought from Laura Marnier, was rather dismayed when she found that the place had an orchestra and a dance floor.

Evidently David had ordered the food and wine in advance as, a few minutes after they had been ushered to a table, he asked Diane to dance with him. She was wearing a long dress with a white duchesse satin skirt, and a black lace bodice which accentuated the beauty of her pale, lovely neck and shoulders. The next to rise was the Captain and, as he and Mary left the table, Julien asked Justine to dance.

'I told you, I don't know how to,' she said regretfully.

'It's easy. I'll show you. Don't be nervous.' He took her hand, and made her go with him.

With him it was easy, she discovered. The first turn round the floor was rather agonising, but then she discovered that it wasn't really necessary to know the steps, as she had supposed. If she relaxed, and let Julien guide her, and concentrated on the rhythm of the music, the right movements seemed to come naturally.

It was even easier partnering Captain Stirling, because he didn't know the steps either, and simply walked her backwards and forwards in a kind of zig-zag pattern, as if he were tacking in a dinghy.

When she returned to the table with him, the others were already seated, and Mary was choosing delicious titbits from the *hors d'oeuvres* trolley.

Between the *hors d'oeuvres* and the smoked trout, David danced with his sister and, between the fish and the *Blanc de Volaille Maréchale*, he danced with Diane again.

Justine was dreading the inevitable moment when he would ask her to stand up with him, because she knew it would be impossible to relax with his arm round her.

'You seem very pleased with yourself tonight,' she said to Julien, in an effort to distract herself from the ordeal ahead of her.

Julien laughed. He had been joking and playing to the gallery ever since they set out from the yacht, and now the wine he had drunk had made him even more ebullient.

'Today is a good day for me,' he told her, with a wink and a grin. 'From today everything will be different.'

Justine remembered that he had once expressed the hope that David might offer him a place in the Cassano organisation.

'You mean David has offered you a job?' she asked.

'No, no—much better than that. Now I don't need a job. Grand'mère has at last agreed to sell Pisano.'

'*Sell Pisano?*' The shock made Justine stop dead.

A couple, dancing close behind them, narrowly missed bumping into them. Julien gaily apologised, tucked Justine's hand through his arm, and led her off the floor not far from their table.

'It surprised me also,' he said wryly. 'I was afraid she would refuse to consider it. It has taken her more than a week to make up her mind—but at last she has done so. Pisano is for sale, and very soon I shall be rich.'

'I suppose I needn't ask who's going to buy it,' Justine said, in a hollow voice, as he drew out her chair for her. 'The well-known entrepreneur, Monsieur David Cassano!'

'But naturally—who else? It was a lucky day for me when I lost all my money at

Cannes. I would never have seen that Pisano had commercial possibilities,' said Julien, tossing back some more wine. 'But David saw them immediately. He is going to make the island an exclusive resort for those who do not wish to mix with *les excursionnistes*. It will be similar in character to the Aga Khan's development on the Costa Smeralda in Sardinia.'

'I see,' Justine said dully. 'Excuse me a moment, Julien.' She pushed back her chair, and got up, and asked a passing waiter the way to the ladies' cloakroom.

When she got there, she found it was full of chattering women, so she slipped outside again, and went along a shadowy path leading through a shrubbery. She had to have five minutes alone before she could face the others without showing how upset she was.

It was dreadfully clear to her now why Madame looked as she did.

"Oh, how could you? How *could* you?" she exclaimed aloud, her heart wrung with pity for the old lady.

It was not Julien she was apostrophising. Julien must bear some of the odium, but he was young, and weak, and easily influenced. He would never have thought of such a scheme if it had not been dangled in front of him, tempting the selfish streak in him, suborning the best in his nature.

David was the person she blamed. He was the author of the deal. He was the one she despised.

"I thought you loved him?" a voice seemed to whisper inside her.

"I do . . . I did!" she cried soundlessly. "But I can't love a man I don't respect—and how can I respect him now? This thing he has done is unforgivable. It's mean, and greedy, and heartless. He must know what the island means to Madame di Rostini. Even before this happened, she couldn't have lived many years. Couldn't he have waited? Couldn't he have spared her this cruelty? He doesn't need any more money. He's rolling in it already. I think he's utterly despicable!"

David was alone at the table when she returned to it. When, still some distance away, she saw that he was alone there, she considered keeping out of sight until he was joined by the others. Then, squaring her shoulders, she went forward.

He saw her before she reached him, and rose to his feet. 'Would you care to dance, Justine?' he asked, as she came up to him.

'I'd rather not, if you don't mind,' she answered frigidly.

His eyebrows went up. 'Is something the

matter?'

'Yes—but I doubt if it's something you'd understand.' She moved past him to her chair, and sat down.

A moment later, she was on her feet again, her arm held in a grip which made her wince. 'If you don't care to dance, shall we stroll round the gardens?' he said silkily, his expression belying the painful vice of his fingers.

There were waiters nearby. If she struggled, there would be a scene. She did not want to embarrass Mary and the Captain. Seething, she let him propel her away from the table.

In a far corner of the gardens, they came to an old stone wall where water dripped from the mouth of a gargoyle and splashed into a fluted basin.

David released her arm, and thrust both hands into the pockets of his dress trousers. 'Now, perhaps you'll explain that remark.'

Justine rubbed her bruised arm. She said, in a shaking voice, 'Julien's just told me the news—that you're buying Pisano.'

'So?' he said interrogatively.

'You didn't expect me to be pleased, did you?' she asked, with stinging disdain.

He was wearing a white dinner jacket, and

he looked very dark, and very foreign. At that moment, it was hard to believe that he was half English.

He said, with infuriating blandness, 'No, I didn't expect you to be pleased . . . or annoyed, for that matter. Perhaps I am being obtuse, but I fail to see why the sale should concern you at all.'

'No, you wouldn't!' she flared hotly. 'I suppose you never bother about people's feelings? *Your* only concern is making money. You—' She stopped, almost choking with anger.

'Oh, please, do go on,' he urged. 'You needn't mince words with me, you know. I'm sure some home truths will be very salutary for me. No one else has the courage to point out my failings to me.'

If he had not mocked her, she might have controlled her temper. But his tone, and the curl of his mouth, were like petrol dashed on the fire of her anger and bitter disillusionment.

'Yes—you're very popular,' she flung at him. 'But only because you're so rich, *m'sieur*. This must be a great coup for you. How much are you paying for the island? Enough to ruin Julien, no doubt. But only a fraction of the profit you expect to make eventually. I suppose that's why you want our dig finished? I should have guessed it before. Some Roman remains will give the place an extra cachet.'

She paused, dangerously close to tears. 'I don't care about that,' she went on huskily. 'But I do care for what you've done to Madame di Rostini. I think it's hateful . . . contemptible. It's ironic—everyone says that you hate your mother's people for what they did to her. But nobody seems to have noticed that you're just as unfeeling yourself.'

After a pause, he said softly, 'Is that all? Have you finished your indictment, Miss Field?'

She nodded, her eyes full of tears which, in a moment, would spill down her cheeks.

'In that case, you will excuse me if I return to my other guests,' he said, with velvet-smooth courtesy. 'I suggest you stay here for a time . . . until you have composed yourself again.'

He bowed, and walked away and left her.

CHAPTER SIX

AT six o'clock the next morning, Justine rang for Battista. She had never used the bell before, and was not sure if the kindly old steward would be on duty yet. But if he was not, no doubt one of the others would be.

As it turned out, Battista did answer the bell. He looked very surprised at finding her up and dressed an hour before her usual rising time.

'You wish for breakfast, *mademoiselle*?'

She shook her head. 'No, thank you. I'm not very hungry this morning. I'll just have a cup of coffee, if there's some made. Battista, I want to go to Ajaccio. Would you find out if there's anyone to take me over there?'

'Now, *mademoiselle*? So early?'

'Yes—if it's possible, please.'

He eyed her with some curiosity. 'Just as you wish, *mademoiselle*. I'll make enquiries for you.' He bowed, and withdrew.

When he had gone, she went to the bathroom, wrung out her flannel in cold water, and pressed it against her eyes again. She hoped no one would notice the tell-tale pinkness of her eyelids.

Remembering last night, and what an ordeal it had been to rejoin the others and behave as if nothing had happened, she shuddered. Mercifully, the party had not gone on late. They had returned to the yacht about midnight, and she and Captain Stirling had retired, leaving the others to sit up, talking.

"I expect they'll sleep for another couple of hours yet," she thought, laying down the flannel, and peering at her reflection to see if a second cold compress had made her look a little less haggard.

It was five or six minutes before Battista came back. He said—or she thought he said—'The Captain would like to see you, *mademoiselle*.'

'Oh . . . yes, very well,' she agreed. Probably Captain Stirling wanted to know how long she would be away, in case the *vedette* was needed for some other purpose.

Battista led the way along the corridor, turned a corner, and knocked on a door not far from her own. Indicating that she should enter the room within, he said, 'Please wait here, *mademoiselle*. He will come to you in a moment.'

It wasn't until he had closed the door behind her that she realised she was in a bedroom. It struck her as rather odd that the

Captain should have summoned her here. Then, from behind a slightly open door, came the sound of a tap being run.

"I suppose he's only just up," she thought, and hoped he would not be annoyed at being disturbed while he was still dressing.

The room was exactly as she would have visualised his private quarters, if she had ever thought about them. The bed was a single divan, already made up, with a cover of tailored grey linen. On the wall above it hung several finely chased Corsican daggers. She guessed that they were vendetta knives which, on one side of the blade, were inscribed with the motto *Death to the enemy* and, on the reverse, *May my wound be deadly*. A macabre collection to hang over one's bed, she thought, with a slight grimace.

She was looking at an antique terrestial globe which stood on the desk below the portholes, when the bathroom door opened. She turned, and her heart gave a lurch. For it was not Angus Stirling who stood, watching her, from the threshold. It was David.

Too late to escape, she realised that what Battista must have said was not "*Capitaine*," but the Corsican "*Capu*"—meaning the Chief. The two words were easily confused— especially as Battista spoke French with a

271

strong Midi accent—and, stupidly, she had misheard him.

'I'm afraid it isn't convenient for you to take the motorboat this morning. May I ask why you want to go to Ajaccio at this early hour?' David asked.

He was wearing a short, dark silk dressing jacket over a pair of plain grey pyjamas. His hair was wet from the shower, and he had evidently just finished shaving, as he was drying the vicious-looking blade of a cut-throat razor on a white huckaback towel.

'I want to see Father,' she answered constrainedly.

Battista came in with a breakfast tray, which he placed on a low table in front of a couch.

'*Mademoiselle* wishes only for coffee this morning, *m'sieur*. Shall I serve it here?' he enquired.

David nodded, and the steward went back to the door, and took another smaller tray from someone waiting outside. He set this down next to the first tray, assured himself that everything was in order, smiled at Justine, and left the room.

David closed his razor, and dropped it into the pocket of his dressing jacket. The towel he tossed on to a chair. 'Won't you sit down?' he invited.

Reluctantly, Justine seated herself on the extreme edge of the couch.

'You've made a conquest,' he said. 'Battista has lost his heart to you. In fact all the crew seem to be in your toils, little one.' He sat down beside her, and began to peel his morning orange.

Justine shot a quick sideways look at his autocratic profile. He caught the suspicious glance, and his fingers stilled.

'I'm not being sarcastic. It's true,' he said, looking amused. 'Don't you sense their liking for you? No doubt it's because you appeal to their protective instincts.'

She didn't know what to say. She couldn't fathom him. Last night, she had said things which—deserved though they might be—she had thought he would never forgive. Yet now his tone and manner were as if last night had never happened. Why? she wondered distrustfully.

He finished peeling the orange, and filled his cup with black coffee. 'So you want to see your father?' he said consideringly. 'Presumably to tell him what an infamous character I am, and to urge him to sever all connection with me?'

His percipience made her flush. 'Yes—

something like that,' she admitted shortly.

'Aren't you going to drink your coffee?' He leaned back and ate the orange, putting himself at the advantage of being able to watch her, while she, unless she half turned, could not see him.

When he had eaten the fruit, he wiped his hands on a linen napkin, and lit a dark-leaved cheroot. 'How unfortunate that the boat won't be available today, and possibly not tomorrow either,' he said lazily.

She did turn and look at him then. 'Is that a veiled way of saying you won't *let* me go to Ajaccio?'

'I think it would be unwise to embroil your father in our differences until he is at least out of hospital. In any case, he may not share your indignation. He isn't as sentimental as you are.'

'It has nothing to do with sentiment. It's a matter of principle.'

'Well, I regret that, for the moment, you'll have to swallow your principles,' he said, with a touch of impatience.

'Haven't you forgotten that your sister will be going back to the mainland some time today?' she pointed out. 'If I can't go this morning, I'll go over with her later on. You can't very well stop me, can you?'

David raised an eyebrow. 'You think not? You underrate me. I can very easily stop you. Nothing could be simpler.' He glanced at his watch. 'None of the others is up yet. When they are, I can tell them you've had a slight tummy upset, and are spending the day in bed. If anyone asks to see you, you'll be sleeping and better not disturbed.'

He was joking—he must be, she thought. And yet there was something in his face which sent a queer tremor through her.

'I don't believe you,' she said flatly. 'For one thing, it wouldn't work. You don't imagine I'd submit to being locked in, do you? I'd shout the place down.'

He shrugged. 'In that case I should have to give you another sedative.'

She said, with more nonchalance than she felt, 'What would be the point? You couldn't keep me shut up indefinitely.'

'No, not for more than a day or two,' he agreed. 'Your father would wonder why you hadn't been over to visit him. But you won't dispute that I could easily keep you confined today and tomorrow?'

Justine did not reply for a moment. If only she could be certain that he was pulling her leg. But she wasn't certain . . . she wasn't certain at all. There was a glint in his eyes which made her afraid he might really mean his threat.

'I suppose you could—if you went to such extraordinary lengths,' she conceded, trying to sound casual. But she was suddenly intensely aware that she was alone with a man she had known only a very short time, a man who had already demonstrated his ruthlessness. Perhaps this was how he meant to punish her for the things she had said last night.

He answered—and his hardness made her flinch—'Oh, I'll go to any lengths to get my way. I thought you knew that.'

If she had not been awake half the night, she might not have acted so foolishly. But she was tired, and confused, and her nerves were at snapping point. It flashed through her mind that, if only she could reach Diane's room, she would be free to leave the yacht when she pleased. That would spike his guns! He wouldn't be able to bend her to his will in front of Diane.

Without stopping to consider what reason she could give for bursting into the other girl's room at half past seven in the morning, she jumped up and dashed to the door.

Because her flight took him by surprise, she reached it and wrenched it open. But, a few yards along the corridor, he grabbed her and swung her round. He pushed her against the wall, gripping her arms above the elbows. She had never seen him look so menacing.

'My God! You believed it!' he said, in a savage voice. 'You little fool. What kind of swine do you take me for? Have I suddenly become such a monster that you have to run away from me? Of course I can't keep you here—and wouldn't, even if I could. I'm not yet entirely depraved—though you obviously think so.'

He let her go, and stood back, and controlled himself. The fierceness went out of his face, and left it coldly impassive. He said, in his normal quiet tones, 'I apologise for frightening you. I thought you would know I wasn't serious. I assumed—mistakenly, it seems—that you still had some vestige of trust in me.'

A steward came along the passage, and David beckoned him to pass them. When the man had gone by, he went on, 'You can refuse, if you wish, but I'd like you to come up to the villa with me later this morning. After that, if you want to go to Ajaccio, the *vedette* will be at your disposal. In the circumstances, I'll tell the men that you won't be working today.'

He walked away to his door, and disappeared.

⋆　　⋆　　⋆

It was about eleven o'clock, and Justine had not been outside her stateroom again, when Battista brought her the message that *M'sieur* was waiting on deck, if she wished to accompany him ashore.

She did not look at David when she joined him at the head of the gangway, and neither of them spoke on the short run across to the jetty.

On the terrace, they found Julien eating a late breakfast, and looking as if he might have a hangover. He had not yet shaved, and was wearing a flamboyant brocade robe over equally gaudy pyjamas. David explained tersely that, if Madame di Rostini was up, they would like to see her.

'She's in her sitting-room,' said Julien, getting up to go with them.

'Alone, if you don't mind,' said David.

Julien blinked, and shot an enquiring glance at Justine, who pretended not to notice.

They found Madame lying on a day-bed. She seemed surprised that Mary Ghilardo
278

was not with them. David said his sister would be coming to see her later.

Listening to their conversation, Justine even more puzzled about his purpose in bringing her here. She was not kept in suspense much longer.

He said suddenly, 'Madame, Miss Field is very disturbed by the news that you have agreed to sell the island to me. She feels I've taken advantage of you, and that she can't go on living under my aegis. I would be glad if you could convince her that there's been no coercion in this matter.' He bowed, glanced briefly at Justine, and left the room.

'Why does the sale of Pisano disturb you, my child?' Madame asked, when he had gone.

Justine looked down at her hands. 'I know how much it means to you, *madame*,' she said, in a low voice. 'It's belonged to your family for so long. I can't believe you really wish to sell it.' She raised her eyes, and met the old lady's dark ones. 'Julien may not want to live here now. But he's young and restless. He'll change in a few years' time.'

'Ah, there you are wrong, my dear,' Madame said, shaking her head. 'It is true that some wild young men become sober in later life. But the fundamentals of character—strength or weakness, selfishness or

279

generosity—are inborn in us. I have known since my grandchildren were young that they took after my daughter-in-law, and had little of my son's strength of character. Julien is very dear to me, but it would be misguided to hope that time will make him wise and strong. There is much that is good in him, but he lacks the highest moral qualities.'

She paused, and toyed with the rings on her thin white fingers. 'As you say, Pisano has been owned by di Rostinis for many years,' she went on. 'But there are families in the village whose forebears came here with Ludovico di Rostini. The island is their heritage too. In coming to this admittedly painful decision, I had also to consider their best interests. One can never resist progress, child. Times change, and we must change with them. The present mode of life on Pisano is in many ways admirable—and there can be no doubt that, in some respects, it is a happier and saner way of living than that of many people in the so-called modern world. But the islanders, particularly the younger ones, are beginning to tire of the old ways. They want more money to spend, and work that is not as hard as fishing. They want a cinema, and the television. They want more shops, and the girls want fashionable clothes. They want electric power and *gaz de ville*. If they cannot have these things here, they will leave the island. Soon, there will be no young ones left, only the old people like myself. But, if Pisano becomes a resort, they will obtain their desires, and stay here.'

Justine had never considered the islanders' prospects before. She had thought only of Madame, and of her personal feelings.

'Yes, I suppose you are right,' she said reluctantly. 'There are places off Scotland where that's happened. All the young people have gone to the mainland and, gradually, the communities have died out. I'm afraid I hadn't thought of that aspect of it. But surely—' She stopped, and looked uncomfortable.

Madame guessed the thought in her mind. 'You are wondering why I do not keep possession of Pisano until I die?' she enquired.

'Well, yes—yes, I was,' Justine admitted. 'Won't you hate seeing it changed and built over?'

The old lady pursed her withered lips. 'No, I believe—since it must be done—it will interest me to see the future take shape.'

Her black eyes twinkled suddenly, and she gave her gentle chuckle. 'If I chose to leave the matter to my improvident grandson, he

281

might not drive such a hard bargain. He would certainly waste the money. He is very extravagant. I shall leave him a generous income, but the capital will be in trust for his son, if he has one. Perhaps the next di Rostini will be like my husband and Pietro.'

'What about this house?' Justine asked. 'Will you be able to go on living here, *madame*?'

'Yes, Monsieur Cassano has agreed to my retaining this house for whatever short time is left to me. He has also accepted my condition that a clinic must be built in the village, so that the people can have medical attention without going all the way to Ajaccio.' She put up the gilt lorgnette which she used for reading. 'Will you bring me that box on the table, please?'

Justine fetched the Florentine leather casket, and placed it gently on her lap.

'There is something I wish you to have,' said Madame, before she unlocked it. 'A memento of your time here. It is very old-fashioned, but I think it will appeal to your taste.'

The casket was a jewel case. From it, she took a necklace which made Justine draw in her breath.

'I haven't worn this for thirty years. It

needs cleaning,' the old lady said critically. 'But the stones are good ones, and well matched.'

'It's beautiful!' Justine exclaimed. 'But aren't those amethysts, *madame*? I can't possibly accept such a valuable family heirloom. It's exceedingly kind of you, but—'

'Nonsense!' she was told briskly. 'I wish you to have it. If I leave it to Diane, she will sell it, or have it re-set.'

'This setting is lovely,' said Justine, examining the intricate silver filigree.

'It will become you. Take it, my child. It pleases me to think of you wearing it.'

Justine saw that the old lady would be offended if she persisted in refusing the gift. 'I don't know how to thank you. I shall treasure it always,' she said warmly.

Madame put the casket aside, and lay back on her cushions. But when, seeing that she was tiring, Justine got up to go, she said, 'I am touched that you should feel such concern for me, my dear. But I am surprised you should have thought Monsieur Cassano might have dealt unfairly with me. He is an honourable young man. You misjudge him if you doubt his integrity.'

'Yes, I see that now,' said Justine, flushing. 'I was wrong. I'll apologise to him.'

But when she left the room, and returned to the terrace, Julien told her that David had gone back to the yacht.

'He's in a strange mood today,' he said, with a grimace. 'Why did he wish to see Grand'mère in private with you?'

Justine avoided answering this question by showing him the amethyst necklace. 'I feel I ought not to have accepted it, but I was afraid of offending her,' she said worriedly.

He pooh-poohed her misgivings. 'She is quite right. Diane would never wear anything so old-fashioned,' he assured her.

As she waited for him to dress, so that they could return to *Kalliste* together, Justine's cheeks burned at the memory of the charges she had flung at David the night before.

It seemed to her now that it was she who had behaved contemptibly. How, loving him, could she have been so ready to believe the worst of him? Trust was the keystone of love, yet her trust in him had been so tenuous that, at the first test, it had evaporated. In his actions, if not always in his words, he had shown her nothing but kindness and consideration; and, in return, she had denounced him as an unscrupulous profiteer.

When Julien came back, he said, 'Aren't you working at the dig, today?' And, when she had shaken her head, 'Good—this afternoon I'll teach you how to ski on the water. David has all the equipment. You'll enjoy it. It's a wonderful sport.'

She said, 'Not today, Julien. I don't feel like it.'

They went down the stone staircase to the jetty, where a seaman handed her into the motor-boat. After his own return to the yacht earlier, David had sent the man over to wait for them.

By now, it was nearly one o'clock, and they found the others having drinks on the main deck.

Justine walked up to David, who was talking to Captain Stirling. When he broke off his conversation to look at her, she said, in a strained voice, 'Could I speak to you for a minute, please?'

'Excuse us, will you, Angus?' He put down the glass he was holding, and led the way along the starboard deck until they were out of earshot of the other.

'Well?' he said, without expression.

Her mouth was as dry as the palms of her hands were damp. She swallowed, and cleared her throat. Looking down at the decking, she said, 'I want to apologise for all the things I said last night.'

David crossed his arms, and leaned back against the safety rails. He didn't say anything.

After a moment, she went on, 'I'll get my things together, and leave at once.'

'Leave?' he queried. 'You still want to go to Ajaccio?'

'You can't possibly want me to s-stay after this,' she said unsteadily.

There was another pause, and then, as he had done once before, by the waterfall pool in the pine forest, he put out a hand and tipped her chin, making her look at him.

'Can't I?' he asked dryly. 'What should my reaction be? A vow of eternal vengeance on all who bear the name of Field? My dear girl, I may be a Corsican, but my pride is not so sensitive that it's injured beyond repair by a little spirited abuse. If Madame di Rostini has succeeded in allaying your qualms, I suggest we forget the matter. Come along—it's time for lunch.'

★   ★   ★

Mary Ghilardo decided to spend a second night on board, and did not leave until the following morning, some time after Justine had gone ashore with her working party. So it was

286

not until after lunch, when Julien came up to the dig, that Justine learned that David and Diane had also gone to Ajaccio for the day.

Speaking in French, as he always did when he wanted to express himself freely, Julien said, 'Tell me, *chérie*, has it struck you that those two have a particular interest in each other?'

Justine, who was coating some coins with bedacryl, did not look up from her task. 'What makes you ask that?'

He lit a cigarette. 'Because I happened to overhear a rather interesting conversation this morning, just before they went. Madame Ghilardo was asking David when he would be going up to see them again, and he said he would try to be there for one of her kids' birthdays, in a couple of weeks' time. Then she said it was time he settled down and raised a family of his own.'

He paused and, since he evidently expected some comment, Justine responded with what she hoped was a non-committal 'Oh, yes?'

'Then *he* said,' and here Julien paused again, to emphasise the significance of his next words, 'He said, "As it happens, I'm considering doing just that." Madame Ghilardo made that sort of squeaky sound that women of her age do when they're excited about something, and David said, "But it's no use grilling me about it, my dear sister, because I don't propose to discuss it until it's *fait accompli*." Now, what d'you deduce from that?'

What Justine deduced made the hot day seem suddenly cold.

Fortunately, Julien's question had been a rhetorical one and, without waiting for an answer, he went on, 'Of course I know Diane is a good-looking piece, but it never occurred to me that she might be the one to catch him. Frankly, I thought she didn't care much for David—but maybe that's just a crafty bit of strategy on her part. He's so used to women flinging themselves at him that it could be her coolness which has hooked him. I wonder if that is her game? She's never breathed a word to me.'

Justine turned away, ostensibly to inspect some other coins which were immersed in a bath of diluted formic acid.

'If that is what she's up to,' Julien continued, 'she may be overplaying her hand. David also told his sister that she needn't start planning a wedding because, at present, the affair wasn't progressing too well. Perhaps I'd better drop a hint to Diane that it's time to hot things up a little.'

'I should mind your own business, if I were

you,' Justine answered, rather abruptly.

'I thought she'd had enough of marriage,' he said contemplatively. 'She had the devil of a life with that old brute, Mathieu St. Aubin, and one of the conditions of his will was that, if she marries again, she'll lose the fat income he left her. But of course that wouldn't matter if she hooked a big fish like David.'

'I should have thought that what mattered most is whether she loves him—and he her,' Justine retorted, in a brittle voice.

Julien laughed. 'Depends what you mean by love, *chérie*. They've both knocked around too much to work up a grand passion. Diane's already in love—with herself. As for David, if he offers marriage, it'll be because he knows that's her price. It's no use dangling some chunks of carbon under her pretty nose. She's got plenty of rocks already.'

Justine whirled round, her face pale under her tan, her grey eyes bright with disgust. 'How can you talk like that? It's revolting. I wish you'd go away. I'm busy.'

'I'm sorry,' he said, taken aback. 'There's no need to bite my head off. I was only speaking the truth. You're too idealistic, *petite*. It's not *my* fault if real life isn't as romantic as you'd like it to be. Oh, come on, be your age, Justine. You don't really see David and Diane

289

as a twentieth-century Aucassin and Nicolette, do you?'

'I credit them with some decent feelings,' she countered fiercely. 'The way *you* talk about him, anyone would think David was as debauched as . . . as Caligula.'

'Oh, I wouldn't go as far as that,' he said, with an impenitent grin. Then: 'You're very hot in his defence. *Diable!* You haven't a *tendresse* for him, have you?'

She could have thrown something at him, but she managed to check the impulse. 'Don't be silly,' she said, with a creditable attempt at insouciance. 'It's merely that I think you're unfair to him. I think you're more of a . . . a *roué* than David is.'

She moved to another tank in which some small bones were soaking in bedacryl-tolual solution. 'If you really think so poorly of him, I'm surprised you want your sister to marry him.'

Julien shrugged. 'His peccadilloes won't trouble Diane. She's no angel herself. You ought to see her in one of her wild moods. She can rant and rave like a fishwife. Look—d'you see this scar?' He showed her a thin white cicatrice on the inside of his right upper arm. 'She did that to me. We were having a row one day, when we were both kids—she was about thirteen, I think—and suddenly she grabbed a knife from the kitchen table, and came at me like a hellcat. If I hadn't managed to dodge, she'd have had my arm off. As it was, I bled like a pig. When Sophia came back, she nearly had hysterics, poor old thing. And don't think Diane has changed since then, because she hasn't. Oh, she's as sweet as sugar when everything's going her way. But if something riles her— whoosh!' He flung up his hands, indicating all hell being let loose.

Just then, one of the crew came to ask Justine to inspect a metal object which had come to light. As she was gone some time, she hoped Julien would grow bored and go away. But he was still hanging about under the awning of the field laboratory when she returned there.

'How about coming to the *dancing* in the village with me tonight?' he suggested.

She shook her head. 'I can't tonight, Julien. After I've been to see Father, I must do some work on our records. It's taking me all my time to keep them up to date. Now, please, do go away. I can't get on, and talk to you at the same time.'

But Julien was in a determined mood, and he coaxed and wheedled until, finally, worn down by his persistence, she agreed that, if he would only go and leave her in peace, she would go to the *dancing*—but only for an hour or so.

He was waiting to take over the wheel of the motor-boat when one of the crew brought her back from her visit to the hospital.

'How is your father getting on?' he asked, on the way to the island's harbour.

'Oh, he's making excellent progress. He's so anxious to get out of hospital that he's being a model patient now,' she said.

She had not yet told her father that his discharge would have to be followed by a long period of convalescence. Nor did he know about her shorn hair, and the money she had spent. Apparently he saw nothing remarkable in the fact that she always wore a scarf over her hair when she visited him. All that concerned him was the progress of the excavation.

The *dancing* was taking place in the largest of the three café-bars in the village. Before they arrived there, Julien explained some of the local etiquette. None of the village girls would dream of going to a *dancing* on her own, he said, but it was perfectly correct for them to attend in pairs or trios, and they must dance with whoever asked them. To refuse a partner—however politely—was considered

292

offensive, and the girl who was unwise enough to do so was likely to be ignored for the rest of the evening.

'If you dance with anyone else, don't be indignant if he walks off and leaves you when the music stops,' he warned her, with a grin. 'It isn't correct for our girls to talk to their partners, or to be escorted from the floor. And they never permit a man to take them home, however much they like him. That would be considered most scandalous. It's not so many years since men and girls were not allowed to speak to each other at all in public.'

The music for the *dancing* was provided by a gramophone, and most of the records were of the tango and paso-doble variety, interspersed with some waltz-type music for a dance which consisted of all the couples on the rough concrete floor whirling round like spinning tops. To Justine's relief, none of the villagers asked her to dance, although there were many more men than women present. This, she learned from Julien, was because it was acceptable behaviour for married men to attend *dancings* on their own, leaving their wives at home to mind the children.

The part of the evening she liked best was when the dancing stopped for a time, and a very old man, with half an inch of silvery stubble sprouting from his deeply creviced cheeks, stood up and sang two songs. Considering that he looked at least eighty, his voice was astonishingly resonant and true. Julien whispered that he was a famous improviser, and that she was lucky to hear him as he rarely performed in public nowadays.

After the old man had been loudly applauded, she insisted on going back to the yacht. It had been a long day, and her eyelids were beginning to smart with fatigue.

When they were back on board, Julien was not at all pleased when she thanked him and said goodnight. But, even if Captain Stirling had not appeared, and spared her an argument, she would have resisted Julien's efforts to persuade her to stay up.

On the way to her stateroom, she wondered if the Captain would tell David she had been out with Julien, and if David would be displeased with her. She hoped not, for it had not been her intention to annoy him.

★   ★   ★

Julien's elation at the success of his scheme to persuade his grandmother to sell Pisano gave place to sulky umbrage when he discovered that the capital was to be tied up in a trust, and that all he would get was the income which Madame di Rostini had decided was adequate for him.

'It's not fair!' he protested bitterly, venting his resentment on his sister. 'I'm the heir to Pisano. The money is mine by right. Why should I live on a pittance when I'm entitled to all of it?'

'Sixty thousand francs a year is scarcely a pittance,' Diane answered tartly. 'I'm not getting a sou out of the deal.'

'You've got Mathieu's money. You don't need any more,' he retorted. 'And if you hook David, you'll have twice as much as my income for your clothes alone.'

'Oh, be quiet . . . go away . . . you bore me,' she said impatiently. 'You ought to think yourself lucky the old girl has agreed to sell at all. When you sent for me, you were afraid she wouldn't hear of the idea. I didn't think you had much hope of getting round her. But, apart from keeping you in suspense for a bit, she's been no trouble at all. If I were you, I'd be crossing my fingers that she won't change her mind at the last moment. Nothing is signed yet, remember.'

'You don't think it's likely, do you?' he demanded in alarm.

'It's possible,' Diane said maliciously.

Then, because she was anxious to get rid of him, 'No, no, you fool—of course she won't change her mind. Go away—I'm sick of your whining. I want to rest.'

When he had gone on deck, she lay down on her bed, and gave herself up to the almost physical pleasure of contemplating her future as Madame David Cassano. Forty-eight hours ago, she had been in a very different state of mind. Then, she had reached the infuriating conclusion that David was merely amusing himself with her. But, yesterday morning, Julien had reported what he had overheard David saying to his sister. Now she knew it was only a matter of time before her scheme, too, was *fait accompli.*

She smiled to herself, her blue eyes glittering. So David had told Mary Ghilardo that the affair wasn't going well at present. It must be a novel experience for him to be unsure of himself. No doubt that was why, every time he seemed on the brink of making love to her, he kept shying off. Well, it would do him good to cool his heels for a change. Far from taking Julien's advice to be more encouraging, she planned to be cooler with him for the next few days. The more she tantalised him, the more readily he would accede to her plans for their life together. For one thing, she had no intention of living on a boat, however luxurious. No, he would have to buy a house . . . perhaps a *château* within easy reach of Paris . . .

★ ★ ★

For four days, life on *Kalliste* ran smoothly. Justine reverted to her habit of having a dawn bathe. One morning, she came on deck to find David there ahead of her.

'May I join you?' he asked, smiling. 'Or do you prefer to have the sea to yourself at this hour?'

She shook her head, her heart hammering. When he smiled at her like that, with only friendliness in his eyes, she felt half-way to heaven. She knew it was madness to let herself be so exalted by a smile from a man whose interest was in someone else, but she couldn't help it.

They walked to the head of the gangway, and David stripped off the terry robe he was wearing over his swimming shorts. The stairway leading down to the water-line was taken up last thing at night, and had not yet been replaced for the day. He unfastened the length of chain which spanned the gap in the rails when the gangway was not in use, and waited for her to go first.

She pulled on her bathing cap, hoping that nervousness would not make her muff the dive. David had disappeared when she surfaced, and trod water. Then he came up a few yards away, and struck out for the beach. She did not attempt to race him. As she had surmised, he swam superbly, his powerful shoulders giving him twice the speed she could achieve on her best form.

They swam until the sun was up, and *Kalliste's* white hull was patterned with shifting golden reflections from the surface of the sea around her. The water was so clear that when, from some distance away, Justine swam down into the depths, she could see the yacht's keel as clearly as if she were close to it.

The gangway was back in place when David signalled that he was going aboard. He waited on the platform at the bottom of the steps and, when she reached it, hauled her easily up beside him. There was a delectable aroma of fresh coffee mingling with the scent of the *maquis*, and Battista was waiting on deck to put Justine's towel round her shoulders, and to ask, 'An English breakfast this morning, *m'sieur?*'

David looked enquiringly at Justine. 'Bacon and eggs today?'

'Oh, yes, please. I'm ravenous.' She pulled off her rubber cap, and ran her fingers through her hair. She had washed it since her visit to the hairdresser, and managed to set it herself with hairpins and rolls of cotton-wool.

David towelled his head, and gave himself a cursory rub down. He did not put on his robe. Although his hair was probably as curly as Julien's Byronic black locks, he kept it so closely cropped that it did not need combing into place as the younger man's would have done.

While they were having breakfast together, Justine found herself wishing that time could come to a stop. The blue sky, the shining emerald sea, the icy coldness of the orange juice, the crispness of the grilled bacon rashers, and—most of all—the nearness of the tall, bronzed man, hungrily intent on his food on the other side of the table, gave her such an intense sense of happiness that she would have been content to spend the rest of eternity re-living these perfect moments.

David glanced up and saw the look on her face. He put down his knife and fork, and leaned back in his chair, appraising her ruffled hair and her white swimsuit, now nearly dry again.

'You should have been called Alexandra,'

he said lazily.

'Oh . . . why?'

'My mother was fond of poetry, particularly Tennyson's. You remind me of that poem about Alexandra—"the sea-king's daughter from over the sea."'

Her pulses quickened. 'I like Tennyson too,' she said. 'But I should have thought he was too florid for your taste.'

'I can't say I ever thought much of "Come into the garden Maud,"' he agreed dryly. 'But I approve of his views on the proper relationship between the sexes. You know the lines I mean, don't you?'

She wrinkled her forehead. 'I don't think so.'

A teasing gleam lit his eyes. '"Man for the field and woman for the hearth . . . man to command and woman to obey; all else confusion,"' he quoted.

Justine sipped her orange juice. 'Do you also approve of—"He will hold thee, when his passion shall have spent its novel force, Something better than his dog, a little dearer than his horse?"' she asked innocently.

He laughed, and made the sign of a fencer acknowledging a successful riposte. '*Touché!*'

But he did not answer the question and,

before Justine could press him, one of the crew came hurrying along the deck and handed her a sealed envelope, at the same time speaking to David in Corse.

'We've just received a telegraph for you from England,' David explained, as she looked blankly at the envelope.

'From England?' She slit open the envelope, and drew out a single sheet of paper. Her frown cleared. 'Oh, it's from my Aunt Helen. My cousin has had her baby. It's another boy. She says "Most concerned Richard's illness. Are you sure you don't need me? Feel I should come. Certain Richard impossible invalid."'

'Now that her grandchild has arrived, are you sure you wouldn't like her to come?' David asked. 'There's plenty of room for her, you know.'

'Oh, no, thank you. You're very kind, but it really isn't the least bit necessary. Father is well out of the wood now. There would be no point in her coming.'

'Well, you'll want to send a reply. Lend Mademoiselle your pen, will you, Antonio?' he added, in French.

Justine thought for some moments, then wrote on the back of the paper—*Delighted your news. No need to worry. Father recovering fast. Everything under control. Love.*

301

Justine.

'Don't forget to put your aunt's name and address,' David reminded her, as she was about to hand this to Antonio.

'Oh, yes. Mrs. Charles Hurst, The Rectory, Little Farthing Green, Suffolk, *Angleterre.*' With a smiling word of thanks, she returned the pen to its owner.

When they were alone again, David said, 'Tell me about your aunt. You said once that she and your father don't get on too well, but I get the impression that you are very attached to her.'

'Oh, yes, she's a darling,' said Justine. 'So is her husband, Uncle Charles. I've often—' she hesitated, 'I've sometimes wished that Father had let them bring me up, as they wanted to. It would have been fun to live with my cousins. Not that I was at all unhappy as a child, but it must be nicer to be part of a large family—especially at Christmas, and on the Fifth of November and so on.'

He said, 'Perhaps the poem which suits you best is the one about the girl who was shut up in a castle, and was only allowed to watch the world through a mirror.'

'You mean *The Lady of Shalott?*' she said, startled and flurried by the unwonted gentleness in his voice.

'Yes, that's the one.' His mouth twitched slightly. 'But, if you remember, one day a knight rode past, and she couldn't resist having a look at him, and the spell was broken.'

Justine looked away at the horizon. 'You've got it muddled with some other story. When the Lady of Shalott left her mirror, it cracked and a curse came upon her. It wasn't a happy ending.'

'Wasn't it?' He leaned forward, and she was astonished to feel his hand close over her smaller one which was resting on the table beside her glass.

She turned her head, her breath catching in her throat.

'Don't look so despondent,' he said quizzically. 'I'm sure, when your knight comes along, the ending will be a happy one.'

'Good morning. I see you have both been swimming,' Diane remarked pleasantly, making Justine jump at the suddenness of her appearance.

David released Justine's hand, and quickly got up to draw out a chair for the older girl. 'Good morning. Yes, we were up early. Did you sleep well?' he asked, as she seated herself.

'Very well, thank you.' She put on the

tinted glasses she always wore on deck.

A few minutes later, Justine excused herself to go and get ready for work. She did not see David again before she went ashore, but all that day, the feel of his strong brown hand seemed to linger on hers, and the bliss she had felt during breakfast kept welling up inside her again.

She ate her lunch under the awning where she had been sitting on the day she first saw him. And she thought, "I don't care what happens next week . . . or next month . . . or next year. I don't care if it's folly to think about him, to dream impossible dreams about him. I shall never love anyone else the way I love him. It's no use trying to fight it any more. Even if it worsens the misery later on, I've got to make the most of this time. It's all I shall ever have of love. But I must be careful not to let him guess how I feel about him. That's the one thing I couldn't bear."

When she returned to the yacht, after the day's work, she had a shower, and lay down on her bed to rest for half an hour. She had just closed her eyes, when a tap at the door made her open them again.

Raising herself on one elbow, she called, 'Yes, who is it?'

'It's Diane. May I come in?'

Justine rolled off the bed, and quickly put on her underclothes before padding across the room to unlock the door.

'Oh, have I disturbed you? I'm so sorry,' Diane apologised.

'It doesn't matter. Come in,' said Justine, wondering what she wanted.

Diane walked in, and sat down in one of the armchairs. Looking at her lovely, serene face, it was impossible to believe Julien's allegation that she still had a violent temper.

She said earnestly, 'Justine, I must talk to you. What I have to say may make you angry—but please listen to me. Believe me, I wish only to spare you pain.'

Justine sat down in the other chair, and tucked her legs up beside her. 'What do you mean?' she asked warily.

Diane toyed with the gold link bracelet she was wearing, a faint frown between her beautifully shaped eyebrows. 'I asked you once if it was for David or Julien that you had changed yourself,' she began. 'I thought then—although you denied it—that it was my brother who attracted you. But, this morning, when I came on deck, I could see I had been mistaken. You are in love with David. You may say it is not so, but I know it is, *ma chère*. Another woman can always tell.

305

He was holding your hand, and it was as if . . . as if there was a light inside you. That look is unmistakable.'

Justine said quietly, 'Well, go on.'

Diane bit her lower lip. 'I don't like to tell you this, because I know how much it will hurt you, but I think David will soon ask me to marry him. Perhaps it will happen tonight. You see'—she looked embarrassed—'he has been making love to me for some time. But until this week I was not sure of my own feelings.'

'Are you sure now?' Justine asked, her voice still empty of expression.

'Yes, I have decided to accept him,' the older girl admitted reluctantly.

'I see. Well, you needn't worry, Diane. I never imagined that he would propose to me, you know.' Justine jumped up, and moved to one of the portholes. 'This look you say you saw on my face . . . did he see it too, do you suppose?'

Diane followed her, and put a comforting hand on her shoulder. 'I don't know,' she said gently. 'Perhaps—he is clever about women. But this morning was the only time *I* have seen that look in your eyes. So perhaps, if you also are clever, you can make him think he was mistaken. Only a few days ago, he was still worried that you might be in love with Julien. He asked my advice about it.'

'What did you say?'

'That it was best not to interfere.'

'And what did he say to that?'

Diane didn't answer for some moments, and something in the quality of her silence made Justine look sharply at her face. It was clear that the Corsican girl was even more ill at ease now.

'What did he say?' she insisted.

In a low voice full of compassion, Diane answered, 'He said he had been unwise to discourage your friendship with Julien. He said it would have been more subtle to ensure that, if you became infatuated with anyone, it was with him.'

'What?' Justine whispered disbelievingly.

'I am afraid it is quite true,' Diane assured her. 'He also said it was not too late for that to happen. I think that is why he swam with you this morning, and held your hand.'

'Oh, God—how could he?' Justine felt physically sick.

'Lie down, *petite*. I will get you a glass of water.' Diane steered her to the bed, and then disappeared into the bathroom.

When she came back with the water, she said, 'Try not to hate him too much, Justine. I know this is difficult for you to understand now, but he does not mean to humiliate you. Men are such strange creatures. I think perhaps David is the type who, although he has had many *affaires*, has a great respect for girls like yourself—girls who are innocent. I have heard Sophia tell the story of a man who took his daughter into the *maquis*, and shot her, and buried her there because she had been disgraced by some young man. Such a thing would not happen today, but Corsican men are still very jealous of the honour of their wives and daughters. David feels responsible for you while your father is in hospital. I don't know why he is so suspicious of Julien. My brother is a flirt, but he wouldn't harm you.'

Justine sat on the edge of the bed, and drank some of the water.

'What are you going to do now you know the truth?' Diane asked sympathetically.

'Do?'

'You surely can't wish to stay here. I would not. My pride would not permit it,' said Diane, with a sparkle in her eyes.

Justine's mouth twisted. 'My pride has become very resilient lately,' she replied, in a flat voice. 'Thank you for telling me all this, Diane. Is Julien about at the moment?'

'Yes, he is somewhere on the yacht. He had

lunch with us. Why do you ask?'

'Would you do me a favour? Would you find him, and ask him to come here?'

'Very well, if you wish,' Diane consented, looking puzzled. 'Are you sure you don't want me to stay with you for a little while?'

'No, thanks. I'm all right.' Justine got up, and went to the wardrobe to take out her yellow dress.

When, some minutes later, Julien knocked, she called him in and gave him a wide, bright smile.

'If you took me to Ajaccio this evening, instead of one of the crew, after I've been to the hospital we can dine somewhere in the city,' she suggested.

Julien accepted the idea with enthusiasm.

'Good—let's go now,' she said gaily. 'I'll just write a note to David, explaining that we may be late back.'

The sailor who usually took her over was already waiting in the boat at the foot of the gangway. He raised no objection when she said he would not be needed because Monsieur di Rostini was going with her. Justine gave him the note to deliver to David, and hoped that, by the time he read it, they would have too good a start to make it worthwhile sending the big launch in pursuit of them.

Although she did not suggest that they should hurry, Julien hurtled the motor-boat over the water at a speed which made Justine thankful she was never likely to ride in a car driven by him. He kept the engines at full throttle all the way, and would have gone faster, she guessed, if the boat had been capable of it.

When she came out of the hospital, after seeing her father, she half expected to find David lying in wait for her. But he was not, so presumably he had decided to wait until they returned to castigate her for the deliberately provocative note she had left him. Well, he would have a long wait, she thought hardily. She had every intention of staying out till two in the morning.

In fact, it was a little after one o'clock when, at a more moderate speed, they made the return trip. Julien steered with one hand, his other arm round Justine's waist. Submitting to this embrace, she felt rather guilty about making use of him to retaliate against David. Poor Julien. If he was looking forward to some more ardent caresses on board, he was due for an unpleasant surprise. David would probably send him packing before he could even set foot on the gangway.

But in this conjecture she was wrong.

When they drew alongside *Kalliste*, the decks appeared to be deserted.

Climbing the gangway, Justine began to regret that they had not stayed out longer. If David and Diane had also gone to Ajaccio, and were still there, she would have spent an extremely wearing evening to no purpose.

As they walked along to the main deck, Justine wondered if she would be able to manage Julien adroitly if he became too amorous. She did not want to be kissed by him at all, but she felt sure he would not be content to say goodnight as decorously as he had done with Captain Stirling present.

All the lamps in the main deck area had been switched off, and it seemed that everyone on board, except the night watch, had retired. Julien caught Justine's wrist, and drew her expertly down on to a couch with him. But, just as she was bracing herself to receive her first proper kiss from someone who, dashing as he was, no longer had the smallest attraction for her, several lights blazed.

'Hello. Had a good time?' David asked amiably, from a few yards away.

Julien stifled a curse, and let her go. 'I thought you were in bed,' he said crossly, looking very much like a small boy caught red-handed at some misdeed.

311

Justine expected David to say something sardonic. But he only said, 'No, I haven't been back long myself. I've been walking up on the cliffs.' He glanced at his watch. 'However, it is rather late, so perhaps we should get to bed now. See you tomorrow, Julien.'

The younger man reddened, and glanced uncertainly at Justine. It was amazing how his *boulevardier* manner wilted when David was about, she thought, with a flicker of impatience. She willed him to assert himself, to say something like, "Don't let us keep you up. We shan't be long."

But, after some seconds of palpable indecision, he muttered, 'Goodnight, Justine.'

'Goodnight. Thank you for a lovely evening,' she said brightly.

Julien gave David a glowering nod, and disappeared. A few minutes later, they heard him rowing away in the dinghy belonging to the villa.

'Would you care for a nightcap?' David asked, his tone still bland.

'I don't think so, thank you.' She rose from the couch, and pretended to smother a yawn. Inwardly, she felt as if she were standing in range of a time-bomb. But she was determined to maintain an outward poise until the explosion actually happened.

312

David switched off the lights. 'Thanks for leaving a note. We might have been worried if we hadn't known you were planning to stay in town. Where did you dine?'

'At La Côte d'Azur, and then we went on to Roi Jérôme.'

He escorted her to her stateroom. It occurred to her suddenly that perhaps he wasn't going to flare up. Perhaps, while they had been gone, he had asked Diane to marry him, and was in too euphoric a mood to care what she, Justine, did.

Nevertheless, when they reached her door, every nerve in her body alerted. He stepped forward to open it for her. Then, with his hand on the lever, he paused.

'You know,' he said mildly, 'you had a remarkably unenthusiastic expression on your face when I switched on the lights and disturbed you and Julien just now. I have the impression that it's not so much the man you're interested in, as the experience of being made love to. The unknown always has a compelling fascination for the young, particularly when it's by way of being forbidden fruit.'

Justine said nothing, but her heart had begun to pound against her ribs, and she had difficulty in breathing evenly.

David let go of the door handle. There was

only one subdued wall lamp lighting this part of the corridor, and it was some distance behind him. He could see the look on her face, but his own expression was veiled by the rosy dimness.

'I'm sorry I butted in before you could satisfy your curiosity,' he went on, and there was mockery in his voice now. 'But if it's merely the experience you want—well, I can give you that, little one.'

He moved closer, and put his right hand on her slim, bare throat. His touch was light, but she could feel the latent strength in his fingers. She trembled, but she did not recoil. She couldn't—she felt literally paralysed.

He bent his dark head and kissed her, lightly and briefly, on the corner of her quivering mouth. His lips were unexpectedly soft, and warmer than her cheek, still cool from the spindrift flung up by the bows of the motor boat.

He let go of her throat, and drew her into his arms.

'That's how I would have done it, had I been in Julien's place,' he murmured, close to her ear. 'But this is what he would have done.'

His arms tightened, his mouth came down hard on hers, and he kissed her in a way which should have made her struggle to fight him off, but which, instead, seemed to make her bones melt, and her body tingle with response.

At last he let her go, and stepped back, and opened her door.

He said, with a rasp in his voice, 'Well, now you know what it's like. Was it up to your expectations? Goodnight, Justine. Sleep well.'

And he strode off along the corridor.

*   *   *

Battista did not call Justine the next morning, and it was nearly eleven o'clock before she woke up. She pressed the bell and, when he answered it, said, 'Why didn't you wake me, Battista? Have the men gone to work without me?'

'No, *mademoiselle*. M'sieur Cassano gave orders that you were not to work today. He also gave me this note for you. He was called to Paris during the night, and left for Campo del Oro—the airport, you understand—at six o'clock.'

Justine opened the note, and read—*A friend of mine is in trouble and needs my help. I shall be away two or three days.*

The two lines of bold flowing hand were initialled *D.F.C.*

315

'Shall I bring your tray, *mademoiselle*?' the steward enquired, when she looked up.

She shook her head. 'It's too late for breakfast. Just coffee, please, Battista.'

When he brought the coffee, the steward informed her that Madame St. Aubin had gone up to the villa, but would be back for lunch.

Justine quailed at the thought of lunching with Diane, and probably Julien as well, and she asked Battista if it would be convenient for her to go to Ajaccio.

'I—I want to have my hair done,' she explained, this being the only feasible pretext which occurred to her on the spur of the moment.

Half an hour later, she was on her way to the capital. Luckily, since she could not very well return without a set, the hairdresser who had cut her braid was able to fit her in among his other appointments.

Without thinking, she had put on her newest dress—a shantung Empire style, with a band of smocking defining the high waistline. As her father was sure to notice it, she decided that the time had come to stop hiding her short hair from him. He was well enough to stand the shock.

When she walked into his room in the

apricot dress, with her hair newly set, and coral lipstick on her mouth, Professor Field reared up in bed with a glare which would once have terrified her.

'What the devil have you done to yourself? You look like some cheap little strumpet. Have you lost your senses?' he demanded, in a thunderous voice.

'Don't bellow at me, Father,' she said quietly. 'Other people may be asleep. And it's no use getting worked up, because it won't have the least effect on me. I'd rather look a strumpet than a frump, which is how you like me to look.'

'How dare you take that tone with me!' His face was purple with rage. 'And wipe that red muck off your lips. I won't have you painting your face.'

'I'm afraid you can't stop me,' she said calmly. 'I'm twenty-three, Father, not thirteen. In future, I'm going to dress like everyone else. I'm tired of being dowdy and unfeminine. You've brought me up as if I were a boy, or had no sex. Well, I have. I'm a girl—and from now on I'm going to look like one.'

'My God! I might have known this would happen. It's that damned young lounge lizard, isn't it? He's put you up to this brazen

317

defiance of my wishes. He, and that vulgar harpy, the St. Aubin woman.'

Justine sat down, and let him vent his choler unchecked. For nearly five minutes, he scarcely paused to take breath.

'You're like your mother!' was his final, most bitter sneer. 'I've always been afraid you'd take after her. I hoped I could spare you her vanity and stupidity. But it seems I've failed. My efforts have been in vain. You're as shallow and frivolous as she was.'

'Are you washing your hands of me, Father?' Justine enquired evenly. 'Or do you still want me to work with you? If you do, I shall need a proper wage. I've already drawn some back pay out of the bank.'

This sparked off another outburst, and again she listened in unmoved silence.

'Well, I don't suppose you want me to stay,' she said, when he appeared to have finished. 'So I'll go now, and come again tomorrow. We'll discuss the future when you've had more time to think. I don't want to stop working with you, but it must be on my own terms. If you can't accept that, I'll have to work for someone else.'

To her surprise, as she was leaving the room, Professor Field called her back. 'I wrote to Fuller Agnew about the caves

Cassano once mentioned,' he said gruffly. 'I had an answer from Agnew this morning. He'd like us to inspect the caves for him, and send a report. If you're not too busy bedizening yourself, I'd be obliged if you'd attend to the matter.'

'Yes, certainly,' she agreed. 'I'll do it tomorrow. Goodbye, Father.'

*   *   *

The following afternoon, Justine called a halt to work at the dig at three o'clock. The crew returned to the yacht, and she and Julien set off inland on their way to explore the caves on the far side of the island. When she had mentioned them to him, the previous evening, he had said he knew them well, having often played in them as a boy.

The caves—one large one, and two smaller ones—were on a part of the island overgrown with dense, high *maquis*. It was half past four when they reached the mouth of the largest cave, and it was so well hidden by scrub that, had she been alone, Justine would not have detected it.

Julien hacked the scrub down with a *machete*-type knife with which he had cleared the long-disused track to the place.

The entrance chamber was about twenty feet high, and twelve feet wide, and then the cave narrowed into a winding tunnel with about eight feet of headroom.

With the aid of a powerful torch, Justine examined the rock faces, and scribbled notes. Julien said that the farthest he had ever ventured was to a point where the passage forked in several directions. He had never dared to go farther for fear of losing his way out.

They were nearing the junction when, without any warning, he suddenly seized her and tried to kiss her.

Justine fended him off, and said sharply, 'Oh, not now, Julien. It's cold and creepy in here. I want to get on and get out.'

'Don't you want me to kiss you?' he said sulkily.

'No, to be honest, I don't.' She had not meant to be quite so blunt, but for some minutes past she had been feeling an unpleasant sensation which she thought must be mild claustrophobia.

'I thought you liked me?'

'I do . . . as a friend.'

'But I am in love with you,' he burst out.

'Oh, Julien, of course you aren't. You're just bored, and at a loose end. You wouldn't look at me twice if you were in Paris.' She moved farther along the passage.

'I know why you are so cold to me,' he said angrily, following her. 'It's David's fault. I suspected the other day when I told you he was going to marry Diane. I could tell you were upset. You have fallen in love with him, haven't you?'

At that moment, Justine's only concern was to make him be quiet and to get back into the open again.

She said recklessly, 'Yes, I have!'

The effect of this admission was the reverse of what she expected. Julien lunged at her again, grabbed her, and made her drop the torch. The glass protecting the bulb was unbreakable, but the torch must have fallen on its switch as, when it hit the ground, the light went out.

In darkness, they struggled—he to pinion her arms, she to escape from his.

'*Let me go!*' she demanded furiously.

'Not until I have kissed you,' he said, through clenched teeth.

Justine kicked his shin, and he cursed and began to be rough with her. Then a sound like distant thunder made them both freeze.

'Dear God! The roof's coming down!' she whispered in terror, clutching him. 'Run, Julien—run!'

'Which way? I don't know which way,' he cried, panic-stricken.

But, even if they had not lost all sense of direction, there would have been no time to escape. Within seconds of that first ominous rumble, the whole mass of hillside overhead seemed to come crashing down on top of them.

CHAPTER SEVEN

'JUSTINE . . . Justine . . . *Justine!*'

The urgent repetition of her name woke Justine from sleep—or so she thought. When she opened her eyes, the room was dark, pitch dark. That was odd. She always drew back the curtains before she climbed into bed. And even if she had, for once, forgotten to do so, surely they would not shut out every glimmer of daylight? Was it still night-time? Who had roused her? What was happening?

'Oh, my God! She is dead!' a voice exclaimed hoarsely, in French.

'No, I'm not. Who are you? What's going on?' she asked bewilderedly.

A cold hand brushed her arm, and felt its way up to her face. 'Holy Mary be praised! You're alive. You lay so still. I couldn't wake you. I thought you were dead. I was frantic. Are you hurt? It's me . . . Julien. The roof collapsed. Don't you remember?'

She coughed. Her throat and her nostrils seemed to be full of dust. 'Oh, it's you. I'm sorry—I couldn't think where I was for a minute. Yes . . . yes, I remember now. At least I remember being hit on the head by

something. It must have knocked me unconscious. Have I been out long?'

'I don't know. I was knocked cold too. I
came round some time ago. At first, I couldn't
find you. We must have been thrown different
ways.'

'How cold you are,' she said, taking his
hand from her cheek, and chafing it with her
own warmer ones. Then she realised she was
still lying down, and struggled up into a sitting position.

'Ouch! I feel as if I've been scalped. My hair
is all wet and sticky. I must be bleeding.
There's a lump the size of an egg.'

'Can you move your legs?' Julien asked.

'Yes—I'm all in one piece except for this
crack on the head. What about you? Are you
all right?'

'I think I've sprained my ankle. When I
came round, there was stuff piled all over my
legs. I managed to work myself clear, but I
doubt if I can walk. Never mind: we're lucky
to be alive. I thought we were going to be
crushed like a couple of ants.'

'So did I,' Justine said, with a shudder.

He shifted his position, and she heard him
hiss at the pain from his injured ankle. Then
his arm came round her shoulders.

'I'm sorry about what happened before the

roof fell. Don't be frightened. I won't hurt you. I swear it.'

'I know. Forget it. I'm glad you're here.' She found and pressed his other hand. 'If I were alone, I'd be petrified. Do you think there'll be another fall?'

'No, it's over now,' he reassured her. 'The question is—which side of it are we? If it fell behind us, you'll be able to grope your way out. But if we're behind it, we're stuck for some hours, I'm afraid.'

'The torch!' she exclaimed. 'What a fool I was to drop the torch. I'd better start crawling around to see if I can find it. If it hasn't been smashed to smithereens.'

'No, wait,' said Julien, restraining her. 'I'd forgotten . . . I've got a cigarette lighter. I could have used it when I was trying to find you. I forgot all about it. Here it is. Luckily, I refilled it this morning. It should keep alight for some time.'

The little tongue of flame did not illuminate their surroundings, but it did reveal their faces to them.

'We look like a pair of golliwogs,' Justine said, in English. Then, reverting to French, 'Am I as filthy as you are? I suppose I must be.'

'Yes, as black as a chimney-sweep. I can

hardly recognise you. But the dirt will soon wash off. We need more light. What can we burn to make a blaze?'

'I've got a hanky,' she suggested.

'Ah, yes—so have I. We'll burn them both.'

The flames from the two handkerchiefs did not make much of a blaze, but it was enough to show them how narrowly they had missed being pulped under the tons of rock which blocked the passage not more than twenty feet away.

'My God! We've been lucky,' Julien said, in an awed voice, as they gaped at the jumble of jagged boulders.

'Give me the lighter, and I'll see if we're on the outside,' said Justine, scrambling up.

She took the lighter and, keeping close to one wall, made her way along the winding passage, praying that soon she would find herself back in the entrance chamber. When, instead, she came to the junction of three narrower tunnels, a thrust of horror stabbed her. They were trapped. There was no way out, except through that impenetrable rockslide.

"I mustn't panic," she thought. "I must keep calm. I mustn't scream." And then she was rackingly sick.

'So we're stuck here, are we?' said Julien, when she got back. He must have guessed from her silence what she had found.

'I'm afraid so.' She tried to sound casual. 'Well, we'll just have to make the best of it till we're rescued. If we're not back for dinner, Captain Stirling will send out searchers. They don't know where the caves are, but someone from the village will show them.'

'Oh, yes, it's only a matter of a few hours' wait,' he agreed cheerfully. 'Once they're here, they'll have us out in no time.'

'Let me look at your ankle. If I tear my shirt into bandages, perhaps I can strap it and make it less painful,' she said.

'No please—don't touch it,' he said sharply. 'It's not sprained, Justine. It's broken. Unless you're an expert on fractures, it's best left alone.'

'What? Are you sure? Oh, Julien, you must be in agony.'

'It's not too bad. I'll survive. Better put the light out. We don't want to waste it.'

She knelt beside him. In her absence, he had dragged himself close to the wall so that he could lean against it. She capped the lighter, and put it carefully in the pocket of her ruined blue trousers.

Feeling for his hands, she said, 'You're freezing. You're in shock. You should be swaddled in blankets, sipping hot tea. We've

327

got to get you warm somehow. I know—I'll be a blanket for you.'

She slid sideways into a sitting position, close beside him and face to face, and put her arms round him, and pressed herself against his chest.

He held her, his cheek on hers. He was so cold and devitalised, and she so worried about him, that they were like children clinging together for comfort.

She knew, and she knew that he knew, that their rescue could take several days. To break through that mass of rock would require expert knowledge, and special equipment. In the meantime, they would have no food, no water, and no warm clothes. She could survive the ordeal, but what about him? The pain from his ankle must be excruciating. What happened to a broken ankle if it went untreated for forty-eight hours or more? Would gangrene set in? Would he lose his leg? Perhaps his life?

"Stop it," she told herself sharply. "It's no use looking on the black side. Try to remember all you've ever read about survival techniques. You've got to start thinking constructively."

Some time later, when Julien had

become a little less alarmingly cold, something suddenly occurred to her which made her sit up, and exclaim, 'Julien, perhaps we aren't trapped. Haven't you noticed the smell?'

'The smell?' he echoed blankly.

'The *maquis!* Can't you smell the *maquis?*'

He sniffed, then sniffed again. 'Yes . . . yes, I believe I can. Yes, I am sure I can.' He stiffened, gripping her hands. 'Which means there is another opening somewhere.'

'There must be,' she said excitedly. 'I'm sure there's no air coming through that great barricade of rock. And if this cave was sealed now, the air would be sour and stuffy. But it isn't. It's still quite fresh.'

'Then why are we sitting here? Come on: let's get started,' he said.

'You can't move with a broken ankle. I'll go and find the way out, and then run and fetch help. Should I go to the village, or the yacht? The yacht, I think. They may not have a stretcher in the village, but I'm sure there'll be one on *Kalliste*. Oh dear, it means leaving you alone for at least an hour, I'm afraid. I'll need the lighter to find my way to the opening. Can you stand being left here on your own?'

'I am not a little boy, afraid of the dark,' he

329

said shortly. 'But anyway I'm coming with you. You don't think I'd let you explore those tunnels alone? You might lose your way, or fall, or even faint. You also were hurt, remember. A blow on the skull can cause concussion. If you passed out somewhere up there, how would I find you? No, we have to stick together.'

'But how can we? You can't hop. The pain would be torture,' she expostulated.

'I can stand it,' he insisted stubbornly. 'Light the lighter, and help me up.'

When they reached the place where the passage forked in three directions, Julien slumped against the wall.

'Let's rest for a minute,' he muttered.

Justine found it incredible that he had managed to get so far. Every lurching step must have been like treading barefoot on red-hot coals. But, using her as a crutch, and never once even moaning, he had hauled himself forward, his injured foot crooked off the ground.

Sweat had poured from his face and body, washing his face almost clean again. Watching his laboured breathing as, with closed eyes, he mustered his stamina, Justine thought, "You were wrong, Madame di Rostini. He has more mettle than you think."

Aloud, she said, 'I'll go a few paces along each passage, and see if the air smells fresher in any one of them. I shan't go far. You wait here.'

When she returned from the third tunnel, she said, 'I may be wrong, but I think the *maquis* scent is stronger in the right-hand passage, Julien.'

He nodded, his jaw clenched. 'Right—let's try it.'

The passage seemed to have no end. When they stopped, to rest again, she said, 'If this is the wrong way, you're being tortured for nothing, *mon cher*. Please let me go on alone. We can keep in touch by shouting.'

But he would not let her go without him and, soon, they set off again.

They must have travelled at least a quarter of a mile, and Julien's teeth were grinding and his face was glistening, when the flame of the lighter began to flicker and dwindle.

"Now we're really sunk," she thought desperately. "We'll never get out this way, and we'll never get back in the dark, and if they can't hear us shouting they'll think we were killed in the rockslide."

And then, just as he gave his first sobbing groan of anguish, the passage turned, and she saw a faint radiance ahead.

'We've made it!' she cried, in English. 'Oh, Julien, look! We're safe. We're nearly there!'

Fortunately, the way out of the cave was not as densely overgrown as the entrance had been. Justine was able to push her way through the shrubs growing outside the opening, and trample them down and make a way clear for Julien.

For her, it was ecstasy to be safely in the open air again. No doubt because she had been so long in darkness and near-darkness, the colours of the sunset sky seemed more vivid and beautiful than any she had seen before.

'Now you lie down and, before you know it, I'll be back with a stretcher party,' she said to Julien.

But the last stretch of tunnel had taxed his endurance to its limit. Before she could help him to lower himself, his body sagged, and he fainted.

When after three or four minutes he showed no sign of coming round, she judged that the best thing to do was, not to wait any longer, but to get to the yacht as fast as possible.

Stripping off her grimy trousers, she folded them into a pillow for Julien's head. Her shirt was equally dirty, but the part which had been tucked inside her trousers was still bright pink. She shinned up a nearby tree, and tied it to a branch as a marker flag, in case she had any difficulty in leading the men back to the spot where Julien lay. Then, with no clothes left but her bra and nylon briefs, she began the rough cross-country race to fetch help.

She never knew how long it took her to get from the cave exit to the beach of the bay where *Kalliste* lay at anchor. On the way, she remembered that the dinghy belonging to the villa was tied up to the yacht, so she knew that, unless someone on board saw her scrambling down the cliff path and realised something was amiss, she would have to swim the last lap.

This, as it turned out, she had to do, for there seemed to be no one about on deck when she arrived, panting and almost exhausted, on the beach.

However, someone aboard must have spotted her as she plunged into the sea, as most of the yacht's company were craning over the rails when she reached the bottom of the gangway. By now she was so worn out by her exertions that she couldn't have hauled herself out of the water unaided if there had been a shark at her heels. One of the crew hoisted her on to the platform, lifted her into his arms and carried her up the steps.

'Good grief, lassie, what a state you're in!' Captain Stirling exclaimed, arriving on the scene just as the seaman stepped on deck with her.

Two of the stewards had already had the forethought to hurry for a couch from the main deck. Before the Captain could ask any questions, they returned to the gangway, carrying the couch between them. Gently, the seaman laid Justine down on the cushions.

'What's happened, Miss Field? You look as if you've been through a shipwreck. Where's young di Rostini?' Angus Stirling asked, bending over her.

Justine was shaking with reaction. Even her teeth were chattering. She said, as coherently as she could, 'The roof of the cave fell in. Julien's broken his ankle. We got out of the cave, then he fainted. I left him unconscious. If someone could fetch me some clothes, and a glass of brandy, I'll show you the way to where he is. Is there anyone on board who knows how to splint a fracture? When we get him back, you'll have to take him to hospital. He's badly shocked, and his foot will have to be X-rayed.'

The Captain rapped out orders, and men

hastened off to obey them. He turned back to Justine. 'We'll find the lad, if you can tell me roughly where he is. You can't come with us, Miss Field. You're in no condition to move. You're prostrate yourself, lass.'

It was only then that she realised she was bleeding from head to foot. Blundering her way through the scrub, thinking only of Julien, she had scarcely felt the briars and thorns which had scratched and gashed her bare flesh. Her swim had washed most of the blood off, but now she was covered with it again. It trickled and oozed from a score of painful lacerations.

Someone covered her with a blanket, and someone else brought her a mug of hot, sweet coffee. As she drank it, she felt so weak and giddy that she knew the Captain was right. She couldn't return with the rescuers. She would need a stretcher herself.

She told Captain Stirling the area Julien was in, and about the marker she had left.

'Right, I'll go along myself,' he said briskly. 'As soon as we get the laddie back here, we'll take the pair of you to hospital.'

At this point, Diane hurried up. When she saw Justine's condition, she gave a little scream of horror.

'What's happened? Where's Julien? Is he

hurt?'

Briefly the Captain explained. 'I'll leave you to see to Miss Field while we're gone, *madame*. Never mind dressing her cuts. Keep her warm—that's the most important thing. She's had a nasty crack on the head. She may be concussed.'

By the time he had given orders for the big launch to be standing by to rush Julien and Justine to Ajaccio, the rescue party had assembled with all the necessary equipment.

'You lie still and rest,' he told Justine. 'Don't worry, we'll soon find the lad and fix him up. You're a plucky girl, Miss Field. You deserve a medal.'

As the motor-boat roared away to land him and his men on the island, Battista brought along some more blankets to wrap round Justine. It was some time before her shuddering abated, and she began to relax and feel warm again.

Diane was more hindrance than help. All she did was to harry Justine with questions until, quite brusquely, the steward told her that Mademoiselle was too spent to answer them yet. It was he who gently examined the lump on the back of Justine's head, and who sponged away the blood and dirt, and put on a temporary dressing.

'We must contact M'sieur in Paris. He will wish to return immediately,' he said, as he ministered to her.

'Oh, no, Battista—he's busy,' she objected. 'There's no point in bothering him. He'll probably be back tomorrow anyway.'

'I agree,' Diane said haughtily. She looked crossly at the younger girl. 'If you ask me, it was extremely foolish of you to go into the cave. You should have known it might be dangerous. And, as neither of you seems to be seriously injured, there's certainly no need to call Monsieur Cassano away from important business in Paris.'

Presently, in spite of the steward's indignant objections, Justine insisted on going down to her stateroom to put on some clothes.

'Don't fuss, Battista,' she said, smiling at him. 'I'm perfectly all right again now, and I'd feel a fool arriving at the hospital in blankets when I'm only suffering from a few scratches and bruises.'

'They are more than scratches, *mademoiselle*. They must be cleaned and dressed,' he said anxiously.

'Well, that's no reason why I shouldn't put on some clothes,' she replied stubbornly.

When she saw her reflection in the mirror-glass doors of the wardrobe, her jaw dropped.

She had realised she must look very bedraggled, but she had not known that her eyes were still rimmed with black dust, or that she had a large bruise on one cheekbone and streaks of dried blood across her forehead. As Captain Stirling had said, she looked like a survivor from a shipwreck.

She put on some dry underclothes, and her other shirt and trousers. But before she had time to deal with her hair, which was drying in untidy wisps, or to clean up her face, Battista came to tell her the rescue party had been sighted on top of the cliffs.

Although he had been only semi-conscious when they reached him, Julien was sufficiently recovered to give her a feeble grin as they lifted him from the *vedette* into the launch. Seconds later, accompanied by the Captain and Diane, and two of the crew, they were on their way to Ajaccio.

Julien's face was still a very bad colour, and during the crossing he was sick.

'I'm afraid his ankle is badly smashed up,' Captain Stirling murmured to Justine. 'To be frank with you, I'd regarded him as a rather spineless young man until today. But he's come through this like a Trojan. Getting out of that cave must have given him hell. He's not the weakling I took him for.'

338

An ambulance was waiting on the quay for them and, as soon as they reached the hospital, Julien was borne away on a trolley as Professor Field had been on the night of his collapse. The casualty department was busy that evening, and a nurse showed Justine to a curtained cubicle, and asked her to wait there until someone was free to attend to her less urgent hurts.

She was sitting on the examination couch, trying to ignore the stabbing headache which had started during the crossing, when the curtain was swished aside.

'*David!*'

For an instant, she gaped at him. Then, slipping off the couch, she flung herself into his arms. 'Oh, thank goodness you're back!' she exclaimed with her face pressed against his chest.

The words were scarcely out of her mouth before she realised what she was doing, and recoiled in chagrined confusion.

'I—I'm s-sorry,' she stammered, backing away. 'It's just that it's been such a day. I'm a bit shaken up, I'm afraid. What are *you* doing here? I thought you were still in Paris.'

'I got away earlier than I expected. When we landed at Campo del Oro, I rang through to *Kalliste* to ask them to send a boat over, and they told me about the accident.'

'Oh . . . I see.'

Before either of them could say any more, a doctor arrived to examine her. David seemed about to speak, then changed his mind and disappeared.

She did not see him again until after her cuts had been tended and her skull X-rayed. And then Diane was with him.

'Is there any news of Julien yet?' she asked them.

David said, 'Yes—they've set his ankle, and admitted him for a few days, in case there's concussion. I've also been up to see your father, and told him what's happened. How are you feeling now?'

She avoided his eyes. 'Oh, I'm fine. My head aches a bit, but that's not surprising. Otherwise I'm as right as rain.'

'We'll see what the doctor has to say about that,' he said.

The doctor's verdict was that she must rest for a few days, but that it would not be necessary to detain her.

'What about concussion?' David asked, frowning. 'Surely she should be kept in overnight?'

'Any fall or blow which results in a period of unconsciousness causes a degree of

340

concussion, *m'sieur*,' the doctor told him. 'But in the case of this young lady, I don't think it's necessary to keep her under observation here. If her headache is still severe tomorrow, or if she finds her vision affected, she must be brought back. But, at present, there is nothing to suggest that any treatment, other than rest, will be needed.'

David drew him aside, and had a low-voiced conversation with him. Then the doctor went away, and David returned to the girls.

'I don't think you should come back to the yacht tonight,' he said to Justine. 'No doubt the doctor is right, but to be on the safe side, I'm arranging for you to spend the night in a nursing home.'

She knew that tone. It would be useless to argue with him. 'Very well—if you feel it's best,' she agreed docilely.

He and Diane took her to the nursing home in a taxi. Half an hour later, she was tucked up in bed, and they were on their way back to Pisano.

*　　　*　　　*

When Justine woke up the next morning, her headache had gone. There was still a tender lump on her scalp, and she was a little stiff, but otherwise she felt perfectly normal.

After breakfast, she was visited by the director of the nursing home, who took her pulse and temperature, and tested her blood pressure and her sight.

'Surely I haven't got to stay in bed, have I?' she asked him. 'There's nothing wrong with me.'

'No, I see no reason why we should confine you to bed,' he agreed. 'You can rest equally well in a chair on the balcony. As you see, there is a delightful view.'

While she was dressing, a nurse came in with a vase full of white carnations.

'These have just arrived for you, Miss Field. There was no card with them, but no doubt you will know who sent them.' She smiled at Justine's heightened colour, little guessing that the two dozen exquisite blooms gave the English girl more pain than pleasure.

When the nurse had gone to fetch a radio and some magazines for her, Justine stood gazing at the carnations through a blur of tears.

"He knows," she thought miserably. "After last night, he must know. Oh, *why* did I have to give myself away like that?"

And she wished with all her heart that she

342

was free to go to the airport, and catch the first flight out of Corsica.

*   *   *

At that moment, far away in England, her Aunt Helen was speeding through the village on her high-saddled vintage bicycle.

'Morning, Mrs. Hurst,' someone called to her.

She pedalled past without replying. She had just received a telephone call which had made her rush out of the house in search of her husband, her mind in such confusion and excitement that she had even forgotten to take off her nylon overall.

She found Canon Hurst in the church, chatting to the Langham children while they started work on a brass rubbing.

'Oh, Charles, thank goodness you're still here. I was afraid you might have gone,' she burst out breathlessly.

'What on earth is the matter, Helen?' the Rector asked, in astonishment. He had never seen her looking so agitated.

'You won't believe it. I can't believe it myself. It's incredible . . . quite incredible!'

Deducing that whatever had happened was not of an unpleasant nature, her husband

343

steered her to the vestry, and made her sit down to get her breath back.

'Now, what is incredible?' he asked, curious to learn what had put her in such a fluster. She was normally so placid and imperturbable.

'Justine is getting married!' she announced, still panting.

'What?' His eyebrows shot up. 'Well, that is a shock. When did you hear? There was no letter this morning, was there? Have you had a wire from the child?'

She shook her head. 'No, no—a telephone call. But not from Justine herself. She doesn't know, you see. He says he hasn't asked her yet.'

Canon Hurst sat down himself. 'You're not making sense, my dear. Start at the beginning. Who was it who rang you up?'

His wife drew in a deep breath, and became a little more composed. 'This Monsieur Cassano who's been putting her up on his boat while poor Richard has been in hospital. I thought, from what she said in her letter, that he was a man of your age. But he's young . . . at least his voice is young. Oh, really, it's all most bewildering.' She discovered she had her overall on, and began to unfasten the buttons.

'Go on . . . go on,' the Rector urged, greatly

344

intrigued by what he had learnt so far.

'Well, the first thing he said was that Justine is in hospital as well now. It's nothing serious, apparently. She got trapped in a cave with some other man, and they thought she might have concussion. She was hit on the head by some rocks, he said. However, they've had her X-rayed, and it seems there's no damage done. She'll be out tomorrow, or the next day.'

'What was she doing in a cave?' Canon Hurst enquired.

'I don't know. He didn't explain. But anyway it isn't important. We'll hear all about that when we get there.'

'We? There? What *are* you talking about?'

'He wants us to fly there at once, to attend the wedding. I said we couldn't possibly go today, but that we'd go on Wednesday. That will give us time to—'

With commendable restraint, in the circumstances, her husband broke in, 'Really, Helen, you must know we can't afford—'

'You needn't worry about the expense, dear,' she interrupted. 'David insists on paying for everything. All we have to do is to ring up some office in London, and tell them when we can go, and the whole thing will be arranged for us. You can get old Whittaker to take the services on Sunday, can't you? How lucky there are no weddings this Saturday.'

'I'm beginning to feel as if *I* were suffering from concussion,' said the Rector, closing his eyes for a moment. 'I don't like to appear obtuse, Helen, but who is this fellow called David?'

'Oh, Charles—*David Cassano* . . . the man she's going to marry, dear,' said Mrs. Hurst, in the tone of someone explaining a point which should need no explanation.

'But you said he hadn't asked her yet.'

'Well, no—but he obviously knows she's going to say "yes." He sounds simply charming, Charles. You'd never guess he was a foreigner. His English is perfect. I could tell from his voice that he's nice.'

'Could you indeed?' the Rector said dryly. 'The whole thing seems very extraordinary to me, I'm afraid. How long has she known this man? Who is he? Why all the haste?'

'Oh, what does it matter who he is, as long as he loves her. I can't wait to meet him. I wish I'd asked him how old he is. He *sounds* about thirty-five . . . not a boy, but not middle-aged yet.'

'What I can't understand is why he's arranging the wedding before he's asked Justine to marry him,' Charles Hurst said perplexedly.

'Yes, it is rather odd, I suppose. But perhaps that's the way they go about things in Corsica. Oh, Charles, it's like a miracle, isn't it?'

Her husband stroked his chin. 'You are quite sure it isn't some kind of cruel joke?' he asked dubiously.

'Don't be silly, dear. Of course it's not a joke. Do you realise what it must cost to phone all the way from Corsica, and he was on the line for at least ten minutes,' said Mrs. Hurst rather crossly. 'I can't understand you, Charles. I know it's a shock—I was flabbergasted myself—but I should have thought you'd have been delighted. I certainly am. It's exactly what I hoped would happen . . . though I must admit I never thought it would.'

'What about Richard? Does he know? I can't see *him* being delighted at Justine rushing into marriage with a man she can't have known very long.'

'Richard doesn't know anything about it yet. David is going to get his consent before he proposes to her this afternoon. He said he'd telephone again tonight, and we'd be able to speak to Justine too. He rang up this morning to give us as much time as possible to arrange

347

getting away. The wedding will probably be on Friday.'

'He seems a very assured young man. What if Richard refuses his consent?' the Rector suggested.

'How can he?' said Mrs. Hurst. 'Justine's not a minor. Asking his permission is merely a courtesy. He will have to agree, whether he likes it or not.'

'My dear Helen, he may have no legal right to prevent her marrying, but you can't seriously suppose that he'll give them his blessing? As you said yourself, when we were discussing her future some time ago, your brother will never willingly release his hold on her.'

'And you said that one day she would meet someone whose influence would be stronger than his,' his wife reminded him.

*　　　*　　　*

When the nurse found that Justine had scarcely touched her lunch she scolded her like a nanny admonishing a faddy child.

'I'm sorry—I'm not very hungry. It's too hot to eat much,' said Justine.

'And it's too hot to sit out here. You must come into the shade and rest on your bed,

Miss Field,' the nurse said firmly.

Justine argued that she was used to the afternoon glare, but the woman was adamant, and made her lie down on the bed, and drew the curtains.

'I will call you at four. Until then, you must sleep,' she instructed, before she bustled away.

Justine closed her eyes, and tried to empty her mind of thoughts. But the room was full of the delicate scent of the carnations, and she was tormented by a mental picture of David and Diane relaxing on loungers in the shade of the yacht's awning. Perhaps by now there was a ring on Diane's left hand; a ring bought yesterday at some exclusive jeweller's in the Faubourg St. Honoré in Paris. In her mind's eye, Justine saw David lean from his chair to capture the other girl's hand and press his lips against her knuckles as, that very first night on the terrace, he had kissed Justine's.

And, remembering how, only two nights ago, he had held her hard against him, and kissed her mouth, Justine moaned and rolled over, and buried her face in the pillow.

When, some time later, she heard the door open, she thought it was the nurse, looking in to make sure she was obeying orders. She lay still, waiting for the door to close, and footsteps to fade away down the corridor outside.

The door did close, but the footsteps approached the bed. Someone sat down on the side of it.

She tensed. Who was it? Not him . . . please God, not him . . . not now, not yet.

'Justine,' David said quietly. Gently, he tapped her shoulder.

Did he know she was awake? No, how could he? Perhaps, if she didn't stir, he would go away. "I can't face him," she thought. "I can't."

After several interminable moments, he rose from the edge of the bed. But he did not leave the room and, to her consternation, she heard him sit down in the visitors' chair. There was a scratching sound, the faint rasp of a match struck. He was lighting a cigar.

Cornered, knowing it was impossible to go on feigning sleep while he sat there, watching her, she waited a few minutes, then pretended to be waking up.

'Oh . . . David. How long have you been here?' she murmured, simulating drowsy surprise when she turned over and saw him.

'Not long.' Before she had a chance to sit up, he came over and sat beside her again. 'How are you feeling today?'

Her clothes were crumpled, her hair was dishevelled, her face was hot from being pressed into the pillow. She had never felt more unhappy, and hopeless, and angry than she did at that moment.

'Oh, fine, thanks,' she said hollowly.

She attempted to sit up, intending to slip off the bed, but he shook his head, and pressed her back against the pillows. 'No, don't move. You're supposed to be resting.'

She turned her face towards the carnations on the locker. 'I imagine you sent the flowers. Thank you—they're lovely. How much longer have I got to stay in here?'

'Only until Wednesday. Then you can move to the Hotel des Etrangers for a couple of nights. That's where your uncle and aunt will be staying.'

'My uncle and aunt?' she echoed blankly.

'I phoned Mrs. Hurst early this morning, and she and your uncle will be arriving some time on Wednesday.'

Justine jerked into a sitting position. 'Why? What for? I'm not ill. What on earth possessed you to send for them . . . both of them?'

He smiled, and suddenly there was a blaze in his eyes which made her tremble. 'A bride must have someone to give her away. Unfortunately, the doctors don't think your

351

father will be up to it by Friday, so your uncle will have to stand in for him. In any case, I assumed you would want them to be present.'

"I *am* concussed," she thought dazedly. "This isn't really happening at all. It's a hallucination. They're one of the symptoms of concussion."

David took her hands in his. 'I'm not mistaken, I hope,' he said quizzically. 'You do want to marry me, don't you?'

'B-but you're going to m-marry Diane,' she stammered, in a stunned voice.

His black brows lifted. 'Marry Diane— God forbid! What gave you that crazy idea?'

'She told me you were,' she said faintly.

His grey eyes narrowed. 'Did she indeed? I see. Well, she was wrong. I wouldn't marry the ornamental Widow St. Aubin if my life depended on it.'

Then the grim look left his face, and he laughed, and let go of her hands and pulled her against him.

'I'm in love with you, my foolish Miss Field. And when you shot into my arms last night, I assumed my feelings were reciprocated. Well, are you going to marry me, or aren't you? A fine fool I shall look if you say no.'

This rocketing ascent from the depths of

wretchedness to a pinnacle of happiness far above her wildest day-dreams was too much for Justine. She burst into tears, and clung to him.

She was calming down, and David had just given her his handkerchief, when the nurse came in to wake her, and administer some tablets.

'Oh, excuse me . . . I did not know you had a visitor, *mademoiselle*,' she apologised, looking rather flustered.

Evidently she did not approve of David sitting on the bed, and as soon as Justine had swallowed the pills, she suggested that Monsieur should wait outside on the balcony while the patient tidied herself. Then she would bring them both refreshments.

David had brought Justine's clothes with him in a suitcase. She was glad to change into a dress, and attend to her hair and face, but it was with renewed shyness that she joined him on the balcony.

'I'm afraid we've shocked your nurse,' he said, turning round from the balustrade, and holding out his hands to her. 'In Corsica it isn't proper for unmarried people to be alone together, particularly in a bedroom with the curtains drawn. You'll have to marry me now, *ma mie*, if only to redeem your reputation!'

She laughed, and blushed, and put her hands into his. 'Oh, David, are you sure? I'm not at all the sort of person you ought to marry.'

He lifted an eyebrow. 'Why not?'

'Well . . . your world is so different from mine.'

A curiously sombre look came into his eyes. 'Most people would say I'm not to the sort of man you should marry, Justine. I'm thirteen years older than you are, and my life hasn't been an ascetic one.'

'I know that,' she said candidly. 'You don't have to tell me. I've heard it already from Diane and Julien. According to them, no woman is safe with you. If it's true, you've been amazingly circumspect with me—at least until the night before you went to Paris.'

His hands tightened on hers, and she saw amusement tugging at the corners of his mouth. 'Did you enjoy what happened the night before I went to Paris?'

'Yes. I didn't want to—but I did,' she admitted honestly.

He laughed. 'So did I. I'd like to repeat the experience, but unfortunately it isn't very private here. There are several convalescents sitting about in the garden. We don't want to be the cause of any relapses. For the moment, I'll have to be content with this.' He lifted her hands in turn, and pressed his lips against her palms.

The nurse reappeared with iced coffee and cream cakes.

'You weren't serious about getting married on Friday, were you?' Justine asked, when they were sitting down with the width of a wicker table between them.

'Certainly I was serious. You have no objection, have you?'

'No . . . but I'm sure Father will have,' she said, frowning. 'It's only two days since he found out I've cut my hair and started to use make-up. This is going to be an even worse shock for him.'

'And if he objects?' David asked.

She studied her hands for a moment. 'You're the most important person in my life now,' she answered steadily.

'Don't worry, *mon coeur*. I've already told your father. I saw him this morning.'

Her eyes widened. 'What did he say?'

'Well, I didn't announce that we were going to be married. I asked his permission to address you. It's still the custom here in Corsica. As a matter of fact, he took it very well. He even wished me luck.'

'Wished you luck?' she repeated disbelievingly.

'He said you had lost your head over "that damned young whipper-snapper"—which I took to refer to Julien—and, if I could bring you to your senses, he'd be grateful to me.'

'He wouldn't call Julien a whipper-snapper if he had seen him getting out of the cave yesterday,' Justine said shortly. 'I can't imagine why he thinks I'm infatuated with Julien.'

'You can hardly deny that you have been at some pains to give me that impression,' David said dryly.

'Only because I didn't want you to guess the truth, David—' she stopped, colouring. 'David, when did you begin to like me?'

He smiled. 'I liked you from the first. You gave me such fierce looks, but you were so easy to rout. I realised I was in love with you that day we met near the dig, and I saw you'd been crying. I told you I was going to marry you the night your father was taken ill.'

'You told me?'

'The night I "drugged" you, and put you to bed. Surely you haven't forgotten that?' he said, with a mocking gleam. 'You were nearly asleep at the time, and I said it in Corse, so even if you had heard, you wouldn't have understood.'

'But if you wanted to marry me as long ago as that, why were you so nasty to me, and so nice to Diane? That day you took me to lunch with your sister, for instance. You didn't say a word on the way home, and when I was coming back from the hospital, I saw you going off with Diane.'

'My dear child, when a man touches a girl and she flinches, as you did that day, you can't expect him to be in a very good mood.'

'That was the day I knew I was in love with you,' she said huskily. 'I didn't mean to flinch. But it still doesn't explain why you took Diane out.'

'Were you jealous?'

'No—not jealous exactly. I didn't hate her. I envied her for being so beautiful, and sophisticated, and . . . well, your kind of woman.'

'My kind of woman!' He sprang up from his chair and went to stand at the balustrade, his brown hands gripping the rail with a force which frightened her.

'What have I said?' she appealed. 'David . . . darling . . .'

He swung round, his dark face set. 'I took Diane out that night—and other nights— because it amused me,' he said savagely. 'If you think she offered to chaperone you out of disinterested kindness, you're mistaken. She's

357

more subtle than most of her kind, but I'm too experienced not to recognise an opportunist when I meet one.' He paused, and went on less fiercely, 'When I was a boy in my twenties, I didn't want marriage. I was too restless and ambitious to have time for more than casual relationships. By the time I'd achieved my objectives, the only women I met were like Diane. But by then I wanted what my father had—a woman who wouldn't give a damn if I lost every cent and went back to fishing for a living.' His mouth took on an ironic twist. 'Well, finally, I met someone like that—a prim English girl who not only didn't care about my money, but showed all too plainly that she didn't like me much either.' He came to her, and went down on his heels beside her chair. Very gently, he touched the bruise discolouring her cheek. 'When they told me about the accident—before they said you were safe—it was the worst moment of my life. You are my kind of woman, Justine. Can't you believe that?'

Five days later, at three in the afternoon, the *Kalliste* left Ajaccio for a destination known only to her owner and her captain. Even the owner's bride had no idea where the yacht was bound, nor was she particularly curious to know. As she took off her short white wedding dress, and hung it tenderly away, all that concerned her was that five hours earlier she had ceased to be Miss Field and begun to be Madame Cassano.

She had changed into a cotton sun-dress, and was dreamily brushing her hair, when there was a tap at the door. She called 'Come in,' but no one came. Puzzled, she went to the door. The passage outside her stateroom was empty. Then, when the knock was repeated, she realised that it was coming from the other door—the one communicating with David's room. For the first time since she had occupied the room, there was a key in the lock. Smiling, her heart beginning to bump, she went across and turned the key.

'Well, did you enjoy your wedding, *madame*?' David asked, as he came through the doorway.

'Yes, it was lovely,' she said shyly. 'But at the moment it all seems rather unreal. Everything's happened so fast that I feel I may suddenly wake up and find it's only a dream.' She went back to the dressing-table, and took up her hairbrush again.

'Perhaps I should have given you more time. Perhaps it was selfish of me to rush you like this,' he said.

'Oh, no—I don't *mind*,' she said. 'I expect I

should feel the same if we'd been engaged for several months. I expect all brides feel a bit strange to themselves at first. Don't you feel odd . . . being somebody's husband, I mean?'

'It would help me to adjust to my new status if you came over here and kissed me,' he said, sitting down and beckoning to her.

She put down the brush and went to him, trembling a little. The preparations for the wedding, and the arrival of her aunt and uncle, had left little time for them to be alone together during their brief five-day engagement. And, when they had been alone together, he had never made ardent love to her, but had conducted himself rather formally, as if she were a strictly reared Corsican girl.

'I hope my plans for our honeymoon aren't going to disappoint you,' he said, as she sat down beside him on the end of the bed. 'I've rented an empty fisherman's cottage on one of the Greek islands in the Aegean. *Kalliste* will drop us off there, with enough supplies to keep us going for three weeks, and then we'll be virtually marooned until she comes back for us. There's nothing to do there but fish, and swim, and lie in the sun. Will you mind that? Will it be dull for you?'

'Oh, David, it sounds heavenly. Will we be quite alone there?'

'Yes, which means we'll have to do our own cooking and cleaning.'

'You mean I will,' she said, laughing. 'I don't suppose you can fry an egg.'

'On the contrary, I am extremely competent in the kitchen. My mother believed that boys should be taught such things. I am probably more adept than you are, *ma mie*.'

Her shyness forgotten, she slipped her arms round his neck. 'I'm glad we're not going anywhere grand. I'd rather have you all to myself. Darling David, I'm so happy.'

He caught her close, and kissed her as he had done on the night before he went to Paris, and she felt his heart pounding against hers. And then she knew that it didn't matter that his world had been so different from hers. Because today they had begun to make their own new, private, shared world.